PASSF

"A fine novel of both the triumph and defeat of the human spirit, giving us yet another parallel to the Holocaust story and to all tales of religious persecution."

Booklist, American Library Association

PASS

William Mirza

PORT

THOM LEMMONS

VICTOR BOOKS

A DIVISION OF SCRIPTURE PRESS PUBLICATIONS INC.
USA CANADA ENGLAND

Copyediting:
Carole Streeter and Barbara Williams
Design:
Paul Higdon
Cover Illustration:
Kazuhiko Sano

Library of Congress Cataloging-in-Publication Data

Mirza, William.
    Passport / by William Mirza.
    p. cm.
    ISBN 1-56476-390-0
    I. Lemmons, Thom. II. Title.
PS3563.I722P37 1995
813'.54—dc20   94-33034
                                              CIP

---

1 2 3 4 5 6 7 8 9 10 Printing/Year 99 98 97 96 95

Dedicated to my late wife, who said to me,
"Don't be discouraged; you will make it."

— W.M.

CHARACTER LIST

(in alphabetical order, by last name)

Ahmed Dabirian—a Muslim cabinetmaker and official of the Khomeini regime.

Mullah Nader Hafizi and **Akram Hafizi**— Muslim cleric and his wife who befriend Ezra and Esther.

Mullah Hassan—corrupt mullah who presides at Ezra's trial and carries out covert operations for the Khomeini regime.

Reuben Ibrahim—Jewish rug dealer who meets Ezra in prison; **Jahan** and **Maheen** are his wife and daughter.

Firouz Marandi (alias "Aziz")—Ezra's resentful pharmacy assistant who becomes active in the revolution against the Shah.

Nathan Moosovi—friend of Moosa, son of prominent Jewish businessman Abraham Moosovi. He recruits Moosa into a counterrevolutionary cell.

Ameer Nijat—wealthy Muslim businessman who purchases Ezra's pharmacy.

Khosrow Parvin—Muslim schoolmate and boyfriend of Sepideh.

Ezra Solaiman — Jewish pharmacist of Tehran; **Esther** is his wife, **Moosa** and **Sepideh** ("Sepi") are his son and daughter.

ONE

The leather handle of the carrying case felt gummy, moistened by sweat from his palms. Looking over the shoulder of the taxi driver, Ezra could see, in the rearview mirror, the military jeep bearing down on them from behind. It was directly behind them now, its bumper nearly touching theirs. Ezra's heart was hammering like a caged beast against his ribs, and despite all his efforts to remain calm, he knew his breathing had to be audible to everyone in the car. The jeep's driver started honking. The taxi driver glanced at his rearview mirror and began to pull to the side of the road. Ezra's nostrils flared in panic and his eyes were wide, round discs of fear. . . .

. . . .

IT WAS GETTING DARK. The traffic on Nasser Khosrow Avenue was already bumper-to-bumper, moving scarcely faster than the pedestrians jamming the sidewalks on both sides. The druggist wearily leaned against his shop door and slid the lock home, waving once more at his last customer of the day, an old woman who tucked her parcel under her arm and walked away.

Ezra was tired. The flow of customers into the pharmacy had been nonstop, for which he was grateful. But once again Firouz had called in sick. With no help, Ezra barely had time between prescriptions to gulp down the

9

sandwich he had brought for lunch. Esther was right. He should hire some more assistants, and perhaps fire the undependable Firouz. The business was certainly profitable enough, and this pace would eventually kill him.

He pulled open the cash drawer and began pulling the *rial* notes out of the crammed compartment. He grunted in satisfaction: the day's receipts had been excellent. Swiftly and with practiced motions he sorted the currency into piles by denomination. He would not bother to count it here — he was tired and hungry and wanted to go home. Esther would have dinner waiting, and with the traffic crawling as slowly as frozen molasses through the streets of Tehran, he wanted to leave as soon as possible.

He had just placed the money into a canvas bank bag and shoved the bag into his battered briefcase when a staccato rapping came from the front window of his shop. He glanced up to see a white-turbaned mullah waving impatiently at him through the dusty plate glass, plainly signaling that Ezra should unlock the door and let him in.

Ezra sighed, looking wistfully from the wall clock to the mullah's intent face. The old man's manner seemed urgent. And Ezra always made a practice of paying special attention to the respected, if poor, Muslim clergymen. *Oh, very well,* he told himself. *Surely this won't take long, and then I'll be on my way.* Trying to conceal his chagrin, Ezra went to the door and unlocked it, beckoning the mullah inside.

"I am Mullah Hafizi," said the old cleric, inclining his head toward Ezra. "Thank you for opening to me."

Ezra bowed in turn. "I remember you, *baradar*,*" he said. "And how is your son these days?"

The mullah looked at Ezra appreciatively. "You remember . . ."

---

*brother

10

"Of course, *Aga* Hafizi. Your son was ill, and you needed a prescription. It was my pleasure to be helpful—"

"And you would not accept payment," finished the mullah. "I have never forgotten your kindness."

"How may I help you today, my friend?"

The mullah dropped his eyes diffidently to the floor. "It is my wife," he mumbled. "She has been ill, but intends to go to Isfahan to visit our married daughter. The doctor has said she should not travel, but she is adamant." Hesitantly the cleric pulled a wrinkled slip of paper from his pocket. Handing it to Ezra, he continued, "I...I know it is late, but I hesitated to come to you again, especially during your busy time of day."

"Please, please," protested Ezra, taking the prescription from Hafizi and turning to go behind the counter, "you should not have hesitated. Now let me see..." he muttered, searching among his shelves for the antibiotic the doctor had prescribed. A few minutes later, he handed the old man a vial of small yellow pills. "There, my friend. That should have your wife feeling better in no time."

"How much do I owe you, *Aga* Solaiman?" asked the mullah, reaching into his robe for his wallet.

"Nothing, *Aga* Hafizi, nothing," Ezra said, waving away the proffered *rial* notes. "It was my pleasure to help you. Please do not diminish it by offering payment."

"Once more you do a poor old mullah such a favor," he mused. "Why? You are a Jew, and I am a Muslim. Why should you do me such kindness?"

Ezra shrugged. "I have a great appreciation for all men of God, *baradar*," he said. "Besides, we are both sons of Abraham, are we not?" he chuckled.

"Would that the Shah had a tenth part of your respectful generosity," said the old cleric sadly. "Then we mullahs might not be reduced to such dependence on

11

the kindness of strangers." Suddenly the old man looked sharply at Ezra, a defiant glint in his eyes. "But one day," he said, "perhaps one day soon, things will change. When the Ayatollah Khomeini returns, the blessed faith of Islam will once again take its proper place in the hearts and lives of the people. And in that day . . ." Hafizi left the sentence unfinished.

Ezra glanced nervously about. They were alone in the shop, but one never knew around which corner SAVAK might lurk, how far their ears extended. The Shah's secret police were said to be almost omnipresent; their mission was to crush opposition to the Pahlavi regime wherever they found it. And the mullahs were known to be rigidly antagonistic to the policies and practices of the Shah and his family. From his Islamic acquaintances, Ezra knew that Mohammed Reza Pahlavi was regularly denounced in the mosques. A megalomaniac, the mullahs called him. Perhaps even old Hafizi had a SAVAK informant tailing him, waiting to report on all the mullah's contacts, anyone who seemed friendly with him.

Ezra cleared his throat. "Well, *Aga* Hafizi, it grows late, after all, and I must go home."

The mullah, his reverie broken, grasped Ezra's hand in both his own and shook it gratefully. "*Aga* Solaiman, I thank you again for your generosity. I will never forget your kindness to my family." He paused, looking intently into Ezra's eyes. "If I can ever help you," he said, "you have but to ask."

Ezra returned his gaze for a moment, puzzling over the mullah's words. "Thank you," he said hesitantly. "Thank you very much."

Releasing Ezra's hand, the old mullah shuffled toward the door, then out into the dark street. For a moment, Ezra stared thoughtfully after him, then shrugged and gripped the handle of the briefcase. He walked to the door, glanced back over his shoulder at the shop to reassure himself that all was in order, then switched off the light. He went outside, locked the door, and pulled on the metal cage which rattled down its tracks on either side of the door, banging onto the pavement. Ezra snapped the cage's heavy padlock in place and began walking toward the bus stop, joining the throngs of pedestrians and motorists who slowly made their way through the crowded December evening.

FORTY-FIVE MINUTES LATER, the red British-made bus disgorged him onto the sidewalk, one block from his front gate. He pulled the lapels of his woolen overcoat closer about his neck as he walked home. A light snow filtered down from the turbid sky above Tehran. His key rattled in the lock of the iron gate, and the noise summoned Marjan, who barked loudly as he bounded from his kennel by the front steps of the house. When the large black dog scented his master, his barking stopped and he stood panting and wagging his tail as Ezra clanged the gate closed behind him. Absent-ly he scratched the dog behind the ears as he walked toward the front steps.

The house was a large, red-brick two-story of modern design, set on a lot almost a quarter-hectare in size. A two-meter brick wall surrounded the "estate," as Esther liked to call it. The top of the wall was fortified by sharp iron spikes, to discourage the ever-ready street thieves from attempting a break-in. Even though they lived in one of the better areas of the capital city, this house stood out from its neighbors. Fruit trees grew in the large, well-kept yard, as well as evergreens and oaks. The walk leading from the gate to the front steps was of the same red brick as the house, laid in a curved her-ringbone pattern.

Moosa, their son, had designed the house for them. It was the first project he had undertaken upon completion of his architecture degree from UCLA. Like many well-to-do Iranians, Ezra and Esther had decided that their son's education was best completed in the United States. Moosa was a bright boy, and had no trouble adjusting to life in the West. In fact, the letters they received from him lately sounded less and less like those of an Iranian in a foreign land, and more like an American writing to his relations in the "old country." Ezra sighed. With all the uncertainty these days, who could say? Perhaps it was better that Moosa remain in America. All the same, he missed his son. It had been two years since his last visit home.

As he stepped onto the portico, he heard the bolts of the front door clicking. The door swung open and Esther greeted him.

Despite his fatigue, he smiled when he saw her. He set down his briefcase to take her extended hands. "Come inside," she said. "It's getting colder."

Esther was a handsome woman who carried her forty-eight years well. Her tall, slender build complemented his similar frame; the most frequent comment from those they met was that they were "a distinguished-looking couple." With his salt-and-pepper hair and moustache and Esther's patrician bearing, the epithet was not undeserved.

They had first met at an age when most parents refused their daughters permission to talk to boys without adult supervision. Her mother, something of a free-thinker had been an exception. Ezra had seen Esther sitting alone on a bench in Farah Park, when he was sixteen and she fourteen. She was hesitant to speak to him, but his persuasive speech, combined with a manner slightly older than his years, swayed her.

Her parents had arrived recently from the mountain city of Hamadan, she told him. Her father, a dealer in imported fabrics, had moved his family to the capital to be more favorably located to conduct business — in short, the necessary bribes to government officials were easier to negotiate in person than by post from Hamadan. Her family was middle-class, and her education was superior to the norm—she had even learned some French, which she was proud to employ when the opportunity presented itself.

Ezra's father, by contrast, was relatively poor. He sold fabrics door-to-door, and made just enough money to keep himself, his wife, and their two children, Ezra and his sister, Maryam. Ezra had, at various times, worked to provide partial support for the family. He was very studious, being determined to make the most of the free public education.

After graduating from high school, Ezra went on to college at Tehran University, intending to become a pharmacist. During college, he got a job with a pharmaceutical company, selling drugs to doctors and dentists. He scrimped and saved enough money so that following his graduation, he opened a storefront pharmacy on a small street just off Shahbaz Avenue.

Esther's family attended the same synagogue as Ezra's, so they were able to maintain contact with relative ease. They became friends and, over the course of the next several years, something more. While waltzing with Esther at a wedding celebration, Ezra asked her to marry him and she accepted. Within six months, they broke the glasses beneath their own wedding canopy.

"Why are you so late tonight?" she asked, as he hung his overcoat on the brass coat tree inside the front door.

"An old mullah came just at closing time and needed a prescription filled. That, and the traffic was even more horrendous than usual. Where is Sepideh?"

"In her room, doing schoolwork. She ate earlier, but I waited for you. I'm hungry. Let's go eat."

They went into the kitchen. "What was the news today?" he asked her. "I was so busy I didn't even have time to read the paper."

"More of the same," Esther told him. "The Shah says he is in complete control; there is no need to worry. The American President says he has full confidence in the Shah, and he insists that human rights must be respected. And in the streets the Shiites rant and rave."

"Why doesn't Mr. Carter make up his mind?" groused Ezra. "Can't he understand how all this talk about human rights weakens the Shah's grip? With one hand he builds up the Peacock Throne, and with the other he gives legitimacy to the opposition." Ezra fell silent, frustration and concern curdling his brow.

"My! You're on about it tonight!" commented Esther, as she set a plate heaped with steaming long-grain rice in front of her husband. "Since when have you become so intense an observer of political matters?" She chided him slightly, hoping to nudge him out of his pensive mood. She placed a skewer of marinated mutton kabob atop the rice on Ezra's plate, spooning roasted onions, tomatoes, and peppers over the meat, then she helped herself to a similar serving.

Ezra chewed silently. Esther studied him carefully a few moments, then said, "What is it? Something else is troubling you."

Briefly he glanced up at her, then turned his gaze back to his plate. "Oh . . . probably nothing serious," he mumbled. "The mullah . . . he said something."

Her arched eyebrows asked silently for explanation.

"Not so much what he said, really . . . more the way he said it. As if he *knew* something." A few more silent seconds passed.

"He said, 'When Khomeini returns . . .' "

"And when, since the Shah banished Khomeini, have the Shiites not been muttering about his return?" inquired Esther, pertly. "How long has it been—twenty years? And still he must send his curses long distance."

Ezra looked up at his wife, shaking his head. "I told

you, it wasn't what he said as much as his manner. He offered to help me, should I ever need assistance."

"From a destitute mullah? An interesting notion!"

Ezra took another bite of mutton, chewing slowly and thoughtfully. When he had swallowed, he looked at her again.

"And if the troubles worsen . . . ?" he asked.

Esther studied his face for a long time. Then she dropped her eyes to her plate and took another bite of rice. Outside, the snow began to thicken.

TWO

FIROUZ MARANDI'S first waking thought was, "Today's the day!" His stomach began to tense with anticipation. He sat up on the edge of his bed and rehearsed what he must do.

He had to give his boss some reason for not showing up again. Surely the old Jew was getting suspicious—he had been using the excuse of illness for three days now. No matter; the cause was more important than his miserable dead-end of a job. He would think of something.

Next, he had to gather his cadre and arrive at the agreed-upon place at 9 o'clock sharp. When the operation started, they had to be in position.

After that, the tide of events would sweep them all along. Firouz did not allow himself to think too much about where that tide might carry him; anywhere was better than here. The force of history was on their side, and also the religious fervor of Islam.

Firouz was not overly devout, but the comrades in the movement had long ago recognized the value of Islamic fundamentalism in organizing opposition to the Pahlavi regime. They of the *mujahedin* were more than willing to ally themselves with the mullahs as an expedient means to a just end. So far, the strategy had paid handsome dividends.

Today began the holy month of Muharram. It was a

time of public mourning and self-flagellation, in memory of the martyrs of Sunni repression centuries before. But this year, the devotees would have a strategy other than public displays of piety. Today, the passions of the country would be unleashed, and the gauntlet would be cast down. Firouz's imagination was aflame with the possibilities, the intoxication of life at the nexus of human events. Today would begin the final conflict.

EZRA SAT on the swaying bus, deep in thought. It was early morning, and there were not many passengers. Something in the background slowly drew his attention out of its deep well of contemplation. He looked about him. Someone was speaking, and Ezra seemed to have been the only one on the bus not listening. He realized that the voice was a recording—a cassette tape being played by a passenger holding a small portable tape player in his lap. The voice on the tape was that of an old man. His speech was firm and his words had a resolute cadence. Ezra began to listen.

. . . and in the schools, teachers force boys and girls to hug each other, and to dance in public. That boys and girls should be even in the same school together is scandalous. Women are allowed to forsake the decent *chador*, and to parade their arms and legs before the lustful eyes of men in the streets. These are the perverted ways of the West, which the Shah has imported into our Islamic country. . . .

Rise up, all you faithful Muslims, against the unholy tyranny of the Pahlavis. The Shah, like his satanic father, is an enemy of Islam. Do not be afraid. Allah—may His name be blessed—is on our side.

The tape clicked off. The passengers leaned back in their seats, looking at each other, nodding and smiling.

One of them was a rug dealer surnamed Noori, with whom Ezra was acquainted. Noori looked up, saw the druggist staring back in some confusion, and moved down the aisle to seat himself by Ezra.

"Good morning, *Aga* Solaiman! A beautiful day, isn't it?"

"Indeed, *Aga* Noori. Tell me, what were you listening to?"

The rug merchant looked at Ezra in surprise. "Don't you know?" he asked. "That was the voice of the holy man, Ayatollah Khomeini! How is it you have never heard it before?"

A small, cold ball of foreboding settled in the pit of Ezra's stomach.

"Has the Shah relaxed his ban on the words of the . . . the holy man?" Ezra asked lamely.

Noori chuckled and shook his head at Ezra's naiveté. "Don't be foolish, *Aga* Solaiman. The Shah is as violently opposed as ever to the Ayatollah. But the tyrant's grip is weakening, my friend." Noori scooted closer to Ezra, punching him conspiratorially in the ribs. "Don't you feel it? The people in the streets know it. Mohammed Reza Pahlavi's days are numbered."

Ezra stared at Noori, his face a shifting amalgam of disbelief and worry.

"The Ayatollah's words are heard daily by thousands of the faithful," Noori continued. "Many besides the mullahs are weary of the hypocritical despotism of the Shah. It is a measure of the people's disrespect that banned tapes such as these—" he nodded toward the man who held the cassette player in his lap—"are played on public transportation, in coffee shops, in the covered bazaar."

"But SAVAK—" protested Ezra in a half-whisper.

"SAVAK is a paper tiger," sneered Noori. "Each day their shadow grows shorter. Look at the royal cabinet," he offered. "Every few days, it seems, the Shah denounces the current prime minister, as a sop to the opposition, and appoints a new man in his place. Each time this happens, the SAVAK hierarchy become less concerned about quelling dissent, and more preoccupied with saving their own skins. They smell the blood in the water, just like all the other sharks."

Ezra stared at Noori a moment more, then looked down. After a moment, he said, "Of course, all this is somewhat foreign to me. As a Jew I do not customarily mingle in politics."

"*Aga* Solaiman," warned Noori, looking solemnly into Ezra's eyes, "in the days to come, no one will be able to remain neutral. Either by choice or default, you will be on one side or the other."

Again Ezra's brow curdled. "But I don't understand. My people have lived in this country since the days of Darius and the Persian Empire. This is our home too. We wish only to live in peace—"

"Listen, Solaiman," interrupted Noori curtly, "I didn't ask for a history lesson. I'm only trying to tell you the way things will be." Pausing, he continued in a gentler tone. "I say these things as a friend. A great contest is to be tried in this country, and soon. See that you are on the winning side."

The bus' air brakes squawked as the vehicle slowed. Noori glanced up, then stood. "This is my stop," he said. "Think about what I've said." Gripping Ezra briefly on the shoulder, he walked quickly down the aisle.

As the bus accelerated back into traffic, Ezra leaned back in his seat and closed his eyes. Noori's admonition echoed in his mind, ". . . the winning side . . . the winning side."

SEPIDEH WAITED for him, as she did every day, by the stairs in the bustling main hallway. Ten minutes before their first class, she felt two hands slide down over her face, covering her eyes.

"Guess who," said a mock-bass voice behind her. She giggled and twisted about to face Khosrow, who stood grinning at her, his books stacked on the floor beside him.

He was a strikingly handsome boy, the son of a petroleum engineer. He was slim and athletic, and he wore carefully pressed clothes in the Western style favored by many upper-class Iranians.

"Where were you?" demanded Sepideh suddenly. "The bell for classes is about to ring, and I have been standing here all morning." She stuck out her lower lip and gave him a sidelong pout calculated to produce instant capitulation.

"Ah, Sepi, don't look like that," he entreated, "I couldn't help it. This morning just as I was on my way out the door, my father stopped me and gave me a lecture on which streets to avoid on my way. I would have been here much sooner if I hadn't had to wait for him to finish."

Her look changed to one of concern. "Why must you avoid your usual route?"

"Don't you listen to the news? Today is the beginning of Muharram. The rumor is that some of the radicals will cause trouble in the streets."

"Trouble?" she asked, still perplexed.

"Little Jewish princess," laughed Khosrow, "doesn't your father tell you anything? The mullahs are angry at the Shah, and they're inciting the barefooted ones to make trouble." He shook his head at her innocent puzzlement.

"Does your father hate the Shah too?" she asked, fitting her shoulder into the curve of his arm as they walked toward their classrooms.

"My father? No! If it weren't for the Shah, my father would probably still be selling carpets for Uncle Habib in the covered bazaar. No, we don't hate the Shah," he assured her. "Only the ignorant peasants and the mullahs are against the Shah. And when the army gets through with them, I'll bet they learn to hold their tongues," he boasted.

"Will there be fighting today?" she asked, her eyes round with apprehension.

Khosrow shrugged. "Who knows? I plan to stay out of the way, so I don't really care."

The bell rang in the hallway, accompanied by the sound of scuffling feet, as students hurried to their classrooms. Khosrow leaned close to Sepideh. "Quick! A kiss before I go to class."

She looked at him warily for a moment, a cautious smile flickering about the corners of her mouth. Quickly glancing up and down the corridor, she pecked him chastely on the cheek, then wheeled and strode off toward her classroom.

"You call that a kiss?" he called after her.

Blushing, she ducked into the doorway of her room.

THREE

SHORTLY BEFORE 9 O'CLOCK, the wailing, chanting crowd shuffled along Shah Reza Avenue, filling the broad thoroughfare from curb to curb. Dotted here and there among the roiling mass were the white turbans of the mullahs, shouting their admonitions to the faithful who had turned out to observe ritual mourning for the holy martyrs of the Shiite sect. Along the sidewalks and atop the buildings on the route of march stood army regulars, nervously fingering their weapons and eyeing the huge crowds in the street. Tension crackled in the air with a silent turbulence louder than the shouted Islamic slogans of the wailing marchers.

Firouz and his eight commandos crouched in the lee of a building, just around the corner from the crammed Shah Reza Avenue. The side of the building facing the avenue was windowless, covered with a huge portrait of Shah Mohammed Reza Pahlavi.

Nervously Firouz scanned the rooftops around them. *Good. The army lookouts are preoccupied with the huge throng in the avenue, and the preparations here in the alley go unnoticed. Just as planned.* He glanced at his watch, then quickly around at his cadre.

"Our time has come, comrades," he said, his gaze boring intensely into each face in the circle. "Today we

25

strike the first blow against the corruption and repression of the Pahlavis. History is on our side. Let us never forget this." He gripped the hands of each of them in turn. "Go now. And when you see the signal, do what you have been told." One by one, the others moved out into the crowd. Firouz waited in the shadows, glancing anxiously at his watch and gripping the neck of the glass bottle in his hand.

When the sweep second hand crossed 12, Firouz lit the oil-soaked rag protruding from the bottle neck, stepped quickly around the corner, and flung the gasoline-filled bottle high against the gigantic painted face of the Shah. It struck just below the dark, aristocratic arch of the left eyebrow. The gasoline ignited, spilling quickly down the wall, spreading an orange fusillade of flame across the Shah's likeness. The paint quickly began to blister and curl. "Death to the Shah!" screamed Firouz, and dashed back down the alleyway. His cohorts, by now dispersed among the masses in the streets, took up the cry. "Death to the Shah! Death to the Shah!"

The frenzied crowd of worshipers quickly caught the heady excitement of the moment. The slogan ran like the fire on the wall through the throng in the street. "Death to the Shah! Death to the Shah!" The pent-up anger of decades of repression burst from their throats in a sudden eruption, kindled to the flash point by the burning scar on the mural. With raised fists, they hotly announced the unleashing of the beast, the casting of the die. "Death to the Shah!"

Someone threw a brick through a store window; another followed. A stone caught one of the soldiers in the chest. Shots rang out as soldiers fired their weapons into the air to frighten the mob. Then the burning, choking stench of tear gas burst among the angry crowds. In the street, people began screaming and running back and forth, trampling each other in their panic to escape the acrid fog. A roaring, faceless frenzy swirled through the side streets. Shots rang out as frightened soldiers reacted to the chaotic gangs surging along the avenues.

Six blocks away, in a hidden basement doorway, Firouz heard the commotion of the rioting. A fierce grin gashed his face. History was on his side.

REUBEN IBRAHIM kissed his wife on the forehead. "Time to open the shop, dearest," he said. "Revolution or no revolution, people will need rugs."

"I wish you wouldn't make light of everything," scolded Jahan, shaking her head. "These are dangerous times, and loose lips can be fatal."

"And your lips can be fatal, as well," he crooned, leaning close and pulling her toward him. "Eh? What's this? Who's climbing up my shins?"

He leaned over and scooped his three-year-old daughter into his arms. "So, Maheen? You can't let your papa get a little smooch without wanting in on the act?" He covered the child's face with noisy kisses as she giggled and squirmed.

"Well, time to go," he sighed, placing Maheen in her mother's arms.

"Please be careful," Jahan warned, as he turned to go. "Remember how much we need you."

He turned back to her. "I'll remember, don't worry. The Lord and Savior be with you."

"And with you," she said, completing their ritual farewell.

He closed the door behind him and walked to the corner to await the bus that would take him to his stall at the covered bazaar. He instinctively avoided the knots of men huddled here and there on the sidewalk, trying to make himself as inconspicuous as possible. Since the rioting began a few days ago, he had had few opportunities to engage in his usual bantering with passersby. People were not in the mood for levity.

"I won't let them keep me from my shop," he had told Jahan when the trouble first started, and so far, Reuben had not missed a day, even though Jahan had begged him to stay in the house.

"This isn't a good time to be Jewish," she had pleaded. "Just stay home for a few days and see how things settle out!"

But he hadn't, and it appeared that his decision was vindicated. He had kept to his usual hours, and had even managed to make a little money, since customers who came to the bazaar found few of the other shops open.

Reuben glanced at his watch. The bus was due soon, but that didn't necessarily mean it would arrive. With all the disturbances in the streets, one scarcely knew when the buses would run. He was mildly surprised, then, to hear the approaching rattle and roar of a diesel engine, followed quickly by the sight of the red bus rounding the corner and coming toward him.

Reuben stepped onto the bus and sidled down the packed aisle until he found an unused handstrap. He held on as the bus jerked away from the curb and pulled back into traffic.

"Good day, Ibrahim!" said a voice next to him. Reuben struggled to turn and see who had spoken.

"Ah! Hello, there, Hosseini," Reuben managed. "I didn't see you before."

"No matter," the other man shouted over the din of the bus and the other passengers. "I see you are on your way to work, as usual."

"Of course! As the Americans say, 'Another day, another *rial,*'" he quipped, then wondered if the Western reference had been wise.

"I take it that you haven't given any more consideration to my offer," said Hosseini, swaying with the other standees as the bus swerved in and out of traffic.

28

"I'm sorry, *baradar*," Reuben said, laughing uneasily. "With all the excitement the last few days, I suppose I've forgotten what you're talking about." He hoped he might have a chance to change the subject, but Hosseini was not to be deterred.

"Then allow me to refresh your memory, friend. Why won't you sell me your space in the bazaar? I have offered you my larger space, but—"

"That corner and I have grown very close," Reuben shrugged, grinning. "I'd feel as if I were selling a member of the family. Surely you can—"

"Long live Khomeini! Long live Khomeini!"

Someone at the front had started the chant and it soon enveloped the entire bus. Hosseini joined in loudly, much to the discomfort of Reuben's left ear.

Reuben looked at his feet, wishing for invisibility. He was surrounded by chanting supporters of the Shah's arch-nemesis, and he knew that for safety's sake he should at least make some show of enthusiasm. But he couldn't. Each time he tried to take up the cheer, the words stuck in his throat. And so, he kept his face down and wished fervently for the bus ride to come to an end. He prayed that no one would notice.

FOR ESTHER, cleaning the upstairs bedroom was a weekly ritual, therapeutic in its repetitiveness. She did not allow the maid to clean the master bedroom—it was her domain. First she ran the new vacuum cleaner over all the carpets on the varnished oak floor. Then she dusted the furniture and window sills, lightly brushing the tops and folds of the drapes hanging in the large windows. Finally, she went to the linen closet and removed a set of fresh sheets, redolent with the fragrance of the cedar paneling in the closet. She derived a childlike satisfaction from the crisp creases running at right angles across the pillowcases, the taut white expanse of the bed sheets tucked in neat hospital corners.

Her world was like these bed linens, she reflected on this Friday morning, as the bright winter sun streamed through the polished panes of the bedroom window. Crisp, clean—all right angles and carefully folded corners.

One of the things she loved about Ezra, for example, was his predictability. From their first encounter, his gravity—oddly charming in a boy his age—gave her a feeling of security and safety. And through the years her first impression was confirmed. Ezra knew things, knew how to manage. Competence was his hallmark, and his serious yet kind manner was such that those he dealt with in his pharmacy or on the streets of Tehran trusted him almost instinctively. She supposed it was a result of the early age at which financial responsibility was thrust upon him. Whatever the reason, she enjoyed the world he had built for her—the business, this house, their children—an intricate and thoughtfully woven web of comfort and belonging.

Now this all was threatened by the ominous rumbling in the streets. Even with the news blackouts, word rapidly spread throughout Tehran—indeed, the whole country—about the rioting in Shah Reza Avenue and its aftermath. No longer could she pretend that all would be well. No longer could she scoff at Ezra's worried looks and tense silences. The world was shifting, and all the things she most valued were caught up in the flux. She could not predict what she might lose—perhaps everything. Sighing, she spread the counterpane evenly atop the sheets and blankets, pulling at the corners to smooth the wrinkles. Then she went downstairs to pour herself a cup of coffee.

Sitting at the small wooden table in the kitchen, she was startled to see a workman dressed in shabby clothing striding by the window. She did not remember asking the gardener to come today—and then the kitchen door opened and the man stood looking at her.

"Ezra!" Esther half-shouted. "You startled me! I thought—" A questioning look came into her eyes. "Why are you home today and not at work?"

He gave her a sheepish smile. "Today, I decided to stay here. There is little point in opening the shop. With all the trouble in the streets the last few days, no one comes in. I haven't seen Firouz in over a week. And so, last night when I left, I hung a sign in the door which reads, 'Closed until Monday.' And here I am."

"Why didn't you tell me?"

He shrugged and raised his eyes to the ceiling. "I forgot," he apologized. "And this morning when I awoke, you were sleeping so peacefully that I didn't want to bother you."

She shook her head and gave him an admonitory look.

"I've done quite a bit of work this morning," he remarked, shrugging out of the tattered old coat he wore and helping himself to a cup of coffee as he sat down at the table. "The cherry trees needed pruning, and I've gotten a decent start on that. When I finish, I may work some mulch into the flower beds on the south side of the house." He cupped his hands around the coffee mug. His cheeks were flushed from his exertions and the cold air. He took a slow, careful sip of the hot, black coffee.

Their eyes met.

"What are we going to do?" she asked softly.

He set down the cup, stared into his coffee for ten or twelve heartbeats, and then met her gaze.

"I've been thinking about nothing else," he said slowly. "I don't like the mood of the country. The mullahs grow bolder every day. The people in the streets talk about the Shah as if he were no more than a distant nuisance. No one is afraid of SAVAK anymore. I think . . ." He took several deep breaths, then continued. "I think the Shah is going to lose control."

"What about the army?" Esther asked. "Will they do nothing?"

Ezra shook his head. "Every time a Shiite dies the family and friends begin another of their customary forty-day mourning periods, with all the attendant lamentation and oaths of revenge. Every public funeral is a frenzy of wailing and passion. Is it any wonder that so many riots have started at funerals? It's a vicious cycle, Esther. And bullets serve only as tinder for the flames. Besides, the enlisted men—the ones who would have to do the shooting—are poor. They don't feel the same allegiance to the Shah that the generals and officers do. They don't want to shoot their cousins and uncles. I hear desertions are becoming a problem.

"Even some of my fellow merchants are caught up in the revolutionary fever. The mullahs fan the blaze—" Ezra broke off, looking out the window and shaking his head. "I don't see how this can end well for anyone, least of all the Jews."

Esther kept silent, staring down at the table. Presently Ezra went on, more to himself than to her. "If Khomeini comes back in triumph, the laws of Islam will become the laws of Iran."

"But Ezra! Jews have lived in this country since—"

"—the days of Daniel the prophet," he finished for her. "Yes, I know. But I'm not sure it will matter. If there's one thing Jews ought to know, it's the danger of being in the minority when regimes change." He looked up at her, then took another slow sip of coffee. After a long silence, he said, "I've been thinking about selling the business."

She looked at him, but his eyes wouldn't meet hers. "To do what?" she asked, finally.

He replied without looking at her. "Maybe .. move," he mumbled.

Another long silence.

"Move where?"

He looked up at the ceiling, then out the window. His voice sounded as distant as the moon. "To America."

Esther got up and walked over to the window. She looked out at the back lawn to the pile of branches lying haphazardly near one of the cherry trees. Ezra and his pruning . . . carefully trimming off the nonessential. She turned to face him. "Are you sure this is necessary?" She barely managed to keep her voice from wavering. "*This* is our country. We were both born and raised here, as were our children. Our daughter's friends are here, to say nothing of our own. We are *Iranians*, Ezra, not . . ." She felt her lips beginning to tremble, and she quickly went into the drawing room.

A few minutes later, Ezra found her standing in the middle of the drawing room, hugging her elbows to her sides and staring at the portrait of the Shah which was semiobligatory in every upper-class Iranian home. Mohammed Reza Pahlavi was shown in his gold-colored military uniform, a half-dozen medals decorating his breast. He wore the jeweled crown and at his side was the centuries-old scepter of the Persian royalty. As Esther looked at the portrait, tears coursed down her face. Her chin was wrinkled, quivering with the effort of silencing her sobs.

Ezra sat down on one of the tapestried Louis XVI chairs. He hesitated to break into Esther's silent grieving, and gazed instead at the woven medallion in the center of the Kerman rug which covered the parquet floor.

"There are angry people in the mosques and in the streets, Esther," he said at last, kneading his hands dejectedly. "And sometimes angry people do things they later come to regret. I am grateful to the Shah for all he has tried to do for the country, but . . . if something happened to you or to Sepi, I would never be able to live with my shame."

While he spoke, she looked at the floor. Now she

WILLIAM MIRZA // THOM LEMMONS

turned her tear-streaked face to his. They looked into each other's eyes for several quiet moments. Without reply, she walked past him, retreating to the kitchen. Slowly Ezra left the drawing room, passing through the kitchen where Esther was once more seated at the table, her face in her hands. She wouldn't look at him. He put on his coat while walking out the door, to return to his pruning.

NADER HAFIZI SPLASHED icy water from the ceremonial urns at the mosque entrance on his arms and head, making his ritual ablutions before leaving for his home. The water was so frigid it almost burned his skin, but even such harsh cleansing as this did not wash away the misgivings he felt deep within himself. The Islamic revolution was still in its infancy, but he smelled a rottenness at its heart which disturbed him profoundly.

Nader Hafizi had been born and reared in a small village in the northwestern province of Azerbaijan. His father had died when Nader was sixteen, and he had worked as a day laborer to supplement the meager living his mother eked out from their three-acre farm with its cow and handful of chickens. For Nader and his two younger brothers, it was an austere, harsh life. They rarely went hungry, but there was never anything to spare.

His mother dreamed of a proper education for her oldest son. Despite his day work—carrying loads and digging ditches for anyone who had the price of his hire—she insisted that he continue his studies at night and whenever he failed to find work. Many were the days when his mother would walk to the school, twelve kilometers from their village, to bring him food. In this haphazard, stop-and-start fashion, he managed to complete the course of study to qualify for graduation from high school.

At his mother's urging, he began to seek permanent

employment. "A good job with a desk," was the phrase
she used over and over. Diligently he applied at all the
government offices in the district, waiting for hours in
the summer sun or the winter cold to be admitted to
the presence of some bureaucrat who had the power to
make his mother's dreams come true. And time after
time, he was denied. His application would be placed at
the bottom of the pile, and the job would go instead to
a boy with wealthier parents or better political connec-
tions. Resentment hatched within him toward the corrupt system which gave no consideration to worth—only
to advantage.

At last, he decided to enter the clergy, for it seemed
the only path out of the backwardness his circumstances dictated for him. He spent a year in the mosque
at Tabriz, studying the Koran and learning Arabic. For
thirty-five years now, he had given his life to the service
of Islam. If his dedication had not given him wealth—
he did not even own the small house he and his wife
inhabited—at least it had given him self-respect and a
purpose in life.

The mullah walked slowly along Talleghani Avenue,
almost oblivious to the shuffling masses through whom
he waded in the graying light of the overcast January
evening. The chanting mob of students gathered outside the gates of the American embassy compound dis-
tracted him for a moment; but then the same nagging
questions kept running through his mind, and he trod
slowly homeward along the dun streets, wrestling within
himself for the source of his malaise. He remembered a
conversation he had just had inside the mosque, with
two of his peers.

THEY SAT on cushions in a small side chamber
in the mosque; Nader, Mullah Hojat, and Mullah
Hassan. The other two men were several years his ju-

nior. Hojat spoke of what he planned to do when the forces of Islam achieved final victory over the Shah.

"The first thing I will do, brothers," he announced smugly, "is travel to the village of my family and kill the miserable cur whom Mohammed Reza appointed to administer the land program there."

Hassan nodded in agreement. "When the Pahlavis stole the land from the mosque in Meshed, this alone showed they were no lovers of Islam, regardless of what they may say in public."

Hafizi was troubled by the casual malevolence of his two colleagues. It was true that the modernization programs of the Shah and his father had weakened the grip of Islam upon the wealthier merchant classes. He, like the others, had suffered financial hardship, since many of the most devout, on whose tithes the mullahs depended, were desperately poor. Still . . .

"Brothers," Hafizi began hesitantly, "should we not give attention to the spiritual struggle, rather than the material? Surely you cannot believe that all the ills of Iran stem from the location of her wealth."

"You are too forgiving, *Aga* Hafizi," sneered Hassan. "You cannot expect a people to suddenly become magnanimous, when their rulers have for decades set an example of unparalleled greed."

"True enough," agreed Hojat. "For years the Shah and his family have looted the wealth of this country, using their shell companies and the convenient 'directorates' they hold, while we, the guardians of Islam, are left to subsist on the scraps of the banquet! When the merchants of the country see such rampant avarice, why should they not assume that bribery and extortion are normal costs of doing business? No, Brother Hafizi, we must rise up and claim for Islam what is rightfully owed! It is time to redress the wrongs of the past! It is time to make them all pay!"

In the self-righteous enthusiasm of Hojat's speech,

Hafizi thought he discerned the lurking shadow of cov-etousness. "Brother Hojat," he began, after a long, thoughtful pause, "surely not all the wealthy in this country have prospered at the expense of their poorer neighbors! Should wealth be considered *prima facie* evi-dence of corruption?"

"Are you trying to protect the Shah and his cronies?" demanded Hassan suspiciously. Hojat's eyes were glit-tering slits, waiting for his reply.

Hafizi thought of Solaiman, the Jew who had given him medicine for his son and wife. He looked carefully at the other two mullahs. "I am no lover of the Shah," he began firmly, "but, my brothers, is it possible that you have forgotten? The blessed prophet Mohammed began his ministry after a long and successful career as a merchant in Mecca. He was not a poor man."

Their answer was a hostile silence.

STILL DEEP in thought, Hafizi turned into Javid Street, the narrow thoroughfare where he lived. As he neared his door, he looked up to see a lone figure approaching from Naderi Avenue. The tall, well-dressed man, obviously not at home in this neighborhood, was peering at the small cinder-block houses as he passed them, as if to check the numbers. As he drew closer, Hafizi saw who it was. It was Solaiman, the druggist.

"*Aga* Solaiman! What errand brings you to my poor house?"

FOUR

The taxi driver shunted to the shoulder of the highway, and the jeep accelerated around them in a blast of engine noise. Ezra watched as it quickly shot ahead along the highway, dodging in and out of traffic as the pasdars *rushed along on whatever emergency had claimed them.*

He sat back, trying to relax the screaming cords of tension writhing along his shoulders and neck. He looked over at Esther. She gave him a lifeless smile of attempted encouragement. He saw her eyes stray to the bottom of the case, where the secret compartment was located.

The taxi driver, seeing a small space in the oncoming traffic, jammed the accelerator to the floor. The cab slung gravel and squealed its tires as it reentered the highway. . . .

. . . .

SEPIDEH WALKED THROUGH the front door and slid her schoolbooks onto the table by the staircase. Then she went into the kitchen where her mother was seated, reading a newspaper. With a thoughtful look on her face, the girl drew herself a small glass of tea from the samovar and sat down beside her mother.

Esther glanced up from her reading. "Hello, dear. How was school today?"

"Fine," replied Sepi, without much conviction. A

small plate in the center of the table contained a few dried apricots and almonds. Idly, Sepi nibbled an almond as she sipped her tea.

Again Esther looked up at her daughter. "What's the matter, Sepi? Are you sure nothing happened at school to upset you?"

The girl shook her head. "No, Mother, nothing happened. I was just thinking about . . . everything that's going on." Her eyes dropped to her hands.

The newspaper rustled as Esther folded it and carefully regarded her daughter. Sepi glanced up at her mother, then looked out the window. Hesitantly she began again. "There was a girl at school today, the daughter of a government minister. She was wearing a *chador*. It was the first time I have ever seen one on anybody besides an old woman."

Esther remembered hearing her mother speak with disgust about the heavy black *chador*, a loose, sleeveless draped garment which covered a woman from head to toe. Only a small space for her face was allowed, lest any man other than her husband or father see her hair or body and be incited to lust. Like many women, Esther's mother had celebrated the more liberal policies of the Pahlavi rulers by burning her *chador*. That had happened even before Esther's birth. Esther had a *chador*, kept for the rare occasions when they visited the home of a devout Muslim. She had worn it perhaps five times in her life. But now schoolgirls were wearing the hated symbol of repression. "The moving prison returns," said Esther softly to herself.

"What?"

"Oh, nothing. I just remember my mother talking about how much she despised wearing the *chador*. She called it a moving prison."

Sepi looked at her mother, concern etching deep lines in her forehead. "Mother, are we going back to the past? Will I be forbidden to learn foreign languages or mathematics? Will I have to wear one of those . . . things . . . when I go to school?" Distaste curled a corner of Sepi's mouth as she pondered the prospect.

Esther sighed. "I don't know, my darling. I hope not."

"Me too." Sepi stared at her tea glass, thinking about how Khosrow would react if she approached him wearing the huge black tent. She gave a slight shudder. "I'd better get started on my work," she said, rising from the table and walking toward the staircase.

Esther watched her daughter gather her books from the small table. She thought about the possible consequences of an Islamic hierarchy. With no counterbalancing forces, what edicts might they impose on the country? Things worse than the *chador* could lie in Sepi's future.

Again she picked up the paper, turning to where she had left off. In a lower corner, a small headline caught her attention. Reading, she felt her face freezing in apprehension.

AGAIN EZRA SCANNED the small article. Then he looked up at his wife. "I don't like the look of this at all."

She waited, her eyes flickering from his face to the paper he held in his hand.

The headline, tucked innocuously into a society section of the paper, read, "Minister Announces Vacation for Royal Family." The article contained a blithely worded announcement by the Minister of the Court of an impending foreign junket by the Shah and his wife, Queen Farah.

"It is impossible for me to believe the Shah would go on vacation with all the turmoil in the country," said Ezra gravely. "Whom does he imagine this will deceive?"

Esther looked back at him, her eyes pleading for reassurance, yet expecting none.

"With matters this far advanced, I had better do something about selling the business, and soon," Ezra mused, worriedly. "When the news of the Shah's leaving becomes widely known, the breakdown in the country will go like wildfire. If that happens, our chances of getting a decent price for the store will be almost nil."

"If things are as bad as that, why not just get out of the country and leave the store for the mullahs to run?" Esther asked bitterly.

Ezra's eyes flashed as he looked up at her. "I will *not* leave Iran a pauper," he said in a voice which cracked like a quiet whip. "I have worked too long and too hard to walk away from everything without at least trying to take with me some of the fruit of my life's toil."

Esther held his eyes for a moment, then looked away. Her shoulders sagged and she covered her face with her hands. "I'm sorry," she said softly. "I just find it so hard to believe that an entire nation can go instantaneously insane."

When she looked up again, Ezra was not there. She found him at the desk in his study, with paper and pen, making drafts for a newspaper advertisement. Looking over his shoulder, she read, "For Sale: A Profitable Business in a Prime Location."

Pruning.

EZRA UNLOCKED THE DOOR to his shop and went inside. Placing his briefcase on the desk behind the counter, he unfolded the newspaper he had purchased and turned hurriedly to the advertisements. Running his finger along the columns, he found the ad he had placed.

He heard the tinkling of the small brass bell over the front door and looked up to see Firouz entering. Quickly he folded the paper, sliding it into the lap drawer of his desk.

"Good morning, *Aga* Solaiman," mumbled Firouz, looking at the floor.

"Good morning," returned Ezra. "It's good to see you back at work. Are you feeling quite well?"

Firouz quickly glanced up at his employer, but he could find no trace of irony in Ezra's look or demeanor. Again his eyes fell. "Yes, *Aga* . . . I think I had a case of the flu." He shuffled his feet and thrust his hands into his pants pockets. "But I feel fine now." He coughed slightly, for effect.

Ezra eyed him for a moment. "Good. Then you may begin unpacking the consignment we just received from Sandoz—the large boxes in the back. Be sure to check the invoices against the packing lists."

Firouz shuffled toward the back of the store. From the corner of his eye, Ezra thought he saw his assistant toss a glance at him over his shoulder as he went into the storeroom.

From just inside the storeroom door, Firouz peeked back inside the shop, at Ezra seated at his desk. He wondered what the old Jew was so nervous about and watched as Ezra quietly slid open the lap drawer and carefully produced a newspaper. He eased open a page, looked for a moment, then just as quietly folded the paper and replaced it in the desk drawer.

Thoughtfully, Firouz turned to the task Ezra had assigned him. He decided to keep an eye open around here for a few days. Something was going on.

FIVE

SEPIDEH SOLAIMAN POUTED as she walked along the hallway. Khosrow had not met her by the stairway. She had waited for him for almost twenty minutes, until she feared being tardy.

As she approached the doorway of her classroom, she froze. Khosrow was there, surrounded by five or six other boys who were shoving and slapping him. Just as she was about to whirl and race in search of a teacher, a principal of the school rounded the corner at the far end of the corridor, and Khosrow's attackers vanished.

"Khosrow!" she screamed, dropping her books in a clattering pile as she rushed to him. He leaned against the wall by the doorway, panting. His shirt was torn and blood seeped from the corner of his mouth. "I was going to surprise you here, instead of by the stairway," he gasped. A curious crowd began to gather, students pausing on their way to classes to observe the unusual scene.

Her eyes wide in shock, Sepi gazed about her. Then she saw her desk, just inside the doorway of her room. Someone had carved a series of jagged, angry letters across the wooden desk top, INFIDEL JEW.

The bell for classes rattled in the hallway, but the silent ring of students gathered about Khosrow and Sepi made no move toward their rooms.

Down the hall, the principal took in the scene. He

45

watched them for a moment, then walked away.

In a daze, Khosrow said, "I saw what they were doing, and I yelled at them, but there were too many. One of them I have known since first grade. . . ."

Sepi walked blindly into the classroom, oblivious in her shock to the stares as she passed through the students. She rubbed the heel of her hand across the splintered defacement on her desk, vainly trying to scrub the damning slogan from her life. But the boys had carved far too deeply for such easy removal. This would never be erased, she realized. She looked about her in consternation. Mute, unreadable faces returned her gaze. They seemed to be closing in on her, threatening her. She raced for the nearest door.

"Sepi! Sepi, come back!" Faintly she heard Khosrow's voice through the fog of her panic. Then she was outside.

ESTHER TIPPED the threadbare delivery man, took the letter from his hand, and watched as he walked slowly away. Closing the gate behind him, she glanced down at the return address. The writing was in Moosa's familiar, hurried hand, and she smiled as she eagerly tore open the thin red-and-blue-bordered airmail envelope.

Dear Mother and Father,
Each day the news from Iran is more and more disturbing. On the TV they show scenes of rioting in the streets of Tehran, of chanting crowds holding up posters of Khomeini. I am worried sick about you and Sepi.

I think you should all leave Iran at once. I will help you arrange everything. In fact, I will come there and help you get your affairs in order.

Please write me soon and let me know how you are. And think seriously about what I have said.

Love,
Moosa

46

Esther crumpled the envelope in her fist as angry tears stung her eyes. Now Moosa too! He wanted her to discard everything, as though their lives here were shed as easily as a worn garment! She teased at the thought that Ezra had written their son, enlisting his support in persuading her to accept this hateful uprooting.

Behind her, the gate rattled open and clanged shut. She turned just as Sepi, her chest heaving with great, wet sobs, flung herself into her mother's astonished arms.

"Sepi! What is the matter, my darling? Why are you not in school?"

A wordless wail of fear and pain was her only answer, as Sepideh clutched herself tightly to her mother, her face buried in Esther's shoulder.

EZRA STOOD ON THE SIDEWALK outside the mosque, feeling more conspicuous by the minute. Anxiously he scanned the faces of those entering and leaving the house of worship, searching for Mullah Hafizi. At last the aged clergyman came into view, rounding a corner and crossing the courtyard of the mosque toward Ezra, who now breathed a little easier. Then he remembered why he was here, and again felt the bands of apprehension tighten about his chest.

Hafizi walked up to Ezra, carefully studying the nervous face of his Jewish friend. "Are you certain you are prepared to go through with this?" he asked.

Ezra nodded. "I am, *baradar*. I think it is necessary."

A moment more the mullah searched the eyes of the druggist. "It is possible that your proposal may be received with suspicion, despite all demonstrations to the contrary," he said. "I will do what I can, but . . ." Hafizi shrugged.

Ezra's mind whirled. Like a sheep treading among wolves, he was about to enter the presence of a senior

47

official of Islam. Would Hafizi betray the tenuous confidence placed in him? Would he revoke his intention to aid Ezra, or did he merely try to warn of the very real possibility of failure? Ezra took a deep, quavering breath before speaking.

"My friend," he began in a low voice, "I have opened my mind to you. Already you know enough to cause the failure of my plans. When I spoke with you in your house, by that very act I was committed to this attempt." His eyes darted nervously about for a moment, then came to rest imploringly on Hafizi's face.

The mullah again shrugged, and beckoned Ezra inside. "Wait!" hissed Hafizi, pointing at Ezra's feet. "You must not enter holy ground wearing shoes!"

"Of course," laughed Ezra nervously, when he regained his voice. "You would think a descendant of Moses would remember such a thing!" Cautiously he retraced his steps to the outside, removed his shoes, and reentered the mosque, placing first his right foot inside the portal, then his left, in accordance with Islamic custom. Hafizi took his arm and led him toward the chambers of the *mojtahed*. "In the name of Allah the Merciful and Compassionate," Ezra whispered under his breath as they walked down the colonnade.

THE PHONE JANGLED in its cradle. Firouz paused in his sweeping, leaning the broom against a wall. He picked up the receiver, waiting for the caller to identify himself.

"This is Nijat," crackled the voice on the other end. "I am calling to inquire about the ad placed in the newspaper. Is this the Nasser Pharmacy?"

"Yes," replied Firouz cautiously, "but I am Marandi, the assistant. The owner is not here. What ad is it you speak of?"

"The ad in this morning's paper," said the caller,

impatiently. "When will your boss be back?"

"I don't know," said Firouz, cradling the phone with his shoulder as he opened the desk drawer. The newspaper was gone—the old Jew had taken it with him. "He left about an hour ago—he had to meet someone. He said he would be back before closing time."

After a few seconds of silence the caller said, "All right. Tell your boss that I called. Here is my telephone number." Firouz scribbled a note on the blotter pad atop the desk. The line went dead. His eyes squinted in thought, Firouz replaced the phone in its cradle.

". . . AND SO, AYATOLLAH," finished Hafizi, "I have brought *Aga* Solaiman to you, for I felt confident you would want to know of his generosity."

The *mojtahed* crouched on his carpet like a wizened old lizard. He might have been a painted statue but for his dark eyes which flickered back and forth between Hafizi and Ezra in a mute appraisal that seemed to last for hours. Finally, from within the tangled white bush of his beard, a raspy voice issued.

"You are here of your own free will?" The dark eyes squinted calculatingly at Ezra.

Hesitantly, Ezra cleared his throat, glancing at Hafizi before replying, "Yes, Ayatollah, I am." He fell quiet, his eyes resting on the feet of the *mojtahed*. He reminded himself not to look directly into the eyes of the mullah, for this was considered ill manners.

After another eternal silence, the old mullah asked, "And why should a Jew suddenly have a burning desire to donate one million *tomans* for the expansion of a Muslim graveyard?" The suspicion made the old man's voice brittle. Ezra entreated Hafizi with his eyes.

"As I told you, Ayatollah Kermani," Hafizi said, "*Aga* Solaiman has for some time been known to me for his generosity. I have told you of his kindness to me."

". . . and that is why I wish to help, Ayatollah," inserted Ezra earnestly. "I have always respected the servants of Allah, whether they study the *Koran*, the *Towrat*,* or the *Injeel*.** When Mullah Hafizi told me of the need, I asked him to bring me here."

Another uncomfortable hush fell in the room as the *mojtahed*, still unmoving as a piece of masonry, turned Ezra's proposal back and forth in his mind. Outside in the street, the faint sounds of traffic could be heard. But here, in the darkened room of the mullah, Ezra fancied he could hear the sweat trickling down his back as he awaited the all-important decision of the senior cleric.

Finally the old man stirred enough to signal an attendant who had waited, unseen, behind them during the interview. "Ahmad," he said in his rusty voice, "bring me the stamp and a receipt book."

Ezra felt his insides unwinding with relief. Trying not to grin, he reached into his coat for his wallet. He saw that Hafizi was smiling.

EZRA RETURNED from the appointment with the *mojtahed* to find Firouz's scribbled note on the blotter pad. Not recognizing the name "Nijat," but surmising the call was in response to his ad, he grabbed the phone and dialed the number.

From just inside the storeroom, Firouz listened carefully as the old Jew began speaking.

"This is Solaiman. I believe you called while I was out today. . . . Yes, I placed the ad concerning the Nasser Pharmacy. I see. Yes, *Aga* Nijat, I would most certainly like to meet with you." Ezra glanced toward the storeroom.

---

*Torah
**Gospels or New Testament

Firouz quickly turned away from the doorway, loudly shuffling the invoices on his clipboard. He heard Ezra continue in a lowered voice.

"Perhaps you would care to come to my house? We can discuss the matter at greater leisure. After all, this is a very busy place—customers coming in and out all the time." Ezra gave a small chuckle. "Very good, then. I will look forward to your call." He gave the caller his home telephone number and hung up. Again he glanced toward the storeroom, but Firouz had his back turned, busily matching invoices with shipping labels. Ezra was ecstatic. Two strokes of good fortune in a single day!

In the storeroom, Firouz looked again at the classified section of the paper he had purchased while Ezra was out. He had circled one ad: "For Sale: A Profitable Business in a Prime Location."

S I X

The taxi neared the entrance to Mehrabad International Airport. Two armed pasdars *stood on either side of the gate, looking inside each vehicle as it passed through. The taxi slowed. One of the* pasdars *leaned through the rear window, in Ezra's face. "Who are you and what is your business?" demanded the scraggly bearded guard, scarcely more than a boy, his eyes suspiciously flickering between Ezra and the carrying case.*

Just as Ezra opened his mouth to reply, Hafizi spoke from the front seat. "This man is a friend of mine. He and his wife are accompanying me to the gate where I must meet a plane. Please do not delay us—my business is urgent."

The pasdar *looked at his partner, across the car, and received a slight nod in reply. He stepped back, and impatiently waved the taxi through. He glared after them as they drove toward the customs building.*

. . . .

DIDN'T I WARN YOU something like this would happen? Didn't I tell you it was unwise to continue seeing her?" Khosrow's father spoke quietly, but the anger in his tone was unmistakable. Khosrow kept his face lowered, holding the ice pack to his forehead as much to avoid his father's ire as to reduce the swelling above his left eyebrow.

"Father," he said, "what they were doing was wrong."

53

"That is not what I'm saying, Khosrow. No one knows better than I the injustices being committed in the name of Allah and the so-called Imam Khomeini. Believe me, I know what's going on out there! I deal with it every day at work. It takes all the tact and caution I have to keep my job and stay off the mullahs' purge lists, to survive the craziness in one piece and keep this family from starvation. I only hope you will learn from this, Khosrow. I hope it can teach you the danger of being conspicuous in times such as these. I have learned that I cannot afford rugged individualism just now. You must learn this too."

Khosrow said nothing. His father's advice was nothing new. Since the tide first began to turn against the Shah, most of his parents' conversations with each other, with him, and with his brothers had been variations on a similar theme. He suppressed the flare of indignation burning in his chest. It angered him that he was being chastised for taking a stand. What about the thugs who had carved on Sepi's desk? What were they? Heroes?

"I know you care for this Solaiman girl," his father was saying, "but I am not sure you understand the price you may have to pay for your affection. And not only you, Khosrow. Whole families have been blacklisted because of the activities of a single member."

The silence that followed was a no man's land. Khosrow felt the cold weight of his father's disapproval pressing upon him and knew he was expected to make some apology, some admission of guilt or, at least, of carelessness. He sternly shoved any such words from his mind, his jaw clenched in resentment.

"Think about what I have said," his father finished at last. "Perhaps you will one day see that I have your interest at heart."

As his father rose and walked away, Khosrow slumped lower in the chair, absorbed in the dull ache in his head and the frustration in his mind. When his mother fluttered into the room and fussed over him a bit, he endured it sullenly. He felt relieved when she was gone; right now, he didn't want anyone near him. No one else understood anyway, he thought, grimacing as he shifted the ice pack to the tender place on his cheekbone.

REUBEN IBRAHIM had barely finished securing his rugs for the night. He was just replacing the padlock on his storage closet when a shadow fell across the threshold of his market stall.

"Oh, hello, Hosseini," he said, looking over his shoulder as the lock clicked into place. "I didn't hear you coming. I trust your day was profitable?"

"Not as much so as it might have been," muttered the other man. "But I noticed your trade was respectable, if not brisk."

Reuben tried not to notice the resentment in the other man's tone. "Well, God be praised, yes, it wasn't bad. I sold a number of rugs today, mostly of the smaller sizes. Perhaps, with all the difficulties, the faithful are spending more time on their prayer mats, eh?" He smiled and shrugged.

Hosseini wasn't smiling. He regarded Reuben with a strange, evaluating expression. "These are days when more prayer would not be amiss," he said finally. "In these times, the name of Allah would do well to be on every man's tongue."

Reuben felt his smile wilting. "Of course, my friend," he said, nervously shifting his vision from Hosseini to the briefcase containing the day's receipts. He closed and latched it with more care than he usually felt necessary. "I had no intention of making light of—"

"Of course not," Hosseini remarked in a more normal tone. "You were merely being your usual humorous self. Now, when are you going to sell me this excellent space?"

Reuben gave a mock grimace and held his head in his hands. "Again, Hosseini! Twice today you have put me on the spot!" He picked up the briefcase, walked to the entrance and squeezed Hosseini's shoulder good-naturedly. "And if I sell it to you, my friend, what excuse would you then have to come and talk? I'm afraid I'd grow lonely during the days without your visits."

Hosseini gave him a grudging smile and the two men walked together toward the street.

AMEER NIJAT PRESSED the electric button in the brick wall by the gate. As he waited, he looked about him in the gathering twilight. *Nice area*, he thought. *The fellow who lives in such a place has obviously done well for himself.* Nijat blew into his cold hands as he studied the immaculate grounds of the man with whom he was about to negotiate. He wondered if Solaiman would be difficult to deal with. His son had learned all he could from the druggist he was apprenticed to, and would certainly not get wealthy working for the penurious old scoundrel. The boy needed to try his wings, and the sooner the better. Nijat only hoped that all the money he had poured into the boy's education could someday bear as much fruit as Solaiman's efforts apparently had.

The front door opened and a slender, middle-aged man walked down the brick sidewalk toward him. With the practiced eye of an experienced trader, Nijat began sizing him up.

He was clean-shaven in the Western style, wearing only a neatly-trimmed moustache. He had the dapper air of one accustomed to the finer things. As he walked, he studied the ground in front of him, as if to avoid any potholes which had arrived there since the last time he trod this way. Careful—that was the main impression

Nijat had of the well-manicured man who opened the gate and invited him inside with a genteel bow and spoke in a low, cultured voice, "*Aga* Nijat, I am Ezra Solaiman."

Nijat returned the bow. "And I am your servant, Ameer Nijat." The two men straightened and briefly observed each other, while shaking hands.

Worry. Nijat saw worry unmistakably etched in the creases at the corners of Solaiman's eyes. Then his host turned away, beckoning Nijat toward the house. "Please, *Aga* Nijat. My wife has fresh tea brewing, and some dried figs and almonds. Come in and make yourself comfortable."

Nijat sat at ease in Solaiman's study. As he waited for his host to return, he gazed about appreciatively at the dark paneling, the shelves of richly bound books. Indeed, Solaiman had done well. As Nijat took a deep drag on his Turkish cigarette, Solaiman's wife entered, carrying a tea service for two on a silver tray. Nijat smiled at her. "Thank you, *khanom*,"* he said.

She nodded in return and left the room without further gesture or word. Nijat shrugged. Somehow he had expected a warmer greeting from the wife of a prospective seller. The woman—and handsome she was too— had seemed put off, somehow. Oh, well. She no doubt knew why he was here; and if not, no matter. His business was with the husband.

At that moment, Solaiman came into the room, aiming a worried look back toward the stairs he had just descended. Pulling his eyes away at last, he made a show of briskness as he entered the study. "Good, *Aga* Nijat! I was about to ask you if you cared to smoke, but I see you have already availed yourself, as you should have. And Esther has brought the tea. Is there anything you lack?"

*lady

57

WILLIAM MIRZA // THOM LEMMONS

"*Aga* Solaiman, forgive me, but you seem preoccupied. Is there a problem upstairs you should attend to?"

Solaiman's eyes widened, just before he looked away. "No, *Aga*, not really. My daughter . . . some trouble at school today. It is nothing," he said finally, with a hesitancy which belied his words. "Now," he continued, "what would you like to ask me about my business?"

With practiced deliberation, Nijat reached for a glass of the dark, steaming tea. He placed a sugar lump between his teeth and with elaborate care sipped a swallow of tea through the lump, inhaling the mellow, dusky aroma of the brew. Slowly he set the glass on the table beside the armchair in which he sat. He studied the bookshelves over Solaiman's left shoulder and asked his first question.

"Why do you wish to sell your business?"

A shade too quickly, to Nijat's ear, Solaiman answered.

"*Aga* Nijat, as you can see by our surroundings, the business has done well for me through the years. I have built up a loyal clientele through conscientious service and fair prices. I have worked hard for quite some time, and Esther and I are at the time of our lives when we begin to think of spending more time enjoying what our toil has earned. I want to retire. That is the long and short of it. I am relatively young and in good health, and I want to spend more time with my family." Now Solaiman reached for a tea glass and a sugar lump.

"How long have you been in the pharmacy business?"

"Since college days, some thirty-odd years now." His host took a slow sip of tea. "I opened my first shop in a small storefront on Jabir, just off Shahbaz Avenue. Since then my business has grown steadily."

"Indeed. And have you always lived in Tehran?"

"Oh, yes. My family has always been here."

"How many regular customers would you estimate patronize your store?"

Solaiman's gaze never wavered from Nijat's own as he

set down his tea glass. "Some 300 regulars, and 20 or 30 more who use my services at least once a year." Clearly, the man was primed with all the pertinent facts and figures.

Nijat decided to alter the rhythm of the discussion. After taking a long drag on his cigarette and blowing a leisurely stream of smoke at the ceiling of the study, he leaned comfortably back in his chair and asked, "Do you have children, *Aga*?"

"Oh, yes! We have a daughter, as I mentioned, and a son. . . ." Solaiman's voice seemed to waver for an instant.

"Does your son live here?" asked Nijat quickly.

"No," said Solaiman, after a longish pause. "He lives in America."

Nijat nodded sagely. "It is hard to have one's flesh and blood so far away, *Aga*," he sympathized. *Now we come to it*, he thought.

"I TELL YOU, he is planning something!" insisted Firouz, glaring intently at the man seated across from him. "The old Jew—and probably every other Jew in Iran—has something up his sleeve, and you of the Tudeh sit idly by and do nothing!" Firouz slapped the table in disgust, standing abruptly and striding away to a window.

"We of the Tudeh Party are, at present, content to await the unfolding of developments," agreed the other man, choosing his words carefully. "You must realize, Marandi, that events are still far too fluid to make the sort of assumptions you seem too ready to believe."

"What are you waiting for?" stormed Firouz. "The Shah is all but gone. Thousands desert the army every day. The mullahs crow openly about their imminent victory—"

"Don't lecture me, Marandi!" snapped the party official. "You think because you crouch in alleyways and toss bricks through windows that you *mujahedin* take all the risks. Well, there are battlegrounds other than the streets, my friend. It is far from certain that Tudeh will be able to build a coalition with the Islamic fundamentalists. As you say, the Shah's star wanes. But don't think this means that the Shiites will be any more willing to share the pie with us, simply because the Shah's piece is handed to them."

The politician rose and strode to the window, confronting Firouz. Forcefully he punched the air in front of Firouz's face with his index finger as he continued.

"And don't think I don't understand what this discussion is about. I'm not fooled so easily that I imagine you are motivated by some noble sense of patriotism to report your suspicions of Solaiman's activities. I seriously doubt if you are as concerned with his taking money out of Iran as with getting your hands on some of the wealth. You expect me to use my influence to get Solaiman's property confiscated and handed over to you, Marandi, the loyal pillar of the revolution. Isn't that so? Deny it if you can."

For several moments he glared at Firouz, daring him to contradict the assessment. When Firouz dropped his eyes, the other man snorted as he shook his head. "There are far greater issues at stake in these days, Marandi, than your pocket." Angrily he whirled and walked out the door.

His jaw clenched tightly in anger, Marandi muttered, "And there are other ways to see that justice is done."

NIJAT SNEAKED A GLANCE at Solaiman. His host's gaze was directed toward a dark corner of the study. His eyes had an unfocused, inward look. Nijat rose from his chair and paced slowly to the nearest bookshelf, idly running his finger down the spines of several books. Without looking at Solaiman, he said, "I too have a son, *Aga* Solaiman. It is because of him that I am interested in your business." He glanced over his shoulder at the other man.

With difficulty, Solaiman raised his eyes to briefly meet those of Nijat. "Really?" he managed, with little enthusiasm. "Your son is a pharmacist?"

Nijat nodded. "He's been out of college five years now. He needs to get out on his own and learn what it's like to run a business for himself. I think he's ready, whether he does or not."

Solaiman smiled. "How well I remember the first days, when I was getting started. I was petrified! I feared each prescription I filled would be my last!" He shook his head and smiled.

Casually, Nijat took a string of orange worry beads out of his coat pocket. He began moving two beads at a time along the string. Averting his eyes from his host, he asked, "So, then, *Aga* Solaiman, how much money are you asking for your business?"

Solaiman glanced up sharply. "I don't think it fair to you to quote a price without allowing you a chance to see the store, the inventory, the books—"

"Come, come, *Aga* Solaiman," smiled Nijat, "I'm not asking for an exact figure. All I want is an idea of what you are asking. How else will I know if I can afford to look further?"

Still, his host was hesitant.

"Please, Solaiman," urged Nijat, seating himself again in the chair across from the other man. Earnestly his eyes sought Ezra's. "Don't be so strict with me, eh? For the sake of both our sons—"

Solaiman stiffened, looked piercingly at him, then away. Patiently, Nijat waited. He knew he had struck a nerve. Finally, from far away, Solaiman's voice could be heard.

"Eighteen million *tomans*. And . . . preferably paid in

cash. I am anxious to begin my retirement."

Quickly Nijat calculated in his mind. Eighteen million was no joke. But what he had seen this evening convinced him there was a good living to be made from this business if bought as a going concern. He could afford the store, but it was not in his nature to placidly accept a man's first offer.

"Say twelve million, *baradar*," he pleaded, grasping at Solaiman's hand and squeezing like a bazaar haggler. "Twelve million—I will be a happy man, and you a carefree retiree."

Solaiman turned and gave him a look that was at once stern and businesslike. "Friend Nijat, I will not engage in dickering with you this evening. I have given you the indication you asked for. You are free to come and inspect the store and the inventory, as is anyone else who wishes to make an offer. If, after you have seen the business, you still believe my price is too high, you may say so at that time. But for now, I have said all I wish to say."

Nijat knew better than to push harder just now. He released Solaiman's hand. His host stood. "May I expect you to come soon to the store?"

Nijat stood, pocketing his worry beads. "I believe you may, *Aga* Solaiman. As you can see, I am a man who likes to get on with the business at hand. Would tomorrow be convenient?"

Solaiman gave him a curt nod. "I open at 8 o'clock. Now may I get your coat?"

As HE CLOSED the gate behind Nijat, Ezra heard the telephone. He walked in the front door just as Esther hung up the receiver. As she turned to face him, her visage was white, drained of blood.

"Esther! What is the matter?"

Dully, she spoke as she slid into a chair by the tele-

62

phone stand. "That was Moosa," she said.

"Moosa!" said Ezra. "He barely gives us time to read his letter before—"

"Ezra," she said, cutting him short. "Moosa was calling from the airport. He is here, in Tehran."

SEVEN

THE DILAPIDATED CAB rattled at high speed—the only speed Iranian cabbies use—along Shahanshahi Expressway. The hour was late and few cars were on the highway. In the backseat, Ezra sat glumly, as his son looked at him in hurt confusion.

"But Father, I came only because I wanted to help. . . ."

Wearily, Ezra shook his head. "Moosa, you have done a foolish and dangerous thing. Foolish, not least of all because you have left a good job and an excellent salary to come here. Foolish also because, in the very act of sending your last letter, you may have aroused the suspicions of the authorities." He turned to look at his son. "Have you been in the U.S. so long that you assume all countries have the same sacrosanct attitude toward the mails that Americans have?"

Moosa looked down. Ezra continued.

"Dangerous—need I explain?" He glanced at the cabbie, then went on in a lower voice, barely audible above the groaning, roaring noise of the cab as it rolled down the highway. "Why could you not have simply remained where you were? You were safe there."

They arrived in front of Ezra's gate. Handing Moosa's leather valise to Ezra, the cabbie closed the trunk lid. Ezra paid the fare, including a generous tip for the lateness of the hour. "Many thanks, *Aga*," oozed the obsequious cabbie as he got back in his vehicle. "May Allah grant you long life."

"Indeed," muttered Ezra under his breath. The cab drove off with a clanking of fenders and a squealing of fan belts. They went in the gate, closing it behind them.

THE MORNING sun streamed brightly through the windows of the pharmacy as Nijat sat at the desk, calculator in hand, carefully thumbing through stacks of invoices and shipping manifests. He looked at Ezra over the tops of his reading glasses.

"*Aga* Solaiman, how much did you say you paid for the last shipment from Switzerland?"

Ezra sat in front of the desk, pensively cleaning his fingernails as he stared out the front door. He started and looked at Nijat.

"Pardon me, *Aga,* could you repeat your question?"

Nijat smiled. "Again you are very preoccupied, my friend."

"I'm sorry." Ezra gave a weak smile and spread his hands. "I seem to have a great deal on my mind these days."

Thoughtfully Nijat nodded. "Indeed, *Aga* Solaiman. I asked how much you paid for the shipment reflected on this latest manifest." He indicated the stack of papers in front of him.

Ezra squinted as he tried to recall the figure. "Five million *tomans*," he said, finally, "or thereabout. Of course, that was paid several months ago. I am expecting another shipment from Ciba-Geigy within another month or so, for which I can furnish order forms. Its wholesale purchase price was around three million *tomans*. By now, inflation being what it is, the current wholesale value of the two shipments should be close to . . ." Again he squinted one eye at the ceiling, in calculation. "Eight point three million. Wouldn't that be about right?" he asked Nijat.

Nijat nodded, rubbing his stubbly chin. "I would say so, *Aga*. Or close to it. Do you have a sales ledger?"

"Of course," said Ezra. "Look in the bottom desk drawer, on the right."

Nijat shuffled around in the drawer. "Ah, yes. Here it is." Sliding the manifests to one side, he laid the scarred, black leather-bound ledger book in front of him. He turned a few pages and pursed his lips, nodding in approval. "By the way, *Aga* Solaiman," he asked, glancing up at Ezra, "which set of books is this—the actual sales or the figures you use for tax reporting?"

Ezra leveled a steady gaze at the other man. "I don't keep two sets of books, *Aga*. The figures you see in that book are the actual figures." Ezra held his eyes until Nijat shrugged in acceptance and returned his attention to the ledger.

The bell over the door jangled, and both men looked up. Firouz stood in the doorway, momentarily startled by the sight of Nijat huddled behind the stacks of paper on the desk.

"Come in, Firouz," beckoned Ezra. "I want to introduce you to *Aga* Ameer Nijat." Cautiously, Firouz approached the two other men.

Ezra glanced at Nijat before speaking. "*Aga* Nijat is— a business associate of mine. *Aga* Nijat, this is Firouz Marandi. He has been with me here for three years." Firouz, his eyes downcast, nodded briefly at the other man.

Not to be trusted, thought Nijat. Standing, he said aloud, "*Aga* Solaiman, I believe I have seen enough for now. I will call you within a day or two to continue our discussion."

"I will eagerly expect your call," said Ezra, rising to show Nijat to the door.

When they had reached the doorway, Nijat turned to Ezra. "Tell me, I seem to remember a little restaurant in this area which used to serve an excellent *chillow* kabob. Is it still open?"

"If you mean the small open-air cafe around the corner, yes," answered Ezra. "Perhaps you would care to meet for lunch sometime?"

"Good idea," returned Nijat. "I'll call soon." He left, and the bell rattled as the door closed behind him. Ezra turned around. Firouz was staring at the pile of documents on the desk. He glanced up, saw Ezra watching him, and quickly turned to go toward the storeroom.

KHOSROW LOOKED at himself in the hallway mirror, shaking his head at what he saw. A rumpled young man stared back at him—a far cry from his neat, pressed appearance of only a few weeks before.

This was the accommodation he had made to his father's wishes, to at least try to avoid looking like a Westerner. He had convinced himself that it did no one any good for him to get killed over the cut of his trousers.

His family had made the expected adjustments. When his mother and sisters went out, they wore the drab *chador*. His father had begun allowing his beard to grow out, and had removed the portrait of the Shah which had hung in the living room for as long as Khosrow could remember. Mother had bought a portrait of Khomeini, but his parents, despite their anxiousness to avoid trouble, had not yet been able to bring themselves to hang it.

A part of Khosrow was ashamed of such compromises. To knuckle under, to abandon loyalties when they became untimely—wasn't this the mark of cowardice? Was that what the Islamic uprising was teaching him—that he had no true convictions?

He thought of Sepi Solaiman, and he turned away

from the mirror. Sepi was by far the most difficult question he had to answer for himself. He was quite smitten with her, but . . . could his father be right, after all? Could he afford the luxury of indulging his feelings in these difficult times?

Again he felt the angular fists of his boyhood friends as they cuffed and slapped him, heard the cruelty in their voices as they taunted him for defending an infidel. These were not the faces he had known, not the voices of boys he had played soccer with on bright afternoons. These were young, vicious strangers who attacked him—their faces masks of mob fervor, their voices darkened and curdled by the simplistic hatred of the pack. That had hurt worse than the blows—that the friendship of years and innocence should be so casually swept away by the torrents of hatred flooding this country. He had thought friends were friends. It was a hard thing to learn that this wasn't always so.

His conclusions were very troubling to Khosrow. It was so unfair. Why should anyone else care that he had feelings for a girl of another faith? Why did the world have to intrude on his emotional territory? Why couldn't they all just mind their own business? He felt the old resentment boiling up within him.

And yet . . . why couldn't he make up his own mind about what to do? He looked at himself a final time and turned away in disgust. Grabbing up his schoolbooks, he slouched out the front door.

MOOSA SNORTED as he tossed the newspaper onto the kitchen table. "Whom does the Shah imagine he is fooling?" he demanded loudly. "Vacation, indeed! In the streets the barefooted ones chant, 'Death to the Shah!' What does he do? Climbs aboard his Learjet and flies away to a carefree holiday in the Alps!" Moosa shook his head in disgust as he sipped his coffee.

69

"What would you have him do," asked Esther bitterly, "publish the news that the rightful king of Iran is afraid for his life and is fleeing the country with his family while there is still time?" Angrily she punched and slapped the bread dough between her hands, her back to her son. "He cannot depend on his army or on his own secret service. Would it be better that he stay here to die at the hands of the mullahs? Or escape and perhaps return when the country comes to its senses?"

Moosa heard the resentment in his mother's voice, but her obstinacy galled him. "Mother, this country won't come to its senses. Why can't you accept the fact? Better that you get out and come to America. There, at least, you don't have to be so careful about being Jewish. Iran will soon belong to the mullahs and the Islamic fanatics. Why not leave while you can—like the Shah?"

Esther whirled about, her jaw clenched. "Moosa," she grated, "you may have learned to think like an American, but I have not. This country has existed for over 2,000 years, and for all of that time has been governed by a king. Your promised land across the ocean has been there barely 200 years." She glared at him until his eyes dropped guiltily. "So watch your mouth," she continued. "Others remember and cherish what you have apparently forgotten." She stalked past him, wiping her hands on her apron.

SEPIDEH STOOD by the stairway in the main hallway, feeling hostile stares slide across her as the other students passed. She was afraid to come back to school, but her father told her she would be all right. She wasn't so sure, but he seemed to feel it was important that she maintain a normal routine—avoid unusual appearances, he said. So here she stood, feeling very conspicuous.

The surge of Islamic fervor became more apparent

each day. Some of the boys were allowing their scant whiskers to grow, and several girls wore *chadors* to school now. One of them passed her, the loose black cloth of the shapeless garment swishing about her ankles. From within the folds of the garment, the guarded eyes of the girl stared at her as she walked past. Sepi shivered. Right now she would almost welcome the *chador;* at least it offered a veil of anonymity. Better than being exposed and vulnerable, as she was now.

"Good morning, Sepi."

She whirled about. Khosrow smiled back at her.

"Why must you always sneak up behind me like that?" she demanded.

He chuckled. "I like seeing your eyes when you're surprised."

She squinted at his face. "Are you letting your beard grow?" she asked suspiciously.

Khosrow shrugged, looking away. "Everyone's doing it. Why not?"

"Next I suppose you'll be asking me to wear a *chador.*"

He glanced back at her, then away, saying nothing. A long, awkward silence limped past.

"Well . . . we'd better get to class," he managed, at last.

Sepi held out her hand. Glancing up and down the hall, Khosrow hesitantly took her hand as they walked toward their classrooms. Sepi looked at him questioningly, but he stolidly kept his eyes ahead.

EIGHT

THE FIRST DAY OF February sparkled with the crystalline clarity of midwinter. Sunlight glinted from the wings of the Air France jetliner as it banked to make its final approach to the runway at Mehrabad Airport.

Thousands of people, crammed into the terminal building or peering from cars parked willy-nilly along the expressways around the airport, anxiously followed the plane's graceful, slow-motion descent as its wheels reached from the underbelly of the aircraft, then touched the tarmac. All across Iran, millions of eyes were riveted to television screens, millions of ears anxiously turned toward short-wave radio broadcasts from the BBC, as every nuance of this moment was recorded for posterity. The airliner, now taxiing toward its berth, carried the triumphant long-distance rebel, Ayatollah Ruhollah Khomeini. The victor returned to Tehran to claim his prize.

Devout Muslims rushed toward the aircraft, even before it had fully stopped, hoping to catch their first glimpse of this man whose voice they had heard for so long, yet whose face they scarcely knew. A cheering, jostling crowd greeted the stooped, white-bearded old man who made his way carefully down the steps from the plane, lifting him gleefully onto its shoulders, parading in triumph toward the van waiting to carry him to the first of many speaking engagements. Along the route of Khomeini's entourage, hordes of the Shiite faithful packed the roadsides. For the poor, the devout, and the revolutionaries, this was a day of delirious joy.

Others, watching from greater distances, witnessed Khomeini's triumphal entry with fear and trepidation.

"I have dreaded to see this day," intoned Abraham Moosovi, from the armchair where he sat. A group of friends gathered before the television in Ezra Solaiman's study, witnessing the arrival of the *Imam*, as Khomeini was now being styled. "And yet," continued the rug exporter after a thoughtful pause, "I find that I am also strangely relieved. At least the waiting is over. Now we know for certain who will run the country."

Ezra looked gravely at the other man, then at the somber faces of the rest of the group. "What you say is true, Ibrahim," he said. "And yet I cannot help thinking that things may get worse before they get better. We may look back on the days before this and remember them fondly."

Some of the women wept softly. All felt the stomach-churning malaise of apprehension. No one knew what Khomeini's first acts would be. It was within his power as *Imam* to declare a *jihad*, if he chose. Against whom would the new *de facto* ruler of Iran direct his first assault? The Christians? The Baha'i? The Jews? For all his faults, the Shah had been able to protect the religious and ethnic minorities in Iran. But he was gone. They watched as their new leader, clad in a black camel-hair robe and turban, delivered an emotional speech to a huge crowd gathered at one of the city's largest cemeteries.

"In the name of Allah the Merciful and Compassionate," Khomeini began, standing beside the grave of one of the hundreds of Shiites slain during the uprising. Pointing to the gravestone, he shouted at the admiring throng, "Is this the meaning of 'human rights'? "

The crowd's roar filtered through the speaker of Ezra's television set, filling the room. Khomeini was making an obvious reference to the issue which had helped alienate the Shah from his American protectors.

"Never again," the Ayatollah continued, "will an innocent Muslim die at the hands of the traitors of Islam." Another huge cheer ripped through the increasingly zealous crowd. "Never again will this land be ruled by infidel ideologies. Never again will Iran be ruled by a monarch."

"I would not want to be sitting where Bakhtiar is today," remarked another of Ezra's guests. Appointed prime minister by the Shah before his departure, Shahpur Bakhtiar was charged with the hopeless task of seeking a coalition with the antiroyalist factions. The most optimistic gave him weeks; the more realistic allowed scant days before the tides of anarchy swept aside this last vestige of the Pahlavi regime. Already the crowds in the streets chanted death slogans with Bakhtiar's name attached. "He will be brought down for no reason other than his association with the Shah," agreed another. "And for this crime he will have no defense."

"I have heard people say that the army is defecting en masse," said Moosa, seated by his father. "Barracks are being looted. Rifles are for sale in the covered bazaar at ridiculously low prices, and there is no control whatsoever."

"The war has only begun," mused another. "With the Shah gone, the *mujahedin* and Tudeh will be trying to carve their own pieces from the corpse of this country. We have not seen the end of the bloodshed, by any means."

Another cheer erupted from the crowd on the television screen, as a glum silence fell over the group gathered in the house of Ezra Solaiman.

AMEER NIJAT TOTALED the column of numbers he had written on the note pad, then rubbed his chin thoughtfully as he slowly drew several lines beneath the final sum. Solaiman indeed had a gold mine. As the druggist had correctly calculated, the increase in the market value of his inventory alone was enough to return a decent dividend to a purchaser such as himself.

Nijat leaned back in the chair behind his desk, looking up at the ceiling, which needed paint. He lived in a modest five-room house in an average neighborhood. Years ago he had decided that displaying one's wealth was an invitation to those less willing to work for riches than steal them. But he was a man of more than modest means.

He had started as an apprentice to a printer in Tabriz. Through years of hard work and shrewd dealing, he had built up a very profitable printing business of his own, selling it for a large profit at the beginning of the oil boom of the early '70s. Nor had he allowed his money to remain idle. He had speculated in oil futures and precious metals—both with tremendous success. He knew when to seize an opportunity, and he sensed the Nasser Pharmacy was a plum ripe for the picking.

He reviewed in his mind the salient facts of the business. Solaiman, a Jew, wished to sell his business. The price he asked was reasonable. The inventory, the sales records, the overhead—all were as described.

Nijat glanced down at the day-old newspaper on his desk. Prominently featured on the front page was a large photograph of Ayatollah Khomeini, awash in an adoring mob of supporters. This was the future of the country. Even the children knew it.

So then, whispered Nijat's intuition in his ear, *why does this successful Jewish businessman choose this particular moment in history to liquidate his enterprise and reunite himself with his son in America? Could it be because he is anxious not to live in an Islamic state? Could it be that he senses, as does anyone with an ear to the ground, that Iran will not be a pleasant place while the mullahs, repressed for so long under the rule of the Shah, avenge themselves on their real and imagined enemies?*

Eventually the fury of the mullahs would blow itself out for lack of a target, and by then Nijat's son would be firmly established as the proprietor of a well-known pharmacy. With his son's education and his own business sense, Nijat failed to see how this could be a losing proposition for him. Unfortunate that Solaiman did not have what Nijat possessed—the ability to lie low, to remain inconspicuous. Unfortunate, indeed, for *Aga* Solaiman. Nijat shrugged. Business was business. He picked up the phone and dialed Solaiman's number.

MOOSA PLACED the *rial* notes on the table beside his empty plate and left the cafe. He walked slowly up Pahlavi Avenue, his eyes scanning the newspaper as he strolled along the sidewalk. In these days, it grew more and more difficult to learn what really went on, as the Islamic majority, egged on by the constant propaganda of Khomeini's swelling retinue, gradually tightened its grip on the country. About the best one could do was read the paper and adjust the facts for the blatantly Shiite slant given to every event.

As he walked, he read a story about a woman who had acid thrown in her face by one of the recently appointed *pasdars.* In the article, the armed guard was quoted as saying, "The infidel woman refused to wear the *chador,* according to the Imam's latest order. She had to be punished for disobedience to the laws of decency." The story pointed out that the Imam had decreed that all women, even non-Islamic residents of the country, were obliged to obey the order. If they were seen in public without their heads covered, they were subject to arrest and trial for adultery, since they were presumed to be harlots.

A commotion erupted from one of the shops ahead. Moosa stared at the angry knot of men which boiled out onto the sidewalk. Three *pasdars* shoved and kicked a man Moosa recognized as the son of Abraham Moosovi. One of the guards gave the fellow a final shove which sent him slamming into the door frame of the shop. The three armed peasants turned and swaggered away, laughing among themselves. Moosa rushed up to the beaten man.

"Nathan! What have they done to you?" He bent down and grabbed the slumping man around the waist, pulling one of Nathan's arms across his own shoulders. "Let me help you back inside." Slack-jawed, Nathan nodded as Moosa half carried him into the shop.

When he had slumped into a chair, Nathan looked up at Moosa. "You . . . you are Moosa Solaiman?"

Moosa nodded, then turned to rummage among the cabinets behind the counter for a rag or kerchief.

"I thought you were in America," puzzled Nathan, as he wiped the corner of his mouth with the back of his hand.

"I was, until last week. I came back to help my father leave this crazy country. Why were those *pasdars* beating you?" Moosa asked, handing a damp cloth to Nathan.

The other man winced as he dabbed gently at his cut face. "Last night looters broke into the shop. . . ." Tiredly Nathan gestured toward the center of the store. Moosa turned to look.

Broken glass littered the floor. Nathan Moosovi sold jewelry and curios — vases, chinaware, and the like — but all the shelves were thrown about, the wares shattered on the floor or missing altogether. In the back of the store, a jagged hole gaped in the heavy steel door of Nathan's strongbox, cut by an acetylene torch. Moosa did not need to look inside to know that all the jewelry in the box had been pilfered.

He looked back at Nathan. "Who could have . . ."

Nathan scoffed at him. "Do you seriously wonder? Who else could have brought an acetylene torch unchallenged into a locked shop? The *pasdars* are behind this—you can bet your life on it. Give a stinking barefoot a rifle and a title from Khomeini, and what do you expect? The ignorant fools have become a law unto themselves, Moosa. I've noticed those three thugs hanging around the area for the past several days now— 'on patrol against enemies of Islam,' they said. I suppose they decided they liked some of my merchandise. And since I am a Jew, they saw little harm in taking what they wanted."

Moosa stared back at Nathan, his eyes wide with the enormity of what he was hearing.

"I went to the police—or what is left of them—this morning and reported the theft. I told them my suspicions. Do you know what they told me?"

Moosa shook his head.

"They said, 'Find the looters and bring them to us, and we will arrest them.'" Nathan snorted in disgust as he stared at the bloody rag he held in his hand.

"I'll tell you this, though," continued the shopkeeper, glaring darkly in the direction the *pasdars* had gone. "The next time those Muslim goons come in here, they'll find me prepared."

Moosa's eyes asked for an explanation.

"Guns are not difficult to obtain, even for a Jew," said Nathan. "You should think about it yourself, Solaiman," advised Nathan. "You are as Jewish as I."

Moosa looked from his friend's battered face to the ruined shop, then outside to the sidewalk.

NINE

The huge, low-ceilinged customs building was a bedlam of voices, a shifting mass of bodies. Thousands of men, women, and children stood in long lines before the low counters, attended by the customs officers. Ezra and Esther, their few pieces of luggage slung on straps across their shoulders, moved slowly along the queue. Sepi stood behind them, beside the carrying case. "If only Moosa were here," she began.

"Quiet, Sepi!" admonished Ezra sternly.

Guards behind the counters methodically searched every piece of luggage placed on the counters. Female agents searched the handbags and bodies of the women passengers. As far as Ezra could see, not a single article was omitted from the scrupulous inspection. Again he felt the sweat trickling down his neck.

Esther craned her neck above the crowd, anxiously searching the throng by the entrance. "Where is Hafizi?" she asked. "He came in with us, didn't he? I can't find him!" Panic began to unravel the edges of her voice.

After an eternity, they reached the inspection counter. "Place everything you have on the counter," ordered the official in a bored voice. He glanced over the handbags and the suitcases, then more carefully studied the plywood carrying case. "What is in this case?" he asked.

"An antique rug I am taking to my cousin," replied Ezra.

"I do not see an export permit for this rug," said the officer. "Open the case. I want to look inside."

EZRA HUNG UP the phone, a grimace contorting his face.

"What's the matter?" Esther asked, as she tipped the bowl she held and doled a serving of steamed rice onto each of the four plates.

"That was Nijat. He has made an offer for the store."

"Why the foul expression, then?"

Ezra looked tiredly at his wife. "He has offered fourteen million *tomans,* paid over a year, or ten million in cash, paid immediately."

She paused, the serving spoon poised in midair. "But we must have the money now if we are to—"

"Yes," Ezra interrupted, "I know. And the business is worth almost twice the cash figure he has offered. But he says he cannot possibly raise so much cash on short notice." Ezra rubbed his face, then his temples. He sighed, looking up at his wife. "I thought Ameer Nijat was by far the best prospect for the quick sale of the store. Now I'm not sure."

"You could make a counteroffer, couldn't you?"

Ezra snorted, and shook his head. "We are hardly in any position to bargain, my dear. If we wait too long, we will be trapped in this country, and may well have our property confiscated by the Islamic government. Which is better—to take less for the business, or to stay and perhaps have it stolen from us by the mullahs?"

Esther opened her mouth to reply, then looked away, biting her lip and remaining silent.

"Nijat is shrewd," mused Ezra. "He knows how anxious we are to leave Iran, whether he truly understands the cause or not. I'm afraid the cards are all in his favor."

"Ezra," began Esther carefully, "are you absolutely sure such haste is necessary? Are you certain the troubles cannot be deflected simply by minding our own business and avoiding attention?"

Ezra stared at her in disbelief. "Still you do not see!" he said, standing angrily and turning away from her. "For all our lives we have avoided attention, but camouflage is no longer possible!" He fumed silently for a few seconds.

He whirled to face her again. "Do you think that simply wearing the *chador* is enough?" he said in a quieter, razor-sharp voice. "Do you really believe that we can draw a veil over ourselves and be left alone?" Esther's eyes flared at him, her shoulders rigid with indignation. He bored ahead, too full of the frustration of his predicament to care how she reacted.

"Isn't it funny, Esther?" he said bitterly. "All of my life, I have worn an invisible *chador*—a cloak of meekness, of caution and accommodation. I have ignored the barely hidden smears against my Jewishness, winked at the simmering hatred of the Shiites. I eagerly embraced the principle of the *chador*, even as you decried and hated it. And now, while the women of this country have the obscuring cloak forced upon them, I have my protecting veil of conformity and anonymity yanked from me. Ezra Solaiman, an Iranian Jew, stands uncovered at last, open to the contempt of all. Despite all my planning, all my wariness, all my attempts to blend into the background, I am exposed by the accident of history to the hostile whims of a regime headed by the sworn enemies of my heritage."

He leaned against the kitchen counter, his anger spent by the rushing torrent of words. Slowly he raised his eyes to his wife's. "We're not talking about inconvenience, Esther," he went on in a beseeching tone. "We're talking about survival. Why do you refuse to admit this? Why can I see it and you can't?"

She went into the dining room, her lips pursed tightly in anger. He sat down beside the kitchen table, his face in his hands. Thoughts and emotions tangled inside his mind. Once more the invisible wall had risen between them, but what else could he do? Every day he waited to sell the store, the price of hard currency would increase. And with each passing hour, the chances were greater that he would be denounced before one of the ad hoc revolutionary committees being organized by the mullahs. Firouz was acting strangely; how much longer before he discerned what was going on—perhaps tried to derail Ezra's plans?

With a soft groan of pained resignation, he reached for the phone and dialed a number. He heard the buzzing, then a click as the phone was picked up. Ezra cleared his throat and managed to say, "*Aga* Nijat? This is Ezra Solaiman. I have thought about your offer." He swallowed several times. "I . . . I will meet you at the escrow office at 8 o'clock in the morning, if that is acceptable."

"AGA IBRAHIM, your prices are the highest in the covered bazaar!" the old woman was saying. "How can you expect a poor old woman such as myself to pay 100 *rials* for a rug this size?"

Reuben assumed a pained, sympathizing expression. "Ah, Farnaz *khanom*," he sighed, "how I wish I could help you! To you, I would gladly give this pitiful little piece for, oh, say . . ." His hands circled in the air as he calculated. ". . . a mere 92 *rials*. But, alas! The villains in Isfahan who shipped this pathetic rag to me charged me murderously! If I don't get 100 *rials* for it, I'll barely make my money back, much less afford the extortion which passes as rent for this unworthy hovel they call a shop." He shrugged helplessly and pulled a string of worry beads out of his pocket.

A few moments later, as Reuben knew she would, the woman gave an exasperated little grunt. "Well," she huffed, "if my husband were alive, I'd certainly never stand for this. And that lazy oldest son of mine doesn't give me the help he should."

"Children are a blessing from God," Reuben agreed, "but they can also be a trial from the devil."

"I should say!" she stated with a firm nod of the head. "That, and with all the trouble in the streets these days—"

"Difficult times for all the faithful, to be sure," Reuben murmured.

"Well, at any rate. I just can't pay 100 *rials* for this rug. The most I could pay would be . . ."

Reuben waited patiently, eyes downcast, unmoving.

"Eighty-five."

"Ninety," he countered, quietly.

"Eighty-seven."

"Done." He rolled up the carpet and handed it to the old woman, while she fished about in her tattered handbag for the currency.

"There. Eighty-seven. But I still think it's too much."

"Farnaz *khanom*, your keen perception is matched only by your deep generosity to a poor merchant," he said in a voice that oozed gratitude. "May this small rug bring you much comfort and happiness."

"Yes, well . . . good day to you, *Aga* Ibrahim."

"And to you." He bowed deeply as she left.

He counted the notes again as she walked away down the covered bazaar. Eighty-seven. Not wonderful, but not bad. And Farnaz *khanom* was, after all, a regular customer. At least ten times, over the last few years, they had reenacted the little pantomime just concluded. Reuben allowed her to work him down a few rials each time, listening patiently to all her complaints about her sons, their wives, the difficulties faced by a widow during these days, and whatever else happened to be on her mind at the moment. Reuben had noticed that whatever the political or economic circumstances,

85

they seemed to weigh especially heavily on widows, at least according to Farnaz *khanom*. He noted with some amusement that Khomeini was already the object of many of the same complaints she used to lay at the door of the Shah.

He had just placed the money in his strongbox when he heard footsteps entering his stall. "Greetings, friends! And how may I help—"

Turning around, he was shocked to see three armed *pasdars* standing in his doorway. He forced a smile back onto his face and finished his sentence. "How may I help you today?"

"You are Reuben Ibrahim, Jewish rug dealer?" one of them grunted.

He cocked his head quizzically. "Is that one question, or two, friend?" he chuckled. "Do you wish to know whether I am Jewish, or whether I am a rug dealer? As to the first; yes, I am Jewish by birth. As to the second, well . . ." He gestured about the market stall.

"We didn't come here to pass the time of day, Jew," another *pasdar* grated. "Come with us quietly, or you'll have worse trouble than you already have."

Reuben felt his face going stiff. "Trouble?" he quavered, striving to keep the confused smile on his lips. "Surely there is some mistake? My selling permit is in order, and I can show receipts for every rug in the—"

"Shut up!" shouted the first *pasdar*. "You are accused of being an enemy of the Imam Khomeini and the holy revolution! You're coming with us immediately!" He laid a hand menacingly on the holstered pistol he wore on his hip.

"Very well, very well," Reuben quavered. "Only let me lock up—"

"No time for that," snarled the third *pasdar*, shoving Reuben. "Someone will lock up for you."

The three *pasdars* snickered behind him as Reuben, blind with fear, stumbled down the bazaar.

EZRA GRUNTED as he levered the handle of the shovel back and forth in the hard earth beneath his basement floor. Two or three more spadefuls should do it, he thought. Then the hole would be deep enough. Wiping his forehead with the back of his hand, he glanced over at the canvas bag on the brick floor of the basement. For the hundredth time, he felt chagrin at how small a bulge the *rial* notes made inside the bag. *Ah, well*, he thought, *it was all I could do*. Again he jammed the shovel into the packed dirt.

He placed the waterproof canvas bag in the hole, then covered it with dirt. He tamped the earth down until it was firm, then repositioned the bricks he had removed. He would take the dirt he had displaced from the hole and scatter it in the garden, then pile firewood atop the bricks. He hoped these precautions would be sufficient. Wiping his hands, he climbed the stairs to the main floor of the house.

Ezra went to the desk in his study and slid out the lap drawer. Lying atop the other contents of the drawer was an envelope containing one million *tomans* which he had segregated from the rest of the sale proceeds now buried in the basement. Idly he opened the package and riffled an end of the bank notes. Today he would go to the covered bazaar and buy American dollars. Ten trips he would have to make, to convert all the money in the basement into hard currency. Trying to do the entire job on a single trip would surely arouse suspicion, and probably make him the target of thieves—either official or unofficial.

Moosa came into the study. "What are you doing, Father?"

"Getting ready to go to the bazaar."

Moosa glanced at the stack of *rial* notes, then back at his father. "Why are you going to the bazaar? The exchange rate at the banks is much more favorable."

Ezra looked at his son. "If you were in power, and

you were worried about people like Ezra Solaiman taking money out of the country, what would be your first
act?" Patiently he waited for Moosa's answer.

His brow wrinkled in confusion, Moosa said, "Outlaw
currency conversion?"

Ezra nodded. "Perhaps. Or, even more effective, require the banks to maintain a list of all customers who
request certain transactions—conversions to American
dollars, for example—and to turn this list over to the
government upon request. What better way to monitor
those who are traveling or doing business abroad? How
simple to arrest those whom the government deems
'enemies of Islam' and confiscate their currency."

Moosa scowled at the floor. The phone rang. Ezra
picked up the receiver.

"I must speak quickly," said a muffled voice he did
not recognize. "Others may be listening. *Pasdars* have
come and arrested Abraham Moosovi. The word is that
he will be shot at sunrise tomorrow."

Ezra felt his face going numb. "Why? For what
crime?" he stammered.

"He is accused of giving money to the State of Israel
and of being an Israeli spy."

"But that is preposterous—"

"Yes, but listen," the voice interrupted. "There's
more. Tudeh operatives have been snooping around this
area, asking for the whereabouts of the Jewish and Baha'i families. Your name has been given to them."

Ezra felt his heart come leaping into his throat.

"You must prepare for the worst. That is all I can
say."

"But, wait!" shouted Ezra. "How do you know? When
will they—" The line was dead.

TEN

EZRA HUNG UP the phone. For ten, twelve heartbeats, he could not move.

"Father! What is it?" cried Moosa, seeing the stricken look on his father's face.

Unhearing, Ezra sprang into action. Stumbling across the room to a bookshelf, he threw aside several handfuls of books, uncovering a wall safe. "Go find your mother," he tossed over his shoulder as he frantically dialed the combination. "Tell her to come here." Flinging open the safe door, he scratched through the documents and valuables in the small space, until with an audible sigh of relief, he found the envelope containing the receipt signed by the *mojtahed* for his contribution to the cemetery. He spun about, and saw Moosa still staring, dumbfounded.

"Go, boy!" he lashed, as his son rushed away. As Moosa ran toward the kitchen, he realized it was the first time he had ever heard his father shout.

Esther came into the study as Ezra, seated behind his desk, was spreading the receipt in front of him. Her face went white as he told her of the phone call he had just received.

"Esther, every second is of the essence. This," he said, indicating the receipt, "could save my life."

"What is it?" she asked, trying to see the writing.

"Never mind! There is no time to explain now. But you must know that if the *pasdars* come and arrest me, they will certainly search me, and find anything I might try to conceal in a pocket. You must help me find a way to sew this into my clothing so that it cannot be easily discovered. If it is taken from me, I have no hope."

Esther wavered on her feet, then seemed to catch herself. Nodding, she said, "Do you still have that old pair of black trousers with the watch pocket?"

Slowly Ezra nodded. "I believe so."

"Good. Get them and bring them to me. I'll go get my sewing basket." She turned and half ran from the study.

Ezra was standing to leave as Moosa came back into the room. "Moosa," he said, "I want you to go to an address on Javid Street." He tore off a corner of notepaper and scribbled a number on it. "This is the home of Mullah Nader Hafizi. You must tell him that I need his help most desperately. Bring him back here with you, if at all possible."

Moosa nodded, jamming the paper into his pocket as he turned toward the front door. He grabbed a coat from a rack by the door and was gone.

ESTHER RIPPED at the seam of the watch pocket in a frenzy of haste. She would fashion the pocket into a pouch long enough to conceal the receipt, then baste the flap closed. As she worked, tumultuous thoughts cascaded through her mind. *So,* she thought, *Ezra's worst fears are realized.* With vicious suddenness, she knew the measure of her vain hopes. She felt empty, dead inside. He had been right all along. And she was too foolish to accept it. She tried to push from her mind the thought that Ezra might not return from his arrest. *Abraham....* She covered her mouth with her hand to stifle a sudden sob. Taking several deep breaths, she returned to her work on the pocket.

OVER AN HOUR LATER, the front door opened. Ezra bounded down the stairs to see Moosa coming in — alone.

"Would Hafizi not come?" Ezra asked, the blood freezing in his veins.

Moosa shook his head. "It's not that. He wasn't home. I waited by his door for nearly an hour, but no one came. I left a note for him to call."

"Of course, he has gone with his wife to Isfahan to visit their daughter," mused Ezra. "Why, on this day of all days? Very well," he said, returning to himself. "Perhaps he will come back within the next day or so. You must keep trying to reach him, Moosa."

Moosa nodded. Esther came down the stairs just then, holding the altered trousers for Ezra's inspection. "Get your paper, Ezra. See if this pocket will serve." She had made the pouch of a thick material, to mask the crackling of the paper if the guard passed a hand over the concealed pocket. She hoped desperately that the ruse would work.

Ezra went into the study and came out moments later, wearing the dark, threadbare pants. Thoughtfully he ran his hand over the location of the pocket. "I think this will serve, Esther," he said slowly. "Let's pray it does."

FIROUZ MARANDI TAPPED the driver on the shoulder. "This is the house," he said. The driver stopped the Mercedes sedan by the curb. Behind them, a van pulled over. Firouz rolled down his window, leaned out, and signaled to the van's occupants.

The side door of the van slid back, and four *pasdars* got out, slinging carbines over their shoulders and adjusting their gunbelts. They swaggered up to the gate of the large house. One of the guards reached for the latch.

A huge black dog bounded from a kennel by the door

of the house, barking furiously and showing his teeth. The guard yanked his hand back from the latch, cursing at the top of his lungs as he fumbled for the snap on the holster at his side.

Ezra heard the commotion outside and ran to a window. "They'll shoot Marjan! The fools!" He raced to the front door and threw it open, springing onto the front porch.

"Stop!" he shouted. "Don't kill the dog! Marjan! Heel!"

Growling and licking his chops, Marjan sank reluctantly to his haunches, never taking his eyes off the strangers who threatened his territory.

Ezra turned his head slightly toward the doorway. "Moosa," he said softly, "don't come outside. Don't show yourself. Do you understand me?" He heard the door click quietly closed behind him. Slowly Ezra descended the front steps and paced toward the front gate.

"Marjan," he commanded when he reached the dog, "kennel." Whining and glancing backward frequently, the dog retraced the path to his lair by the front steps, clearly unwilling to leave his master alone with the intruders.

When the dog had entered his kennel, Ezra turned to face the four surly guards. He managed a weak smile. "My apologies, gentlemen," he began. "Marjan is trained to react somewhat suddenly to guests who do not ring the buzzer by the gate." He indicated the electric button set into the wall by the entrance.

"Are you Ezra Solaiman?" growled one of the *pasdars*. "I am."

"We have orders to arrest you and bring you before a tribunal of the Holy Revolution. You are accused of crimes against Allah and the Imam."

Ezra's eyes went wide. "I . . . I don't understand! I have never—"

"Shut up, Jew!" said another of the bearded guards. "We don't have all day to make conversation. Get out here before we shoot you where you stand!"

Ezra felt the world spinning out of control. Darkness was closing in at the edges of his vision before he managed to catch himself, leaning weakly against the wall by the gate. Panting for air, he said, "May I . . . may I at least go into the house and tell my wife good-bye?"

The patrol commander considered a moment. Grudgingly, he said, "All right. But you can't go inside. Stay on the porch where we can see you, or we'll come inside—and we'll do worse than shoot your dog."

Ezra nodded, still trying to regain his breath. He turned and slowly made his way up the brick walkway, climbing the front steps with leaden feet.

The door opened and Esther stood there, her face a red, wet mask of misery. "Ezra," she moaned, "what will happen?"

"They are taking me away—immediately. I'm accused of crimes against Allah."

"Dogs!" hissed Moosa, standing just behind his mother. Fists and teeth clenched, he growled, "I'll kill every last—"

"Stop!" whispered Ezra. "Stay back, Moosa! If they see you, they may arrest you on the spot! There isn't time for threats. You must watch out for your mother and sister while I am . . . away." The eyes of the father locked with his son's. Moosa stood panting as tears of useless rage ran down his face. After almost a full minute, he wheeled and walked away.

Esther came into her husband's arms. "My dearest love," Ezra whispered into her moist cheek, "take heart. I am not entirely helpless, and perhaps Hafizi will return. Listen carefully. You must have Moosa go to the bazaar and convert the money. He must not take more than a million *tomans* at a time. You will find one million *tomans* in a desk drawer in the study. Use this as bribes for the *pasdars*, if they come back. Give them a little at a time, and perhaps they will leave you alone."

He felt her shuddering with silent sobs as he held her. His own throat closing with emotion, he whispered, "There is much to do. Stay busy. When I come back, I will expect a full report." He forced a flickering smile through the choking anguish in his heart, as he gently raised her chin. She managed a tentative nod before burying her face again in his chest.

After a final, lingering embrace, he turned to go. "Wait!" said Esther, ducking quickly into the house. She reappeared, carrying his warmest coat. "You may need this."

He took the coat from her, dragging his gaze away from her weeping face with great difficulty. Slowly he trudged down the walk toward the waiting *pasdars*. Reaching the gate, Ezra turned for a last look at the house. He saw an upstairs curtain move almost imperceptibly. Opening the gate, he stepped outside.

In the car, Firouz watched in satisfaction as the *pasdars* shoved Ezra into the van. He leaned back in the seat. "Drive on," he said, and the sedan slowly moved away from the curb.

ELEVEN

ESTHER WATCHED THE vehicles drive away. She felt as if she were in a trance. *Can this really be happening?* she wondered. All their lives they had been the model citizens — minding their own business, uninvolved in politics, scrupulously sensitive to the mores and customs of the Islamic majority — and for what? All Ezra's caution, all their attempts to make their world safe had come to this. Wretchedly she turned and went into the house.

She wandered into the drawing room, her elbows gripped to her sides. She stared at the blank space on the wall — oblong and brighter than the surrounding, light-faded paint — where the portrait of the Shah had hung. She remembered how she had felt when Ezra took it down, as if they had personally betrayed the ruler and father of Iran. She had adamantly refused to allow him to hang in its place a cheap print of Khomeini. Now, too late, she knew that she would gladly hang a portrait of the hated Ayatollah in every room of the house, if doing so would ensure her husband's return from the clutches of the *pasdars.*

Behind her, the front door opened. She turned, to see Sepi coming in from school. She heard the sound of Moosa's footsteps as he came down the stairs.

Sepi was looking at her strangely. "Mother," she

asked, "what's wrong? You look like you've been crying." Her eyes went from her mother's face to the somber countenance of her brother, standing dourly by the
stair. She glanced about, then asked, "And where is
Father?"

Esther could contain the riptides of her grief no longer. She collapsed onto the divan, sobbing wildly into her
hands. Sepi stared with frightened eyes from her mother to Moosa, who took her by the arm, guiding her into
the kitchen. "Come in here, Sepideh," he said in a
halting voice. "I don't know how to say this. . . ."

THE VAN STOPPED in front of a massive iron
gate in a dingy, gray wall. From the direction and duration of the drive, Ezra surmised this must be the notori-
ous Evin Prison, made infamous in the days of the Shah
by the occupants—robbers, insurgents, political prisoners—who had disappeared into its maw, never to be
seen again. Ezra turned to the commander of the detail.
"I demand to know under what charges I am brought to
this place."

The *pasdar* sneered. "You demand, do you?" He
leaned forward, until his breath, reeking of curry and
onions, smote Ezra's nostrils like a fist. "Let me tell
you something, scum," he growled. "You are done with
demanding anything. You don't matter a spit to me, and
the sooner you get that through your stupid Jew head,
the better."

Still Ezra did not drop his gaze. "Is this the reason for
my arrest, then—because I am a Jew?"

Snarling, the *pasdar* backhanded Ezra across the face
with a blow that sent him sprawling against the door of
the van. "Get this infidel out of here," he barked at one
of his lackeys, "before I kill him."

Quickly the door was yanked open, and Ezra fell
limply onto the pavement. He was tugged to his feet

with curses and kicks, and shoved against the wall beside the gate. A *pasdar* banged the butt of his carbine noisily against the grille beside the gate. A small panel in the grille slid back, and two eyes glittered at them from inside.

"Open up," the *pasdar* said. "We have a prisoner to bring inside." A few seconds more the eyes flicked back and forth, and then the gate began moving with a grinding, grudging noise of electric motors and winch cables.

When it had slid aside far enough to admit a man, Ezra was pushed through, followed by two of the *pasdars*. They marched him through a concrete courtyard to another wall and a gatehouse. A guard came out, his breath puffing steam in the cool air of the early spring day. Methodically he patted Ezra down.

Ezra shuddered as the man's hands passed over the concealed pocket. He felt the muted crackle of the receipt against his skin, but the guard felt and heard nothing. He stepped back, turning his head toward the gatehouse. "He's clean," he called.

Another guard came from the shelter, carrying a clipboard. He began to ask questions in a bored voice.

"Name?"

"Ezra Solaiman," answered one of the arresting *pasdars*.

"Crime?"

"I have done nothing—" began Ezra.

"Quiet, Jew!" threatened one of the *pasdars*. "You were brought here for a reason, be sure of that. We don't arrest people for nothing. You'll get your chance to prove your innocence before the tribunal."

"But," protested Ezra, "I thought a man was innocent until proven guilty."

"You are a traitor to the Holy Revolution," cut in the other *pasdar*. "And if, by some remote chance, you happen to be innocent, you'll go to Paradise as a martyr when you're shot. So stop sniveling."

The guard with the clipboard glanced up at them.

"Cellblock 5," he said, and motioned toward the gatehouse. The gate creaked open, and once again Ezra was marched forward, into the bowels of Evin Prison.

They walked down a dark hallway stinking of urine and vomit. Despite the claustrophobic press of bodies in the cells, the air inside was dank and cold; Ezra silently thanked Esther for remembering the overcoat. They stopped in front of a cell door. Above the door, red paint peeled from a numeral 5 stenciled on the wall eternities ago. As one of the guards fumbled with a key, Ezra looked between the bars.

The place hardly deserved to be dignified as a cell. It was a sty, a pen for human cattle. The enclosure was about ten meters wide by five meters deep. It had been originally planned as a holding place for perhaps ten men, but at least fifty filthy, pathetic prisoners sat crumpled against the walls or sprawled on the bare concrete floor. A bare light bulb dangled from a naked cord, spreading a squalid glare. In one corner was a dilapidated toilet, stained by frequent overflows. Ezra felt the gorge rising in the back of his throat as the guard unlocked the door and thrust him in among the forgotten souls in this wretched purgatory. The bars clanged shut behind him.

MOOSA WALKED among the stalls at the covered bazaar, uncomfortably aware of the press of the *rial* notes in the breast pocket of his coat. He felt eyes boring into his back, as if each shopkeeper, each patron of the bazaar turned and whispered to his neighbor as Moosa passed. He scarcely had the heart to attempt this mission today, after the wrenching events of the morning. But his father had charged him to do the task, and the effort must be made. He had left Sepi and his mother both weeping, and the lump in his own throat was mitigated only by the urgency of completing what his father had asked of him. In fact, it was more critical now than ever that the preparations for leaving Iran be accomplished. Perhaps there would be only three of them. . . . Moosa shoved the thought down in his subconscious as soon as it appeared.

Finally, he located the booth of a moneychanger. At the front of the stall was a vitrine display case, with a few samples each of Swiss francs, Deutsche marks, Italian lira, and a disappointingly small number of American dollars. The merchant squatted behind the case on an Isfahan carpet which looked deceptively old and worn.

"You want to buy dollars," the merchant said. To Moosa, it didn't sound like a question.

"Maybe," he replied in a carefully neutral tone, "but I don't see how you can help me. You have less than $1,000 here."

"Young friend, I am not so stupid as to display my entire stock," the merchant chuckled, as his eyes slid quickly over Moosa's Western attire and recently shaved face. "Come inside. A man who wants to make a substantial purchase should at least be offered a glass of tea." He rose, smiling as Moosa allowed himself to be led toward the gauze curtain at the rear of the booth.

"Ali, mind the front," said the merchant over his shoulder as he turned to follow Moosa behind the drape. A teenage boy shuffled from the corner he had occupied to the carpet behind the display case, sitting with a loose-jointed motion.

The moneychanger seated himself on a cushion, motioning for Moosa to take the place across from him. He swiveled about, filling two small, clear glasses from a samovar. Placing a bowl of sugar cubes between them, he began the negotiation.

"Now, my young friend, how many dollars do you want to buy?"

Moosa wasn't sure he was ready for a tug-of-war with the moneychanger, but there was no alternative. He took a deep breath as he reached for a sugar cube. He placed it between his teeth, sipping a swallow of tea. Slowly placing his tea in front of him, he looked over the merchant's left shoulder. "I'm not sure. I suppose it depends on your price. How much are you asking for dollars?"

The man shrugged. "The going rate—nine."

"Nine *tomans!*" hissed Moosa. "Only a week ago the official rate was seven *tomans,* five *rials!* You are a thief, my friend!"

The moneychanger affected a pained look. "Young man, I am an honest businessman. Feel free to go any-where in the bazaar. You won't find a better rate on dollars, I promise you." Grumbling under his breath, the fellow took another sip of tea, and drew a string of worry beads out of a pocket.

Moosa thought a moment. The old scoundrel was probably telling the truth. Since the Khomeini regime had halted the banks from selling hard currencies, the only sources for foreign exchange were the independent operators in the bazaars. The government did nothing to interfere with the informal, yet quite brisk trade of men such as this. Given the tight supply, and the in-creasing demand by those who wanted to get out of the country, nine *tomans* to the dollar was quite possible, as badly as he hated to admit it. He decided to try a different tack.

Moosa took another sip of his tea. His eyes studiously fixed on his tea glass, he asked, "How much would I have to buy before you would give me a better price?"

The merchant shrugged, his eyes downcast. "You will have to give me a moment to think," he mumbled. "I'm not accustomed to having my ethics impugned by young striplings."

Moosa grimaced inwardly, but said nothing.

In a couple of minutes, the old man looked up, his eyes sliding past Moosa's face to gaze at a dark corner of the room, just under the roof. "Perhaps I can give you some discount for volume. How much currency do you want?"

Moosa avoided answering directly. "I only have about 300,000 to exchange today. But, if I get a favorable rate. . . ." He allowed the end of the sentence to dangle tantalizingly between them.

The moneychanger snorted. "Ah! A big shot! Do you think I can afford to discount my wares for every fledgling financier who swaggers into my booth? Just because you've been across the ocean, boy, don't think I'm a stupid peasant!"

Now it was Moosa who shrugged. "Do as you like, old man," he intoned in a bored voice. "I'll buy my dollars somewhere—if not from you, then from someone else. Thank you for the tea." He rose to his feet as if to leave.

The merchant's eyes widened. He had not expected such a calm rebuff to his offensive. "Wait," he stammered as Moosa turned to leave, "300,000 *tomans?*"

Moosa glanced back at him, nodding slightly.

"Well, if things are as you say. . . ." The moneychanger tugged at his beard, frowning. "How about— eight *tomans*, seven *rials?*" He cut his eyes upward hopefully.

"Eight and five," Moosa shot back, without moving.

The merchant grimaced and looked away. Presently he stood, and gripped Moosa's hand, squeezing as he importuned the younger man. "I like you, boy—you remind me of my oldest son. Won't you take eight and seven? It's below the market rate, and I can give you my oath before Allah for that. . . ."

"Eight and six," countered Moosa, "and I won't pay any more." He tried to pull his hand away from the haggling merchant.

The older man sighed, his shoulders drooping. "Ah, well. You are a stubborn and heartless young man, but . . . all right. Eight and six."

Moosa watched as he went to a padlocked chest in the rear of the room. Glancing back at Moosa a final time, the moneychanger shook his head in regret, took a key from a chain about his neck, and bent toward the lock.

MOOSA WALKED through the bazaar with a spring in his step. He felt elated; he had bargained a better rate for the currency exchange, and felt sure he could squeeze a few more decent trades out of the same fellow. If not, he could use the lower rate as a bargaining tool with other moneychangers.

Just as he reached the entrance to the covered bazaar, his eye fell on a display case near the outside street. It contained handguns: Berettas, Walthers, Kalashnikovs, and a few Smith-and-Wessons. Entranced, Moosa walked over to the case, admiring the dark sleekness of the weapons, the sensuality of their curves, the magnetic aura of nascent danger they emitted. He remembered the helpless feeling he had when the *pasdars* came for his father, and the muttered threat of Nathan Moosovi.

He glanced up at the attendant. "How much for the guns?" he asked.

TWELVE

EZRA STEPPED GINGERLY among the bodies, making his way toward a small vacant space along the far wall. Some of the men on the floor looked like corpses; their jaws were slack, their eyes vacant. Only their faint, shallow breathing gave any indication they still lived.

Ezra reached the far corner of the cell, carefully lowering himself so as to avoid touching the foul-smelling wretch on his right. To his left, a prisoner who looked more alive than most of the others turned his head as Ezra sat down.

"I think I know you," the fellow said slowly.

Ezra looked at his cellmate, puzzled at being recognized by anyone in this hellhole. "Were you speaking to me?"

"Yes, I've seen you somewhere. Are you a doctor perhaps?"

"Not a doctor, but I did own a pharmacy—on Khosrow Nasser."

"Yes! That's it!" the man said, with something like enthusiasm. "You're the fellow who gives medicine to the poor. You helped a relative of mine, some time ago. I brought my aunt to you when a friend of ours recommended you." The prisoner grinned, obviously pleased with himself for making the connection. Then he looked back at Ezra with a puzzled expression on his face. "What are you doing in this rat's nest?"

"I don't know," said Ezra dejectedly. "The *pasdars* wouldn't tell me, other than to say it was up to me to prove my innocence to the tribunal."

"Those motherless curs," spat the other man. "They don't need a reason. Khomeini is their reason.... Khomeini and their bellies." Again he looked at Ezra. "What is your name?"

"Ezra Solaiman."

"Ah!" A look of grim illumination dawned upon the face of Ezra's cellmate. "A Jew. And are you rich?" he queried.

Ezra looked at the man, open-mouthed. "What has that to do with—"

The prisoner nodded to himself. "As I thought. A rich Jew. I figured they'd get around to your neighborhoods pretty soon. You and I are the first minorities they've brought into this stinking place."

Ezra's eyes widened as he studied the other man's face carefully. "Then...you are...."

"Jewish," the other fellow answered matter-of-factly. "*Mazel Tov*, Ezra Solaiman," he said wryly, holding out his hand. "I am Reuben Ibrahim. Pleased to meet you." Incredulous, Ezra shook the hand of his newfound comrade.

Ezra looked around at the tangle of arms and legs in the cell, then back at his comrade. "Why did you assume the *pasdars* would begin arresting rich Jews?"

Reuben shrugged. "Simple. The *pasdars* are controlled by the mullahs, and the mullahs want money. You are rich, so they arrested you. They will try you, shoot you, and confiscate your estate."

Ezra shuddered, remembering the phone call, and the news about Abraham Moosovi. He brushed his hand across his pant leg, feeling the rustle of the paper concealed there. "Why did they arrest you?" he asked. "I presume from what you've said that you aren't rich. What do the mullahs want with you?"

Reuben sighed and looked away. "No, indeed, I'm not rich." He gave a sad little chuckle. "And I don't guess it would make any difference now if I were." He looked up at Ezra. "I am here for not chanting slogans against the Shah."

Glancing away, Reuben continued. "Like everyone else, I've got my opinions, which I kept to myself. But some neighbor or business competitor with a grudge denounced me to one of the revolutionary committees. So here I am." Bitterly he continued, "I don't know the name or face of my accuser, and yet I am trapped in this plague-infested prison, while my wife and daughter cower at home, not knowing whether I am alive or dead." Reuben covered his face with his hands. "This country has gone mad, and I am trapped within its hallucinations."

ESTHER WANDERED through the house like a lost soul. Her throat was raw and sore from weeping, and her eyes felt bruised with fatigue. She had been unable to sleep the night before. Each time her eyes closed, her imagination tortured her with grotesque scenes of Ezra's fate. So she tossed upon her bed, crying until she could cry no more; then she lay exhausted, too overwrought to sleep.

Idly she paced into the study, flipping on the television. As she expected, there was nothing to watch except some wizened old mullah reading the Koran in Arabic—a language neither she nor the majority of the Farsi-speaking population understood. Since Khomeini had come to power, many of the television producers and directors had been arrested, and the remainder were afraid to schedule any programming that could be deemed remotely offensive to the fundamentalist regime. So all one could watch now was the reading of the Koran or brief news programs which were hardly better than Shiite propaganda.

She snapped off the set and went into the kitchen, drawn by the aroma of freshly brewed coffee. Glancing at the clock on the wall, she surmised that Sepi had already gone to school. She thought Moosa had left for the bazaar, or to look for Mullah Hafizi.

As she poured a cup of coffee, she wondered about the wisdom of relying upon a mullah for deliverance from Ezra's peril. Weren't the mullahs responsible for much of the mayhem now tearing the country apart? Why should Hafizi be any different? Yet Ezra seemed to place some trust in the man.

She took a sip of coffee and glanced out the windows toward the side yard. The branches of the cherry trees were beginning to swell with the nodules which would become blossoms in a few weeks. In this season of returning life, she felt nothing but despair and desolation. At this moment, Ezra's trust in his precious receipt and Hafizi's help seemed absurdly remote. She placed her head upon her forearms, as the tears trickled down her cheeks.

The buzzer rudely interrupted her melancholy. Someone was at the gate. Pushing herself away from the table, she went to the front foyer, pulling aside the curtains to look outside. Fear brought her heart throbbing into her throat. Standing at the gate were two armed *pasdars*, accompanied by a mullah. What could they want? Why were they here again? Her hands trembling, she unlocked the front door, opening it only a few centimeters. "What do you want?" she called. "Your people were already here just yesterday."

"In the name of Allah and the Imam Khomeini, I order you to open this gate," commanded the mullah imperiously. "We are here on official business."

"I don't know what you're talking about," she said,

trying desperately to control the hysterical beast inside her breast. Marjan, hearing the tones in her voice the mullah did not, began stalking toward the gate, hackles raised, showing his teeth in a low, rumbling growl.

"You will chain that dog or we will shoot him now!" said the mullah, his voice rising nervously as he measured the height of the gate with his eyes. One of the *pasdars* unholstered his pistol, training it with a two-fisted grip on the threatening Marjan.

Esther looked from Marjan to the mullah and his henchmen. What could she do? Either she would let them in now, or they would come back with more men and force their way in later. Feeling more helpless than ever before, she called out, "Marjan! Heel!"

The dog halted his advance, but kept his rigid, stalking pose. "Marjan! Kennel!" No change. "Kennel, Marjan!" Esther wondered at Marjan's disobedience; perhaps he knew better than she how to respond to these intruders. She walked out to him, gripped his collar in one hand, and tugged him toward the kennel. The sinews along the dog's back and hindquarters tensed, as he momentarily resisted her. Then, with a pathetic, puzzled whimper, he allowed her to lead him back to his shelter. Only when the chain was clipped to his collar did she turn to face the men at the gate.

"Why have you come here?" she asked again. Taking a deep breath, she continued, "Your people have already taken away my husband, for no just cause. What else do you need here?"

"*Khanom,*" the mullah said, his lips curled in contempt, "I'm well aware of your husband's arrest. We're here to collect evidence related to his trial."

Esther felt a faint tendril of hope. If Ezra was to be tried, he could not be dead, could he? Perhaps his receipt would indeed be of some value, if he were allowed to present it as evidence. From the way the rumors ran, she was not at all sure that fairness was a criterion by which the mullahs conducted their tribunals. She went to the gate and unlocked it. The *pasdars* pushed past her, followed by the mullah, who gave her a withering stare as he went by. The three men marched up the sidewalk, glancing edgily at the kennel, where Marjan strained against his collar, still showing his teeth. Slowly Esther followed them into the house.

One of the guards went into the study, immediately going to the desk and yanking out the drawers, spilling the contents carelessly on the floor. With the toe of his boot, he sorted through the piles. Another of the men began tossing armfuls of books onto the floor. Alarmed, Esther said, "Stop it! Tell me what you are looking for, and I will tell you where to find it! Why should you wreck my house?"

The mullah appeared from behind her, carrying an old *chador* she kept in a cedar chest in the bedroom. "Shouldn't you be wearing this, *khanom*?" he asked, smirking.

Esther felt her face flush with anger. "You've been in my bedroom, you animal!"

The mullah chuckled.

"In a civilized country, even a mullah's wife wouldn't wear a *chador* in her own house," Esther raged. "She wouldn't have to fear strangers invading her privacy!" The mullah only smiled in amusement. Another armload of books clattered to the floor behind them.

He turned to his lackeys. "Stop," he ordered. "If they have anything of value, they're not going to hide it anywhere obvious." Turning again to Esther, he asked, "Tell me, *khanom*, do you have any outbuildings—or a cellar, perhaps?"

Esther tried with all her might not to allow her face to show any sign of alarm. "The dog is chained," she said, in a tone she hoped sounded haughty. "Go anywhere on the premises you like." With a final, icy glance, she turned her back on the mullah and walked into the drawing room.

She sat in one of the Louis XVI chairs, wringing her hands as she listened to the search party go out the kitchen door. What if, by some freak chance, they stumbled onto the cache in the cellar? If they did, they would find not only the money Ezra had realized from the sale of the store, but also the American dollars Moosa had obtained yesterday. The dollars would surely tip their hand to the authorities. Had she and Moosa been careful enough to hide the traces of their comings and goings to the cellar? Had they replaced the bricks properly and made the dirt between them look undisturbed? Had they been wise in leaving the cellar door unlocked? Again she heard Ezra's words of warning: *"If a door is locked, they will want to know why. Everything should look innocuous, as though we have nothing to hide."*

Nothing to hide. She felt a manic laugh bubbling upward in her throat. It was almost hilarious—they were tossing a huge *chador* over the whole house, to conceal, to blend in, to cloak. Khomeini had decreed the *chador*, and he was getting it, in ways he would never have imagined.

The search party came back inside after about a quarter of an hour. Esther breathed a silent sigh when she saw that their hands were empty. Sourly, the mullah in charge pointed toward the floor of the study, and the *pasdars* went into the room and began rolling up the expensive Kermani carpet which covered the parquet floor.

"What are you doing?" demanded Esther.

The mullah scowled at her. "Collecting evidence," he grunted, looking away.

"Evidence of what?" she grated. "Admit it—you are stealing. Is this in accordance with the laws of the Prophet?"

"Shut up, Jew!" he snarled. "I don't answer to you! Watch your impudent tongue, woman, or you'll find yourself in want of more than a rug."

The violence in his voice strangled the rage in her breast, replacing it with fear. She turned away from him, gripping her elbows tightly against her sides. She stared in blinded misery into the side yard until she heard the front door close behind the intruders. Hearing a sound like a freight train roaring in her ears, she collapsed onto the kitchen floor in a dead faint.

EZRA STIRRED RESTLESSLY and opened his eyes. So. It was not a nightmare, but real; he was still in the cell. He raised his head and began pulling his shoes on. Remembering Reuben's advice of the evening before, he pulled out the laces and scuffed the toes against the concrete floor, to make the shoes look older and more worn than they were. Reuben had told him that the guards sometimes took a fancy to some of the good clothing worn by certain prisoners. They would come into the cell without warning, stripping the unfortunate one and leaving him shivering in the chill air of the unheated prison. Resistance to such raids usually resulted in summary execution, Reuben said.

As a further precaution, Ezra had turned his overcoat inside out, ripping the lining to make it look less conspicuous. He pulled it about him now, looking next to him to see if Reuben was still asleep.

His bladder was painfully full, but he loathed the thought of using the stinking toilet, and having to creep past all the disheveled bodies between him and it. When he could bear the discomfort no longer, he got to his feet and began making his way toward the grimy commode.

He raised his foot to step over a man and realized, to his horror, that the poor fellow was dead. His chest was still, and his eyes were fixed in a death stare that seemed to be locked on Ezra, as if to say, "Soon, friend.

Soon." Quickly Ezra moved on.

When he got back to his corner, Reuben was stirring. In shocked tones, Ezra related his discovery of the corpse. Reuben seemed unsurprised. "In this place," he said, "everyone dies. Either sickness, torture, or the firing squad. No one gets out of here alive, Solaiman. No one."

THIRTEEN

MOOSA WALKED ALONG Naderi Avenue, his head hanging in dejection. Again he had pounded on Hafizi's door and gotten no answer. He was beginning to suspect the clergyman had wind of his father's arrest, and had left town to avoid a potentially embarrassing entanglement.

A truck rumbled past him along the busy avenue, a troop of *pasdars* seated on benches in the cargo area. With smoldering eyes, Moosa watched them go by, his hand brushing the Beretta concealed by his jacket. With all that was within him, he hated these illiterate, swaggering pawns of Khomeini. They, along with their mullah masters, would be responsible for the death of this nation. Moosa already held them responsible for the persecution and humiliation of his father. And if he died in that prison . . . Moosa's teeth ground together and his nostrils flared in concealed rage.

On his way home, he went into the covered bazaar. He felt more confident today than yesterday, bolstered by his success with the moneychanger. Today he had brought 600,000 *tomans*.

Walking past the gun booths, he saw a familiar figure. Nathan Moosovi stood at a display case, attended by an unctuous merchant who watched eagerly as Nathan peeled off *rial* notes from a wad of currency. Satisfied,

113

the merchant grabbed six double handfuls of ammunition cartridge containers and placed them in a cardboard box, sliding it toward Nathan. "Thank you, *baradar*," the merchant grinned. "May all your enemies perish."

Nathan gave the overly solicitous vendor a withering glance, then grasped the box with both hands, grunting as he lifted it.

Moosa eased up beside him. "Nathan, what in heaven's name are you doing with all that ammunition? Starting a war, or what?"

Nathan's eyes went wide as his face jerked around toward Moosa's. For an instant, the stare was the same one he had given the merchant. Recognizing Moosa, he relaxed slightly. Nathan glanced about him, then back at Moosa. "Come," he said in a low voice. "Help me carry this to my car."

When they were outside, Nathan said, "You scared the life out of me in there. I thought you were a *pasdar* or something."

"Sorry," said Moosa. "I dealt with that same merchant a few days ago."

Nathan and Moosa eased the heavy box into the trunk of a battered green Volvo. Nathan closed the lid, then looked thoughtfully at Moosa. "You bought a gun?"

Moosa nodded. Looking surreptitiously about, he briefly pulled his jacket back to expose the handle of the Beretta, protruding from his belt.

Nathan took a pack of Turkish cigarettes from his pocket. He offered it to Moosa, who declined. With a practiced gesture he shook the pack to expose the end of one of the unfiltered smokes and pulled it from the wrapper with his lips. He cupped his hands around a match as he lit it, then drew the smoke deeply into his lungs, feeling the hot/cool vapor sending its soothing tendrils throughout his chest. He glanced up at Moosa. "What brings you to the bazaar?"

Moosa looked away. "I have come on an errand—for my father."

Nathan's eyes narrowed. "I heard the news about your father last night."

"And I the news of yours," Moosa replied. After an uncomfortable pause, he continued, "I am sorry, Nathan. He was a good man."

Nathan's jaw clenched as twin streams of tobacco smoke issued from his nostrils. "Yes," he said finally. "He was. Far too good to die as he did."

Wordlessly Moosa nodded, scuffing the toe of his shoe on the pavement beside the car.

Nathan took a long, last drag at the cigarette, thumping it into the middle of the street. Decisively he peered at Moosa. "Go and do your errand," he said. "I'll wait for you here. When you're finished, come with me to my place. I want to talk with you about something."

Moosa studied Nathan's intense eyes. After several seconds, he nodded. "All right. I won't be too long." He turned and went into the bazaar. Nathan watched his back until he disappeared into the crowds at the bazaar entrance, then opened the driver's side door of the Volvo and got inside to wait.

THE BACK of Ezra's throat swelled in nausea as he looked into the bowl of filth the guards had given him to eat. Moldy rice swam in rancid pools of grease, and the hunk of cheese in the bowl was old and as hard as shoe leather. Despite the pangs gnawing at his entrails, he could not force himself to eat this slop. As he laid the bowl aside, another prisoner, glancing furtively from the bowl to Ezra, began scooping the rice into his mouth with his fingers.

The sound of booted feet slapped down the corridor outside the cell, and a party of guards halted, looking inside.

115

"Reuben Ibrahim," called one of the guards, "and Ezra Solaiman. Prepare for trial. You have fifteen minutes to make your peace with Allah." The guard detail marched away.

Ezra sat wide-eyed, fear and hope chasing each other in a tangled frenzy through his breast. He was relieved to be leaving this dungheap, and perhaps the receipt would carry the day. But inevitable doom lay like a thick shroud over this place, and it was hard to believe in tomorrow. Suppose the mullahs did not believe his receipt was genuine—suppose it was confiscated in the courtroom?

He heard a soft sob beside him. Reuben was half-weeping, half-praying. Over and over, Ezra heard him mutter a word which sounded like the Hebrew name, "Yeshua."

Ezra reached over and gripped the shoulder of his cell mate. He tried to smile, failing miserably.

Reuben looked at him, tears streaming down his face. "God help us, Ezra," he sobbed. "We are next to die."

Ezra gripped his cell mate by the arms. "You must have hope, Reuben!" he said sternly. "With your last breath, you must cling to hope. Perhaps—"

"It is no use," said Reuben, shaking his head. "The mullahs don't listen to anyone except Khomeini. They do entirely as they please, and justice means nothing to them. They will find me guilty, and they will shoot me, and nothing on earth can change that."

Reuben drew a long, shuddering breath before fixing Ezra with an intent stare. "But death doesn't frighten me, Solaiman, as much as knowing that my wife and daughter will be left alone. I will never see them again." Again Ibrahim's voice caught. He bowed his head, and again Ezra heard the whispered word, "Yeshua."

Drawing a tremulous breath, Reuben looked up at Ezra. "I wonder, Solaiman, if by some miracle you should survive, would you do me a last favor?"

"My friend, you only need to ask," said Ezra with quiet fervor.

"Would you go to my wife, Jahan—she has moved, with my daughter Maheen, to the house of her father—and give them this?" He drew a folded, grimy envelope from his pocket and passed it to Ezra. He muttered the address, which Ezra carefully repeated. "There is a note inside," Reuben continued, "giving instructions about where I hid some money. They will be needing it." He struggled to control his voice. "And . . . one more thing."

Ezra waited, tears seeping from the corners of his eyes.

"Tell Jahan . . ." Reuben's chest heaved with emotion. ". . . tell her that I love her as I have never loved anyone on this earth—to my dying breath this was so. And tell her I have prayed that Yeshua might protect her."

The two men gripped each other's arms. Ezra had time to puzzle only briefly over Reuben's enigmatic last words. And then the guards were outside the door. The lock clicked, and the gate swung open. Ezra and Reuben shook hands, then turned to go.

As they walked down the dark corridor, Ezra, for the first time since his boyhood, began silently reciting a Psalm of David, half-forgotten until this moment: *In You I trust, Oh my God; do not let me be put to shame. Do not let my enemies triumph over me.*

One of the offices in the prison complex was used as a courtroom. Six benches for the accused were lined up on one side of the door. Ezra and Reuben were seated on the front left corner, closest to the trial committee. Thirty-odd wretches crammed the benches already, but they were seated farther back; plainly their cases were to be decided after Ezra's and Reuben's.

The trial committee was comprised of a mullah, who presided, and four civilians. As Ezra looked at his

117

judges, he recognized one of them, Barbar, a porter in
the covered bazaar! How in the name of God could an
uneducated fellow, such as Ezra knew this one to be,
make life-and-death decisions? Yet there he sat, his chin
tilted at an angle which showed he was conscious of his
lofty responsibility and not at all intimidated by it.

On the wall behind the committee hung the ubiqui-
tous oversized portrait of the Imam Khomeini. A table
separated the committee from the prisoners, who were
guarded by six armed *pasdars,* ranged along the walls
near the accused. The room stank of fear and stale
cigarette smoke.

Unseen by Ezra, Firouz Marandi sat at the rear of the
room, impatiently awaiting the beginning of the proceedings. It was he who had arranged for Solaiman's
case to be called early—the sooner to gain what was
coming to him. He fidgeted in his chair, trying to catch
the presiding mullah's eye to urge him to get started.

Mullah Hassan sorted through the stacks of paper on
the table in front of him. As presiding officer of the
tribunal, he had reviewed these brief summaries of the
accusations against each of the men to be tried today.
They were the usual lot: former police officers who had
taken bribes, merchants denounced for lack of charity to
the poor, political operatives of the Pahlavi regime.

He could not find the abstract for the Solaiman fellow, and this was what he sought among the other papers before him. The Tudeh fellow—Marandi, was it?—
had promised him a rich reward for calling this case
early. Hassan was not averse to a reward, but how could
he prosecute the case if he did not have the particulars
before him? Annoyed, he continued to sift through the
documents. Ah, there it was, at last.

The mullah looked up, glanced quickly about the
crowded room, and intoned in a bored voice, "Let the
proceedings begin. In the Name of Allah the Merciful
and Compassionate, on this twentieth day of *Rabi,* Sec-

ond of the 1,357th year of the *Hegira* of the Prophet Muhammad—blessings and peace be upon him—this tribunal of the Holy Revolution is called to order. Summon the first prisoner."

A bailiff consulted the list in his hand. "Reuben Ibrahim, rise, bow to your judges, and take the witness chair."

Reuben stood on unsteady legs, and managed a bow toward the table. He walked stiffly toward the chair to the right of the committee's table and sat down.

The mullah turned toward Reuben. "State your name."

"Your humble servant, Reuben Ibrahim," replied the accused in an unsteady voice.

"Your profession?"

"A small rug dealer, your honor."

Ezra watched the mockery of a trial, horrified. No witnesses were called, no attorneys were present. Only the accused, the mullah, and the four other "judges." No cross-examination took place, nor was the accused allowed to speak in his own defense. The mullah, alone and unchallenged, asked the questions and interpreted the answers.

"Ibrahim, I will ask you a very important question," said Hassan. "Were you a supporter of the satanic Shah, Mohammed Reza Pahlavi?"

The other four members of the committee leaned toward Reuben, awaiting his answer.

The wretched fellow squirmed in his chair. "Your honor, my business was small, and I had to work hard to make a living for my family. I had no time for politics."

"You didn't answer my question," insisted the mullah, his voice rising. "Did you or did you not support the Shah?"

"I have said I did not participate in politics."

"Answer the question!" shouted Hassan, pounding his fist on the table. "Don't waste the time of this

119

court! There are many more criminals to be tried today, and I have no intention of allowing you to make an exhibition of these proceedings! Now answer!"

Ezra groaned inwardly as Reuben seemed to shrink before his very eyes. "No, your honor," came the half-whispered reply. "I did not support the Shah."

The mullah leaned back, a self-satisfied smile flickering across his lips. "Very well," he said. "You have said you did not support the Shah." The cleric sifted through some papers at his elbow, glancing downward, then back at Reuben. "Please tell me how you got to your place of business each day."

Dejectedly, Reuben said, "By bus." He did not look up from the floor.

"And on the bus," continued Hassan, "did you ever hear the patriotic chanting of slogans against the satanic Shah?"

Reuben nodded weakly.

"And did you take part in the chanting to show your solidarity with the revolutionaries of Holy Islam?"

"I . . . I don't remember, your honor. It—so much has happened since—"

"Ibrahim," warned the mullah, "I have here the sworn testimony of two witnesses, as prescribed by Islamic law, that you did not take part in the chanting. They testify, in fact, that you were invited to take part but refused to do so."

"Perhaps," shrugged Ibrahim, sweating profusely. "I can't remember."

With an inward shudder, Ezra remembered Noori's warning: *See that you are on the winning side. . . .*

"Did you go to Mehrabad Airport to welcome the blessed Imam from fifteen years of exile?"

"No, your honor."

"Why were you absent?" pressed the cleric.

"I was one of millions who didn't go to the airport to—" began Reuben.

"The prisoner has confessed his disloyalty to the Imam Khomeini," interrupted the mullah. "What is the verdict of the committee?"

"Death." "Death." "Death." "Death." Barbar held his head high as he pronounced the word, his face a mask of solemn duty. Ezra turned away in disgust.

"Reuben Ibrahim," pronounced Mullah Hassan in a sepulchral tone, "you have been tried by this Committee of the Holy Revolution and found guilty of treason. I sentence you to be shot."

Reuben's eyes pleaded silently with Ezra as he heard his doom pronounced. Ezra shook helplessly in outrage and grief. How had such madness so swiftly infected an entire nation? Iranians had never been so cruel to their fellow countrymen.

Two *pasdars* came to escort Reuben to the prison yard. The wretched man threw himself to the floor. "Please, don't!" he screamed. "For the sake of my wife and child, I beg you!"

The *pasdars* lifted him to his feet and shoved him toward the door. Just before he was pushed outside, he whirled about and faced the room. "Long live His Majesty Mohammed Reza Pahlavi!" he shouted. "Long live the monarchy! Death to the butchers! The day will come when an outraged nation will avenge the blood of innocents like me!" One of the *pasdars* violently jerked the man backward by the shirt collar and he was gone. Moments later, from just outside the window, a burst of rifle fire was heard. Reuben Ibrahim was dead.

"EZRA SOLAIMAN, RISE, bow to the committee, and take the witness chair."

FOURTEEN

NATHAN MOOSOVI PARKED the Volvo in front of his shop. Moosa looked at the storefront—its windows boarded up, a heavy new chain and padlock anchoring the grille which guarded the front door. Nathan got out of the car and walked around in front, motioning with a jerk of his head for Moosa to follow.

They went inside the darkened shop. The shelves were back in their places, but many of the stolen wares had not been replaced. They walked to the back of the store, to the small office space beside the steel strongbox still displaying the jagged hole cut by the burglars only days before.

Nathan reached above him and switched on an incandescent light beneath a shade hanging from the ceiling. As he looked across the scarred wooden table at Moosa, the shadows moved back and forth across his features as the lamp swung like a pendulum. Moosa saw Nathan's eyes now in light, now in shadow. The two men looked at each other for perhaps thirty seconds, Nathan unsure of how to begin, Moosa unsure of what Nathan would say.

"Moosa, we Jews cannot any longer depend on the government to protect us from the hostility of the Muslim majority," said Nathan, at last. "Look at what's happened. My father is dead and your father is imprisoned. These men were not criminals, Moosa, as you know full well. Their only crime was being Jewish. And then, of course, my shop was looted—and that's just the part we know about. The country is destroying itself." He rapped the table with his knuckles to emphasize his last words. Moosa looked down, nodded slightly, then looked back up as Nathan continued.

"And it isn't just the Jews, Moosa. Anyone with a grudge against anyone from before the revolution has to do no more than whisper in the ear of his uncle the mullah, and the accused finds himself sitting in a tribunal, as often as not with the accuser as one of his judges."

Nathan ran a hand through his hair, then stood up, pacing back and forth as he spoke.

"The mullahs and their *pasdar* apes have a stranglehold on us all, Moosa. They are drunk with power as long as Khomeini sits on his mat in Qom, spouting Shiite slogans and egging them on. And now some of the college students are joining the parade. Have you noticed? The crowds outside the American embassy are getting bigger and noisier."

Moosa shrugged. "You're right—but so what? What can we do?"

Nathan stopped pacing and stared at Moosa. "Some of us think that the only language the mullahs understand is the language of force."

Moosa's eyes widened. He had such thoughts himself, but hearing them spoken aloud was, at once, heady and terrifying. Cocking his head sideways, he asked quietly, "How far are you prepared to go?"

In answer, Nathan pulled from atop the ruined strongbox a newspaper, several days old. Opening it on the table in front of Moosa, he tapped with his forefinger at a headline midway down the right column.

"*Pasdar* Killed in Night Ambush," it read. Moosa felt

his face growing stiff with apprehension. His eyes locked with Nathan's. The lamp had almost stopped its swinging, and the harsh light of the bulb etched the lines and shadows of the other man's face in a stark relief of light and darkness.

Something indefinable was speaking to Moosa, far down in the dark places of his soul. Something obscure and terrifying and intoxicating. Something he had not, until this moment, suspected himself of harboring.

Living in the warm congeniality of America, he would never have entertained such a possibility. But the brutality and unfairness of his father's arrest, the casual injustice visited upon Nathan by the *pasdars* and the death of his father—all of these events were chanting within him, evoking something dark and violent. He could imagine the general shape of the invitation being extended to him by Nathan Moosovi. One way or another, Moosa knew, his next words would be a turning point, a Rubicon.

Taking a deep breath, he said, "Who else knows what you are doing?"

EZRA WALKED TO the chair. His legs felt as if they might give way at any moment. He turned around to take his seat and stiffened when he saw Firouz seated at the back of the room. His former employee's face was unreadable, but something in his eyes let Ezra know that his suspicions in the days before the Shah's leaving were truer than he had guessed. *What does Marandi stand to gain from my death?* he wondered. *How much does he know of the dealings with Ameer Nijat?*

"In the name of Allah the Merciful and Compassionate," recited Hassan. Turning to Ezra, he asked, "What is your profession, Solaiman?"

For several seconds Ezra could not make his voice heard. "I am—a druggist, your honor," he said.

"And for how long have you pursued this line of work?"

Ezra looked confused. Where did these questions lead? Would they shoot him for selling his business, or merely for being a Jew? His brow furrowed as he tried to anticipate the shape of the frame the mullah was constructing.

"Answer the question, Solaiman," threatened Hassan.

Ezra began panting. His panicked eyes raced from the mullah to Firouz's hostile face. As he was opening his mouth to reply, the door to the courtroom opened.

Nader Hafizi entered the room, his eyes riveted on Ezra's stricken gaze. It was Hassan's turn to look confused. The mullah stared blankly at Hafizi as the older cleric walked up to Ezra and laid a hand on his shoulder.

"I'm sorry to be so late, my friend," Hafizi said quietly. "We returned from Isfahan only this morning. I read the note left by your son, and I came as fast as I could."

"See here, *baradar*," huffed the presiding mullah at last, "we're running a trial here. What right have you to intrude on these proceedings?"

Hafizi turned to face the committee. "Mullah Hassan, I am here to appear as a witness for the defense of Ezra Solaiman," he said firmly. "I have evidence which will prove that he is emphatically not an enemy of Islam."

An astonished murmur rippled through the room. Ezra glanced back at Firouz, and saw annoyed surprise splashed across his angry face.

Hafizi held Hassan's eyes a moment longer, then turned back to Ezra. "Give me the receipt," he said.

Ezra fumbled at the watch pocket with numb fingers. In a moment, he had ripped loose the basting and opened the pocket, withdrawing the receipt for his donation. His eyes embraced Hafizi with a look of gratitude as he placed the paper in the older man's hand.

Hafizi turned to the committee. "I hold here a receipt,

126

personally signed and stamped by *Mojtahed* Ayatollah Kermani, for a donation of one million *tomans*—" a quiet gasp hissed among the audience—"for the expansion of a local Muslim cemetery. The money was given by the man you see here," he said, pointing to Ezra.

Mullah Hassan's cheeks reddened as he inspected the document placed in front of him by Hafizi. Angrily he glanced up at Marandi, then down again. He would take this Tudeh fool severely to task for placing him in such a ridiculous position.

Hafizi continued, "Ezra Solaiman is accused of being an enemy of Allah and Islam. Yet he donated a large sum of money to honor the hallowed martyrs of our nation. How can this be? I urge you, brother Hassan and members of the committee—release this man. He is no criminal. He has done more good deeds for our people, though he is a Jew, than many Muslims who have the reputation of being devout."

Hafizi stared pointedly at Hassan, who reddened even further. Without looking up, he handed the receipt down the line of the committee for inspection. When each had given the appearance of careful scrutiny, the paper was passed back to the presiding mullah.

Hassan cleared his throat. Still unable to meet Hafizi's eyes, he turned toward the other judges. "Members of the committee," he mumbled, "since this . . . new evidence has come to our attention, I recommend that we . . . that we release Ezra Solaiman, and absolve him of the charges brought against him. How do you vote?"

"Agreed." "Agreed." "Agreed." "Agreed," came the rubber-stamp replies.

Ezra let out the breath he had been holding in a moan of relief. He held his face in his hands as tears of jubilation started from his eyes.

"This tribunal will take a short recess," continued Hassan, rising from his seat. His eyes roved the room, looking for that idiot, Marandi. But he was nowhere to be seen. He had disappeared.

FIROUZ BOUNDED THROUGH the door of the pharmacy, staring wildly about him. The mullahs would be after his skin now, he knew. He would have to hide until their anger dulled with the passing of time. But first he intended to destroy this place. He should have anticipated the cunning of the old Jew—enlisting the aid of a mullah, of all things! But if Firouz could not have this store, neither would anyone else. He remembered an old hatchet Solaiman kept in a dark corner of the storeroom. Quickly Marandi ran to the back of the shop.

As Firouz entered the storeroom, Ameer Nijat, clipboard in hand, looked away from the stacks of merchandise he was inspecting, eyeing the intruder quizzically. Marandi froze, shocked into immobility by the unexpected sight. Just behind Nijat's shoulder was a younger man, looking confusedly from Nijat to the agitated Marandi. Calmly, Ameer Nijat handed the clipboard to the younger man, placing his hands on his hips. Perhaps a full minute passed in silence as the two men stared at each other.

"Ah, yes!" said Nijat at last, "I remember now—you are the helper! Marandi, isn't it?"

Dumbly, Firouz nodded.

Nijat smiled, but his eyes looked as dangerous as a stalking panther's as he spoke again. "And what may I do for you today, Marandi?"

Firouz's brow wrinkled in confusion. Dropping his glance to the floor, he cast about furiously for a suitable answer. "*Aga* Nijat, I . . . I work here," he mumbled.

Nijat chuckled, shaking his head. "No, Marandi. You don't work here anymore. I am not so trusting as Solaiman." The amusement left his voice, replaced by a tone as hard-edged as a knife blade. "I now own this pharmacy, Marandi. And there is no place for you here. Get out."

Marandi glared at Nijat's feet, unable, even in his rage, to meet the other man's gaze. Clenching and un-clenching his fists, he felt his face burning with humili-ation. So—the old Jew had tricked him again. Solaiman had won twice today, but there would be other days, Firouz vowed silently. Nostrils flaring in sullen anger, he slouched out of the pharmacy.

Nijat watched him go, never changing his position. When the bells over the door clattered at Marandi's exit, he spoke to his son without turning his head.

"Yusef, make another note. We will need to have the locks changed on these doors. And perhaps we should install a burglar alarm."

EZRA GOT OFF THE BUS, gazing about him as if he had never before seen the neighborhood in which he lived. His chest pounding with the joy of his release, he almost ran down the sidewalk toward his gate.

He pressed the button in the wall. Marjan's head yanked erect in his kennel, his nose testing the air for the identity of the person at the gate. Slowly, he got to his feet. Just as slowly, the heavy black tail began to wag.

Esther was lying on the divan in the sitting room, so beaten down by depression she was barely able to sum-mon the energy to rise and answer the buzzer. If the *pasdars* were back, she reflected, it was probably to ar-rest her; or, perhaps they had found out Moosa was here. She was so laden with despair she hardly cared which. She parted the curtains in the front windows and peered out toward the gate. A bedraggled fellow stood there. What could he want? She looked closer. Her breath caught in her throat. *Can it be...?*

She yanked open the front door and moved rapidly down the front walk, her hands coming to her mouth. She neared the gate and saw. Then she was running, screaming his name.

"Ezra! Ezra, oh, please, God, is it really my husband? Dear God in heaven! Ezra!"

She threw open the gate and they were in each other's arms.

SEPI AND KHOSROW walked down the crowded hall. Classes were over for the day, and everyone was rushing to gather books and start home.

Khosrow barely seemed to notice her these days. He had stopped holding her hand when they walked together. No more did he meet her by the stairs in the main hallway. When they had infrequent chances to talk, his eyes never met hers. The playful teasing, the delicious flirting she had secretly so enjoyed—these were in the past. Now his face was an illegible tablet of stone, his responses mumbled monosyllables.

The giddy, warm bloom of affection she had felt for him was being slowly replaced by a puzzled frustration. She wondered why he went to the trouble of walking with her. She wondered even more why she clung to the faint hope that he would again be the fun-loving, mischievous Khosrow to whom she had been so attracted.

As they approached the exit, Sepi noticed the boys waiting outside the door. Khosrow and Sepi descended the steps to the sidewalk and the boys drew into a noose around them, two of the boys blocking their path. Sepi's eyes raced around the circle of boys, their faces blank masks of casual malevolence. She felt her stomach freezing as she grasped at Khosrow's arm.

"What do you want?" Khosrow demanded. "Get out of our way."

"I see you haven't listened to the advice we gave you,

Parvin," sneered one of the boys. "You're still hanging around with this trash."

"Shut your filthy mouth," threatened Khosrow.

"Don't," warned Sepi, clutching at him. "There are too many of them."

"You'd better listen to her," growled the other boy. "She's interested in saving her skin, even if you aren't. The Islamic Patriots don't tolerate disobedience."

"Big talk," said Khosrow, his cheeks reddening in anger and fear. "No wonder you Islamic Patriots run in packs like jackals."

The other boy's fist flashed out at Khosrow, but he shied, and the blow landed on his chest instead of his cheek. Sepi screamed, feeling the circle of boys close in. Hands shoved her, grasped at her, slapped her. She fell to the ground and the melee swirled around and over her, closing in on Khosrow in a flurry of dust and curses and blows. Scrambling to her feet, she raced away in mad, unreasoning terror from the circle of hatred.

A teacher rushed outside, staring intently at the scene. He took in the sight of the fleeing Sepideh Solaiman, and Khosrow Parvin encircled by the angry young toughs. He was about to dash forward to break up the fight, when he felt a hand on his shoulder. The principal stood there, looking intently at him. The older man was silently shaking his head. Quietly the two men stepped back inside the school and closed the door.

FIFTEEN

With trembling hands, Ezra reached for the handle of the carrying case. As the official watched, he threw back the latches on both sides, then slowly raised the lid. The customs inspector bent over and peered inside.

"Hmmm," he murmured, "nice rug. And, from the look of it, a fairly expensive Isfahan. But still you have not shown me a permit to take it out of the country." The official leveled his gaze at Ezra.

Ezra felt Esther's fingers digging painfully into his upper arm. He cared not a fig for the carpet, but if they scrutinized the case, they might find the secret compartment. His mind whirled, trying to think, to improvise. . . .

A man shouldered his way through the crowd beside them. Ezra heard a familiar voice speaking to the official. "I am Mullah Nader Hafizi, and this man is traveling with me. Why is he being detained?"

The official stared at Hafizi, before replying, "This rug has no export permit. It cannot be taken out of the country."

"You should read this," said Hafizi, handing the inspector the paper he carried in his breast pocket. Suspiciously, the customs official took the document from the mullah. His eyes roved the page, coming at last to the signature at the bottom. The eyes widened, then looked up with a new respect at Hafizi and Solaiman.

"Very well," he said, closing and fastening the lid of the

133

carrying case. "You may go. May Allah bless your journey." The
inspector chalked an X on each piece of luggage, including the
wooden case containing the carpet.

Hastily Ezra grabbed the handle of the case. With a quick
nod at the inspector and a grateful glance at Hafizi, they passed
through the customs gate and made their way toward the depar-
ture gate.

. . . .

AHMED DABIRIAN THE CABINETMAKER
glanced at the ancient clock on the wall of his
shop. Time for prayer. The devout Muslim laid
aside his tools and went to a nearby counter to get his
prayer rug. He unrolled the rug and laid it in the middle
of the shop floor. Standing, he faced southwest, toward
the Ka'aba in Mecca.

Ezra stopped at the doorway. Seeing that Ahmed was
about to begin his morning prayers, he stayed quiet, not
wanting to interrupt. He heard the tradesman murmur-
ing in Arabic the prayer of Islam: "In the name of the
most merciful Allah. Praise be to Allah, the Lord of all
beings, the Master of the Day of Judgment. . . ." Standing, kneeling, and then face-down on the rug, the cabinetmaker repeated his devotions. When he finished and
was rolling up the prayer rug, Ezra quietly knocked on
the door frame.

Ahmed looked around. "*Aga* Solaiman," he said, smiling. "It's good to see you. How is your family?" he
asked, extending a dusty hand which Ezra shook in
greeting.

Dabirian had made the dining room chairs for Ezra
and Esther's house. He was a meticulous craftsman.
The oldest child of a poor bricklayer, Dabirian had
learned his craft during a seven-year apprenticeship to
an older carpenter, at the end of which he had started
his own shop in the same dusty, shavings-strewn room
where he now worked.

Ezra wished desperately that he could state directly what he wanted from the carpenter, but he forced himself to observe the customary formalities of greeting. Giving Dabirian a tight-lipped smile, he answered, "We are well, *Aga* Dabirian, *Alhmadollilah.** And how are things with your household?"

In the thirty years of his trade, Ahmed had not made a lot of money, and this fact, along with the bitter memories of his poverty-stricken childhood, galled him. Being a devout Muslim, he had welcomed the coming of the Imam Khomeini as the salvation of the poor. And, indeed, his fortunes had improved with the coming of the new regime.

"Much better, *Aga* Solaiman," said the quiet woodworker with a confident smile. "For the faithful, the changes in the country have been beneficial."

Ezra shuddered inwardly, hoping his anxiety didn't show. He decided to broach his business with the craftsman before his nerves got the better of him.

"I need a box built, *Aga* Dabirian," said Ezra. "I want to ship some rugs to my cousin in America, and I want to be certain they make the journey undamaged."

Dabirian nodded, cupping his chin in one hand. "That won't be difficult, *Aga* Solaiman," he said. "I would suggest plywood. It's durable, and far less expensive than ordinary planking."

"Only one thing," interrupted Ezra. "I want the box built in a certain way. I have a rough sketch." Ezra pulled a piece of paper from his coat pocket and smoothed it out on a nearby counter top. Dabirian leaned over the drawing, squinting and scratching his face. After a moment, he looked up.

"What is the purpose of this empty compartment at the bottom of the box, *Aga* Solaiman?"

---

*"God be thanked"

Ezra shrugged. "The hold of the ship may be damp. I intend to place sawdust or cotton in this place to absorb the humidity and protect the carpet."

"Then I will need to drill holes in the partition—" began Dabirian.

"No!" said Ezra. "Leave the bottom solid. I . . . don't think holes are needed," he finished weakly.

Ahmed stared strangely at Ezra for a few moments, then gave a slight shrug as he returned to his study of the drawing. "I don't think this will take long at all, *Aga* Solaiman," he said. "I should be able to have it finished by . . ." He squinted upward in calculation. ". . . day after tomorrow, *inshallah.** I can have it delivered to your house. Will that be all right?"

Ezra nodded. "That should be perfect, thank you very much." Trying to mask the awkwardness of his discomfort about the partition, Ezra asked casually, "And how are things for you now, *Aga* Dabirian—with the . . . changes that have happened recently?"

Dabirian smiled. "Things have never been better for me, *Aga* Solaiman. The blessed Imam will cause the nation to obey the laws of Islam. No more will the poor be downtrodden by the rich. It was a day of great happiness for me when the Ayatollah landed at Mehrabad Airport."

Ezra nodded, with what he hoped was a neutral expression on his face.

"But, *Aga* Solaiman," continued Dabirian in a somber tone, "I understand there have been . . . difficulties for you. I was sorry to hear of your arrest and imprisonment."

Ezra stared at the cabinetmaker, his eyes round disks of shock. "How . . . did you know?" he stammered.

"I have a cousin who is a mullah, *Aga*," explained

*"God willing"

Dabirian. "Through him, I was able to get an appointment as a special agent for the government. As part of my duties, I . . . I hear things."

Ezra struggled to regain control over his features. It would not do to arouse Dabirian's suspicions about the partition in the box—any more than he had already done.

"The system made an error in your case, *Aga* Solaiman," continued Dabirian earnestly. "You are a good man, not a rascal like some of the others. You should never have been put in that horrible place. I am grateful Allah the Merciful delivered you from such a situation."

Ezra looked up at the other man. "Thank you, *Aga* Dabirian. I appreciate your concern." He looked up at the clock on the wall. "And now I really must go. Should I pay you for the box now, or when it is delivered?"

"As always, *Aga* Solaiman, I want to give you the opportunity to inspect my work before I am paid. It is a matter of professional pride, I suppose," smiled Dabirian. "My son will collect the money when he brings the box."

"Very well, then," said Ezra. "Thank you again, *Aga* Dabirian. *Khoda hafez*."*

Dabirian bowed his head slightly as Ezra left the shop. When he had gone, Ahmed looked again at the drawing. Picking up a cedar shaving, he sniffed absently at its resinous scent as he reflected on Solaiman's odd, nervous manner. Why would he want a concealed compartment in a shipping box? Scratching his sawdust-filled beard, he began sorting through his store of lumber for a plywood sheet of the proper size.

Outside on the sidewalk, Ezra wished fervently that he had gone to a carpenter unknown to him.

---

*"May God protect you"

NATHAN MOOSOVI PULLED into the alley and
parked the Volvo. He glanced at Moosa as he pulled on
the door handle. "Here we are," he said. "The door is
just around that corner."

They walked down the unpaved alley, skirting the
puddles of muddy water. In the overcast afternoon
light, the puddles looked gray, like everything else. Nathan stopped beside a rusted metal door and knocked
once, hesitated, and knocked three more times in quick
succession. The door opened perhaps an inch.

"It's Nathan," he said in a quiet voice, "and I've
brought the guest I told you about."

The door opened halfway. The interior was pitch dark,
as far as Moosa could discern. Nathan stepped inside but
Moosa hesitated. The door reminded him uncomfortably
of the gateway to some mythical underworld. Taking a
deep breath, he stepped past the portal.

The room was not completely dark, after all. As his
eyes adjusted to being inside, Moosa could see the
sparse furnishings: a table, a miscellaneous assortment
of chairs scattered about, empty cups and glasses strewn
on the table, a low-wattage lamp in one corner. The air
was heavy with stale cigarette smoke. Several men were
inside, staring at him with looks of appraisal and curiosity.

"We don't use last names here," Nathan murmured
to him. "We think it's better that way, in case . . .
anything should happen."

Moosa swallowed and nodded, his eyes darting to and
fro about the room.

One of the men approached. In the dim light, he
might have been thirty or sixty. His frame was spare
and firm, but his face was careworn and fatigued. Like
many Iranians, Moosa realized, he had aged rapidly in
these last months.

"This is Moosa," Nathan said to the man. "His father was imprisoned in Evin."

"Why did they take him away?" asked the man.

Moosa glanced quickly from Nathan to the speaker. "I . . . I don't know. He had done nothing wrong. The *pasdars* just came and got him."

"Did they shoot him?" the man asked in the same flat voice.

"No. He got out alive."

The man glanced significantly at Nathan and the others. "Why did they let him out?" he asked quickly. "No one comes out of Evin alive, unless he's on their side."

"No, that's not how it is with him!" Moosa replied, louder than he intended. "A mullah put in a word for him—"

"A mullah!" sneered one of the others. "Who is this guy, anyway? What are you doing, Nathan? Selling us to one of Khomeini's lap dogs?"

"My father was kind to this mullah, long before the revolution," Moosa said, trying in vain to keep from clenching his fists. "For the sake of that, the mullah helped him—nothing more. He's not a toady for the *pasdars*, if that's what you're worried about."

"Listen, Ari," Nathan said in a calm voice, laying a hand on Moosa's arm, "I've known Moosa all his life. I'm not stupid. Moosa is just as angry as any of us. Don't hold it against him that his father's still alive."

The others fell silent at this, regarding Moosa with sullen stares.

The man who had approached peered at Moosa for some moments in appraisal. Finally, he said, "I'm Ari. Come on in and have a seat." He turned away without offering his hand.

Nathan guided Moosa to a seat at the table. The others gathered in a loose circle about him.

ESTHER TOOK A SIP of lukewarm tea and carefully set her cup back into the matching bone china saucer she held in her lap. Biting her lip, she looked again at the plywood box sitting in the study. Ahmed Dabirian's oldest son had delivered it early this morning. He told her Ezra had ordered it, and presented her with a bill. Grudgingly, she had allowed him inside and given him the money.

Even a casual glance inside the box showed that the outside area did not match that within. Surely an experienced customs inspector would see that there was space at the bottom of the box unaccounted for by the visible inner dimensions. She doubted the wisdom of Ezra's apparent plans for the hidden compartment. If they were discovered taking hard currency out of the country, no receipt or endorsement from Mullah Hafizi would save them.

Since Ezra's delivery from Evin Prison, Esther's attitude toward emigration from Iran had undergone a drastic change. She was now in an agony of eagerness to leave the country. The distress of her husband's imprisonment, combined with the frank hostility of the search party, had made her a willing accomplice in the plan to escape to the West. As if these weren't enough, their daughter feared for her life if she returned to school. Even Ezra had agreed that keeping Sepi at home was for the best.

Esther was willing to abandon every shred of property and wealth they owned to facilitate their departure. But Ezra still went along with his plans, keeping his own counsel—to protect her, he said—making his careful, studied moves. Now, instead of being angered with his intent to leave, she was frustrated by his tedious, silent preparations, his apparent nonchalance. She wanted nothing more than to quit the churning cauldron of chaos which her country had become. She wanted to scream at him, to tell him to hurry up, to get them out of this cursed place. But Ezra plodded along, ordering a shipping crate with a false bottom, as if they had all the time in the world to pack their goods and make an orderly departure.

Moosa came downstairs, scratching his tousled hair and yawning. Esther looked at him, worry creasing her eyes. Why was he staying out so late, especially in times like these? Every night, rifle fire could be heard in all quarters of the city, as *pasdars* skirmished with resentful supporters of the Shah, or with *mujahedin* guerrillas. Even the mullahs had taken to wearing guns in these days of madness.

Walking home from the bus stop, Esther had seen graffiti sprayed on a wall: "*Qalat kardeem*—We made a mistake." Too late, some had realized the dangers of placing so much power in the hands of the long-repressed mullahs. Yet her son had taken to roaming the streets at night. She didn't know where he went on his mysterious nocturnal trips—and was not certain she wanted to know. Perhaps the insanity in the country was infecting all its citizens. Moosa glanced at her, then away, as he plodded sleepily into the kitchen.

She heard the clink of a cup and saucer, followed by Moosa cursing under his breath.

"Mother," he called in annoyance, "why is there no coffee?"

"The propane tank is empty, and there's no heat for the stove."

Again she heard the mumbled swearing. The fuel oil company had made no deliveries for weeks now, and no one knew when they would resume, if ever. Several evenings the electricity had gone out, due in part to the well-connected but inexperienced workers now in charge of the generating stations. Such was the confusion of these days.

She felt Ezra's hand on her neck, followed by the warmth of his lips on her cheek. "Good morning, my love," he smiled, walking past her into the kitchen. Pensively she watched his back as he moved away. He was dressed as if to go out. Glancing a final time at the wooden box, she got up and followed her husband.

"Where are you going, Ezra?" she asked, pouring the tea down the drain and carefully rinsing the cup.

"I must go and keep a promise I made while I was in prison," Ezra said, a hint of sadness in his voice.

"To whom?" asked Moosa, wincing in distaste as he sipped at the tepid tea which was all he could find to drink.

"To a fellow Jew not as fortunate as I," said Ezra. "He asked me to take a message to his wife and child, and I thought I'd do that this morning, since the weather is warm and clear." Ezra tore off a hunk from a loaf of pita bread Esther had baked the night before. He moved the containers in the refrigerator until he found a jar of marmalade, and began spreading it on his bread.

"What happened to this friend of yours?" mumbled Moosa around a large mouthful of bread.

Ezra paused, knife in hand, and looked out the window toward the cherry trees in the side yard. The echo of rifle shots rattled in his brain, and he closed his eyes for an instant. "He was shot," Ezra said finally, and resumed spreading the marmalade.

Esther looked at him sharply. "Do you think it's safe, so soon after your release, to go to the home of an executed detainee? Surely the mullahs have the place under surveillance."

"I made a promise," Ezra interrupted, his eyes momentarily hardening with resolve as he looked at her. Esther looked away, sighing as she selected a tomato from the produce basket and began slicing it into wedges.

"Besides," Ezra continued, "I have reason to believe the wife is now at the home of her parents."

Esther shook her head in helpless frustration. Did Ezra imagine the mullahs didn't know the locations of all the relatives of this executed Jew?

Ezra chewed the bread slowly, and washed it down with a glass of tap water. Moosa craned his neck around the doorway, looking into the study. "By the way, Father," he asked, "what's the box for? You thinking about going into the smuggling racket?" he joked.

Ezra peered intently at Moosa, then glanced over at Esther. She had stopped paring the tomatoes, standing with her back to him, her face half-turned, waiting for his answer.

"The box is for shipping the Isfahan carpet to America," Ezra answered carefully. "Nothing more." He placed his empty water glass beside the sink and began walking out of the kitchen.

Esther could not contain herself. "Ezra, any customs inspector with one eye and half a brain will notice the dimensions of that box. Please don't tell me you plan to take our money in that . . . that thing." Her eyes challenged him to reply.

He looked at his wife and his son, then smiled ever so slightly, shaking his head. "You two are quite the suspicious types. Perhaps you should go to work for the customs service."

Esther huffed in exasperation as she rolled her eyes. Moosa shook his head and took another bite of bread.

"Well, I'm off," Ezra announced, starting toward the front door. "Moosa, don't worry about going to the bazaar today. I'll change the currency myself for a while."

Moosa grunted and nodded.

"Good-bye, Esther, my darling," Ezra called cheerily.

Esther chewed savagely on a tomato wedge, pointedly ignoring him. She heard the front door open, then close.

SIXTEEN

EPIDEH'S EYES FLUTTERED, then opened. She lay on her bed, sunlight filtering through the curtained and shuttered windows of her room. Without moving, she gazed around the familiar room. Lately, Sepi had wanted to do little but sleep. Like an addict, she sought the black oblivion of slumber as the only refuge from the living nightmare which swirled about her. Yet with each awakening, dread and depression resumed their intimate, dreary vigil within her soul, hovering like carrion birds just beneath her ceiling, awaiting only her stirring to descend and resume feeding. Groaning, she rolled over and closed her eyes, willing herself back toward the bleak refuge of unconsciousness.

But it was already close to noon, and she could not, despite her best efforts, return to the somnolent cave of unbeing. Her eyes fell upon the book resting on her bedside table. It was a volume of poetry, a textbook from her literature class at school. A class she had attended ages ago, in another life, before madness reigned.

Wearily, without consciously willing it, she sat up and opened the book, leafing idly through its pages. Her eye paused. On the page before her was a work of the poet Saadi. Without knowing why, she read:

Human beings are members of one another,
For in creation they are wrought of the same fabric.
When one is afflicted,
All suffer.
You who scoff at the wounds of others,
Are unworthy to be called human....

The words, once only a series of lines to be memorized for a grade, now spawned a dark ache at the back of Sepi's throat. The taunts of the boys' gang resounded in her ears. *"Jew trash. Tramp. Infidel."* She had known some of them, had romped with them on the playground of her primary school. Yet their faces had been as closed, as clenched with hate, as those of total strangers. They felt no empathy for her, no more pity than wild dogs circling wounded prey. Such cold malevolence was beyond her experience, beyond her ability to cope. She could not bring her mind and emotions to accept the possibility of the unimagined dangers now inhabiting the world she had always thought so safe. It was like walking out to Marjan's kennel to feed him and having him suddenly slash at her with his fangs. Or as if her father's flower garden had been overgrown during the night with poisonous thorns.

And Khosrow. Though he had defended her, she had not heard from him since that last, awful day at school. Not a letter, not a phone call—nothing. She felt abandoned, betrayed. Had his feelings for her, his affectionate teasing, all been a sham? A pleasant ruse to be dropped when no longer convenient? Perhaps he did not actually despise her Jewishness, but was he embarrassed by it? Was he secretly relieved that she no longer came to school, that he need not bear the curses of the others as they rebounded from her onto him? To be hated for one's ancestry, or to be an embarrassment because of it—the two appeared much the same in the hopeless, gray world she now inhabited.

A knock came on her door. *It is probably Mother,* she thought tiredly, *come to badger me about being in bed so late.* And then came Moosa's voice. "Sepi? Mind if I come in?"

She pulled her robe from the bedpost where it hung and tugged it on. "Yes, come in," she said, tying the sash about her waist.

Moosa came in, eyeing her thoughtfully. "Isn't it a little late to be in bed?"

Sepi rolled her eyes. *First Mother, now Moosa. No one understands.*

He sat down on the edge of her bed, still studying her listless posture, her vacant expression. "What happened to you at school was a terrible thing," he said finally. "It was unfair and wrong, and the boys who did it should be horsewhipped."

For the first time, her eyes flickered toward him with something that might have been interest.

"And I don't blame you for feeling hurt and abandoned," he continued. "This family has always been law-abiding and loyal; now with the mullahs in control, it seems that counts for nothing. You didn't do anything to deserve what happened to you, just as Father did nothing that should have landed him in Evin Prison, just as Abraham Moosovi did nothing that should have gotten him executed."

She was watching him steadily now, but still said nothing.

"Injustice is the rule of the day for anyone who's not Muslim," he said, his eyes roaming somewhere beyond the walls of her room. "The country is coming apart at the seams, and it's a bad time to be in the minority— any minority."

For the first time, she spoke. "So what do we do? Renounce our Judaism, become Muslim converts? Is that the way?" Her voice was a flat, inflectionless mirror of hopelessness.

"No!" The word came out sharper than he intended. "Sepi," he went on in a gentler tone, "there are three possible responses to what is happening to us right now. And it's very important that we choose carefully, and not simply allow the choice to be made by default."

She said nothing, but her eyes indicated her willingness to listen.

"First, we can despair. Give up, quit. Drift along passively and allow events to knock us about however they may. That's the worst choice of all, I think. It means they've already beaten us. It means we've admitted that they really do have the right to do whatever they want, since we're unwilling to help ourselves."

She would no longer meet his eyes, but her dead expression of moments ago was shifting to one of indignation and perhaps a little anger. *Good,* Moosa thought. *She's still got some fight left, down in there somewhere.* "The second choice is to change to fit the circumstances," he went on. "To make plans, to figure out a way around difficulties—how to get away, perhaps. That's what Father is doing, Sepi. He has felt all the same pain, all the same fear, all the same persecution you've felt—only more. And his answer is to adapt. But at least he's moving, he's doing something. He hasn't quit, not for a second. It means he's still alive, still fighting in his own way."

There was a long silence. Despite her unwillingness, she found herself unable to resist asking the question, "And the third way? You said there were three possibilities."

Moosa turned his head away. Several more silent moments passed before he again looked at her. "You can get angry," he said quietly. "You can push back."

The speed of her reply surprised him. "And which have you chosen?"

He stared at her for the space of ten heartbeats. Then, without a word, he got up and left the room.

EZRA CONSULTED THE ADDRESS on the envelope, then looked again at the numbers painted on the dingy, plastered wall beside the gate. The house stood on Avenue Ismaili, a small street in a slightly rundown neighborhood, and Ezra looked about him nervously as he knocked at the gate. He had not seen anyone following him or observing his movements since he arrived here moments before, but he could not help feeling exposed. Again he knocked at the gate, anxious to get inside, away from passing eyes.

Finally he heard the slap of leather-soled feet on the hard-packed dirt of the courtyard inside the wall. As the steps approached the gate, a low, cautious male voice asked, "Who's there?"

"I am Ezra Solaiman. Are Jahan and Maheen Ibrahim here?"

"Why are you here?" Suspicion hardened the tone of the voice inside the gate.

"I bring a message from Reuben, Jahan's husband."

"Reuben isn't here. For all we know, he's dead. Go away." Ezra heard the grinding sound the man's foot made as he turned to walk away from the gate.

"Wait!" Ezra called. "Yes, you are right. Reuben is dead. We were cell mates in Evin Prison. Just before we went in to the mullahs, he gave me a message for Jahan. He gave me an envelope—here, let me put it under the gate."

He heard no more footsteps. Looking a last time at the envelope, he placed it on the ground, and scooted it under the gate with his toe. For five or six heartbeats there was no sound. Then he heard the man take two paces. His clothing rustled as he bent down to pick up the envelope. Then came a long silence. "Wait here," the man said at last, and he walked quickly back to the house.

Several minutes later, Ezra heard two sets of returning footsteps. He could discern the soft, muffled sobs of a woman, even as the man demanded roughly, "Why have you come?" Ezra decided to appeal directly to the widow of Reuben Ibrahim.

"Jahan *khanom*," Ezra said earnestly, "for me, your Reuben was a blessing sent by the Eternal. His advice was of great help to me in prison. He made me promise to bring this message to you if I got out of prison. And I have brought something else for you and little Maheen. Please let me in. I won't be able to fulfill my promise to your martyred husband if you don't."

A moment more she sobbed quietly. Then a key rattled in the lock, and the latch clicked back. Slowly the gate swung outward, and Ezra stepped into the courtyard of the father-in-law of Reuben Ibrahim.

Jahan was short and slightly overweight. Her round, pretty face was ringed by jet-black curls. She wore a somber gray dress and daubed at grief-reddened eyes with a wrinkled handkerchief. Just behind her stood her father, a round, balding man with a thick, wiry gray mustache. This man now gestured toward the house.

"I am your humble servant, Ismail Menachim," he said. "Come in, *Aga* Solaiman," he said. "I apologize for being rude to you at the gate. These days, one can't be too careful."

"Please. I, of all people, understand your caution," assured Ezra.

"When I saw Reuben's handwriting on the envelope . . ." Jahan began. Her voice caught. After taking several deep breaths, she went on. ". . . I knew for certain he was dead. In my heart I have been trying to prepare for this moment, but . . ." She leaned against the door frame of her house and covered her face with one hand.

Tenderly, Ezra patted her shoulder. "I am so very sorry, Jahan *khanom*. Your husband was a brave man, a true hero. He didn't deserve the treatment he got from the mullahs." He felt sympathetic tears burning the corners of his eyes.

Presently, Jahan's father pushed the door open. "Please come in. Our house is humble, but you are welcome here."

A few moments later, Ezra perched uneasily on one of the two chairs in the sparsely furnished parlor of Ismail Menachim's house. The room was small, but very clean. Floral drapes covered the windows, and assorted rugs, the stock and trade of Reuben Ibrahim, covered the linoleum floors. Seated across from Ezra, Jahan trembled with silent sobs as she held her face in her hands. The sorrow in her parents' faces, as they stood silently on either side of her, was a faint echo of the anguish which covered the grieving young widow like a shroud.

Ezra longed to comfort her, to assuage the pain of Reuben's unjust death, but the only words he could summon to his mind seemed so shallow, so empty. What could he say, after all? That he was sorry? That her husband's death was senseless? How could such inanities heal the raw, gaping wound in Jahan Ibrahim's heart?

He stirred, and heard the rustling of the paper sack in his coat pocket. He had stopped by a candy store on his way here, to get a treat for the child. Now he produced the bag of *gaz-i-Isfahan*.

"Where is Maheen?" he asked. "I brought her a present."

Jahan dabbed at her eyes with the saturated kerchief, struggling gamely to smile. "How kind of you, *Aga* Solaiman! Maheen, come in here, darling. *Aga* Solaiman has brought you a gift!"

The child timidly peeked around the frame of the doorway into the hall. Eyes downcast, she remained where she was, the thumb of her right hand in her mouth. She appeared to Ezra to be no more than three years old. Her face was a heartbreakingly familiar version of her father's, and her mother's dark ringlets circled the shy, pudgy face. Clearly Maheen was uncertain of Ezra

151

and, though intrigued by the notion of a present, was unwilling to enter the room with a stranger.

"Come here, Maheen," her mother urged. "Come meet *Aga* Solaiman."

Maheen glanced worriedly from Ezra to her grandparents and mother, the thumb still lodged in her mouth.

"Please, Maheen, come here," said Jahan. Then, to Ezra, she explained, "The *pasdars* came here looking for Reuben. She was very badly frightened. Even now, when we must go out, she hides her face in my shoulder when we encounter any man she does not know. And sometimes in the night, she awakens screaming. . . ." Jahan's voice faltered.

Ezra felt his heart breaking with pity for this child, this innocent one rendered fatherless by the ruthless ambitions of men. Maheen, hugging the wall, edged into the room, her eyes fixed warily on Ezra. Reaching her mother, Maheen climbed onto her lap. Only from that sanctuary did she extend a hand toward the bag Ezra held on his knee.

Slowly, with what he hoped was a kind smile on his face, Ezra handed the bag of candy to the child. Maheen peered inside, her fear overcome at last by curiosity. Taking a piece of the white, crunchy confection in her hand, she at last withdrew her thumb from her mouth, popping the *gaz-i-Isfahan* inside and chewing noisily.

Jahan smiled down at her daughter, then at Ezra. "Pistachio nut candies are her favorites," she said. Placing her mouth close beside Maheen's ear, she admonished, "What do you say to *Aga* Solaiman, little one?"

"Thank you," the child said quietly, with the briefest of glances in his direction. Then she ducked her head, studiously inspecting the sack of candy.

"Reuben . . ." Ezra began, and stopped. The name was big in the room, made huge by the absence of its owner. He could not say it without feeling a vast draft of sorrow blowing through his heart. His mouth struggled dryly for a way to continue. He realized Jahan was looking at him strangely.

"I'm sorry, Jahan *khanom*," he managed. "I hardly know how to begin. Your suffering . . . it must be unbearable."

"No, *Aga* Solaiman," she said quietly, a look of saddened calm on her features. "It is not unbearable, not quite. I know Reuben is beyond all pain, all suffering. And that is of much comfort to me, even now." She drew a deep, quivering breath, then continued. "And . . . as for Maheen and me, well . . . we will be protected by the same grace which shielded Reuben."

Ezra puzzled the meaning of this enigmatic assurance. Reuben . . . shielded? "I'm sorry, Jahan *khanom*, but I . . . fail to comprehend."

"Death is not the end of the story, *Aga* Solaiman," she said in a quiet voice, husky with conviction. Her eyes blazed with dark fire into his. "Reuben lives, because his Lord lives, and is faithful to His promises."

Ezra felt his face slackening with surprise. He had come here expecting to give comfort, to share the sorrow of a bereaved wife and child. And there was sorrow here, to be sure; anxiety, pain, and longing were evident in the manner and bearing of Jahan Ibrahim. But this . . . this ardent undertone of assurance, this foundation of confidence? So unlike the woeful, resigned fatalism Ezra remembered from the funerals of his parents and friends. Or the vengeful protestations of the Shiite martyrs' families. This was a faith which had nothing to prove to itself, nor to anyone else. For Jahan Ibrahim, it seemed a sufficiency, even in the midst of heartbreak.

"I . . . I heard Reuben speak—or, rather, pray . . . about a Yeshua," he began.

"Yes," said Jahan, smiling through the tears coursing down her cheeks. "We have placed our trust in Yeshua, and He will be with us, no matter what may come."

153

Seeing Ezra's confused look, she continued softly, "Surely you have heard of Him, *Aga* Solaiman. Yeshua . . . some call Him Jesus."

A look of astonishment burst across Ezra's features. "Jesus! But Reuben said he was a Jew!"

"Yes, we are Jews," interjected Jahan. "We are Jews who believe that God came to earth in the person of *Yeshua Mashiach.* That doesn't make us any less Jewish. There is a difference between this belief and the Western Christian heritage which has persecuted and despised our people for so long. That heritage has much in which Yeshua has no part, things which we cannot accept. But we have placed our lives—and our eternal souls—in the hands of Yeshua, the Son of God, the Savior."

Ezra scarcely knew what to say. He was embarrassed, nonplussed, and—he was strangely loath to admit—angry, as if Reuben had somehow deceived him. He had come here to fulfill a promise to one with whom he had supposed himself to have linkage, commonality. And now the man's widow preached to him about some strange, half-Jewish belief in the Christ! Surely the world was turning upside down, when Jews began calling on the name of Jesus! Instinctively, his eyes flew to the face of Jahan's father. Surely a man of his own generation did not tolerate such outlandish notions under his roof. But the intense, unwavering return gaze of Ismail Menachim, the quiet, assured attitude of Jahan's mother, told him that the entire household was of a single mind on this subject.

Feeling more out of place than ever, Ezra stood. "Jahan *khanom,* I . . . I wish, for the sake of your husband's kindness to me, to give you—this." He took an envelope from his coat pocket, proffering it toward the still-seated Jahan. She took it, her brow wrinkling in puzzlement. "That is 10,000 *rials,*" he said, in answer to her unasked question. "Reuben said he had hidden some money for you, with instructions contained in the envelope I brought from him. But, please take this money, as a sign of my gratitude for Reuben's encouragement and bravery."

Her eyes widened, she stared at him in amazement. "*Aga* Solaiman . . . why should you—?"

Ezra suddenly had the desperate need to be away. "Please, *khanom*. Allow me to do this. As for the other things you had to say . . . I . . ." His mouth opened and closed, his fingers made grasping motions, but his thoughts eluded him, evaporating into the thin air of his confusion. ". . . I . . . should go now," he stammered finally, putting his hat on and turning toward the door.

He felt her hand on his shoulder. He turned. Jahan was standing, holding the silent Maheen on her hip. "*Aga* Solaiman," she was saying, "I . . . I hope I didn't frighten or offend you. Perhaps I spoke more freely than I should have, to one whom I have only just met. But, somehow. . . ." Her eyes misted over, her chin quivered as she looked away, then back at him. "You were the last to see my Reuben alive. Perhaps I thought that somehow, in telling you, I was also telling him." Her lips trembled out of control. She brought a hand to her mouth. Hesitantly, her father placed his hand on her shoulder, squeezing slightly.

A moment more her eyes held him. Ezra cleared his throat awkwardly, breaking the spell. "Yes, well . . ." he said, looking away, "I really must go now, and leave you alone. Good-bye, Jahan *khanom*, and good-bye, Maheen." The child managed a little wave, still without looking at him. "I am truly sorry for your loss," he finished. "May . . . may God protect you and Maheen."

"He will, *Aga* Solaiman," she averred quietly. "He will."

After another uncomfortable pause, Ezra smiled weakly and nodded. "Thank you, *Aga* Menachim, for your hospitality." Jahan's father nodded.

Then Ezra was out the door and striding across the small courtyard to the gate. Closing it behind him, he took several deep breaths. After glancing about him, he walked quickly away.

As Ezra rounded the corner, a man who had been leaning against a wall at the opposite end of the block took a final drag at his cigarette and dropped it to the pavement, grinding it with his foot. Glancing back at the small house where he had just met with the revolutionary committee's go-between, Firouz Marandi once again patted the envelope in his pocket. *Not a bad day's pay for informing on an unsuspecting Baha'i scum,* he thought. After a final look about, he sauntered casually along in the same direction Ezra had taken. As he followed at a safe distance, he thought to himself, *What is that old Jew up to now?*

MOOSA PUSHED HIS PLATE AWAY. "That was good, Mother," he said, appreciatively. He stood up from the table and walked toward the front foyer.

"Where are you going?" he heard his mother ask, as he reached for his jacket. Carefully, deliberately, he put on and zipped the leather jacket before turning to face her.

She was standing between him and the table. The others, still seated, were frozen in a tableau of tense anticipation. She gripped her elbows to her sides with the palms of her hands; her face was a tightly pinched portrait of worry and disapproval.

"I'm going out—with some friends," he said quietly. As he was starting out the door, he remembered the gun. He turned and went upstairs toward his room. As he reached the top landing, he heard quiet, terse voices in the dining room below . . . his parents' voices.

When he came downstairs, his father stood in the foyer. Moosa saw his eyes flicker from his face to the bulge in his jacket. "What do you have in your coat?" his father demanded.

Slowly, Moosa unzipped his jacket. "I bought it in the covered bazaar," he explained, closing his hand over the Beretta, bringing it into the open as if it were a precious jewel—or a vial of explosive gas. "I thought... perhaps... it was something... we might need." Holding the gun on his open palm, he displayed it to his father.

Ezra stared at Moosa as if he held a live snake in his hand. "What is the meaning of this?" he asked.

Moosa's stare challenged his father's. "The *pasdars* may come back while you are gone. They came last time for you; they may come for Mother or Sepi. I... I thought it my duty to protect—"

"Protect?" shouted Ezra. "By taking on the *pasdars* single-handedly? This is folly, boy! What could you be thinking of?"

Moosa stared over his father's head, his jaw grinding and his nostrils flaring in silent resentment. "Father," he grated finally, his eyes averted, "I have seen the *pasdars'* interrogation methods. I saw them beat Nathan Moosovi, for nothing other than reporting a crime against his property. They have killed Nathan's father. Perhaps your mullah friend—if indeed he is such— would again intervene, perhaps not. But—"

"Is this what you have learned in America?" said Ezra, incredulous. "To carry such things about like... like some kind of bandit?"

Esther and Sepi sat at the table, their faces white with fear, waiting to hear what Moosa would say.

"In America, Father," Moosa said through clenched teeth, "I never knew the police to drag an honest citizen out of his house and throw him in prison. In Iran, things are different now, wouldn't you agree?" For ten, twelve heartbeats, the father and son stared angrily at each other. Moosa shouldered past Ezra and strode to

157

the entry. He yanked the door open and was gone with a slam into the night.

Ezra stood rooted to his spot at the base of the stairs, feeling as if all the air had just left his body, sucked out by Moosa's belligerent exit. Unbidden, the memory of Jahan Ibrahim floated to the surface of his jumbled emotions. *"We have placed our trust in Yeshua; He will be with us."* Who, Ezra wondered, *will be with Moosa tonight? What dark deity will shield him as he walks in wrath, wielding a weapon of violence?*

Dejection twined his heart like a choking vine. He realized that his escape from the clutches of the mullah at Evin Prison was only a beginning. There were yet many ways for insanity to win the day.

SEVENTEEN

THE SUN WAS just past noon. Ezra was hungry and sweaty in the blazing summer heat, but he dared not leave his place in line. He had already been queuing outside the Swiss embassy for two hours, and at least three dozen people stood impatiently behind him. Ahead, ten individuals waited for an appointment with the consul's representative. Swiss exit visas were in high demand these days.

Tedium finally got the better of him, and Ezra decided to strike up a conversation. He tapped the middle-aged man in front of him on the shoulder. The man turned and looked at Ezra with a pleasant, questioning look. "Yes, *baradar*, what is it?"

"How much longer do you think we will have to wait?" Ezra asked.

The man shrugged. "Who knows? We may have to come back tomorrow."

"And start all over?" asked Ezra, horrified at the thought of repeating his two-hour ordeal.

"Oh, no!" said the stranger. "Unlike our officials, the Swiss are experienced and well organized." Both men chuckled at the unfortunate truth of the comparison. "They will give us a number before they close for the day," the man continued, "and we will keep our places in line for tomorrow. But," he said, glancing at his watch, "it's only 3:30. If they don't close until 5 o'clock, we may yet get in to the consul's representative."

Ezra nodded. Seeing two mullahs close to the front of the line, he nudged the friendly stranger. Pointing his chin at the mullahs, Ezra said, "Obviously this isn't an Islamic Republic office, or those two would already be inside."

"True," agreed the man ruefully. "Well, at least there's one place in Iran where they must wait their turn, like everyone else."

Ezra grunted in agreement, staring warily at the clerics.

"Any guess why they're getting Swiss visas?" asked the man softly, after a moment's silence.

Heartened by the man's apparent mistrust of the mullahs, Ezra snorted scornfully. Leaning closer to the stranger, he said, "Obviously they aren't going there to buy a new wardrobe." The two men chuckled softly together, glancing cautiously about.

Another moment passed, and the fellow whispered close to Ezra's ear, "The Swiss banks."

Ezra reflected a moment, then nodded solemnly at his newfound ally. "I have seen the way they get their riches," he replied quietly. "You think they take their blood money to Switzerland?"

The man looked askance at Ezra, as if to say, "Can there be any doubt?"

As the line moved forward, the man murmured over his shoulder to Ezra, "You are emigrating because you are Jewish."

It didn't sound like a question. After several silent seconds of contemplation, Ezra whispered, "Yes."

Again the line halted and the man turned toward Ezra. Looking carefully about, he said in a low voice, "I'm leaving too."

Ezra glanced curiously at the fellow. "Why? You don't look or sound Jewish. Are you Baha'i or Christian?"

A slight smile skittered across the man's face as he

looked into Ezra's eyes. "The religious minorities are not the only ones who suffer," he remarked sadly.

A silent question was etched on Ezra's face.

Looking over his shoulder, the fellow continued softly, "Until two years before the revolution, my brother was the officer in command of the Shah's bodyguard. Someone denounced him to a revolutionary committee, and he was arrested, tried, and shot."

Ezra shuddered, as the too-present recollection of Evin Prison strangled him with memories of fear and death.

"Who knows how far the net of hatred may widen?" the man asked. "Like ripples on a pool, the circle grows and grows. Today they shoot anyone who had close relations with the Shah; tomorrow, perhaps all who knew yesterday's victims. What is to stop them? I will leave this country and never come back, as long as its only law is the mullahs' greed and ambition."

A silent moment of fearful reflection passed before Ezra said, "Like Scheherazade of the *Alef Laillah,** we could tell a thousand and one tales—of sadness, death, and injustice."

EZRA GLANCED OVER the application form he had just completed. Again he stared hard at the question, "How many people will be in your party?"

He had written a numeral 3 in the blank, after a soul-searching pause. Moosa presumably still had his American visa; Ezra did not want to further alert the Islamic authorities that his son was back in Iran.

Almost daily, the newspapers carried notices about hapless Americans taken hostage when their embassy was overrun by a student faction of the Islamic funda-

---

*the Arabic name for *The Thousand and One Nights*

161

mentalists. Either the press quoted Khomeini, tempo-
rizing about his inability to countermand an order given
the students by Allah, or they printed stories of the
American government fretting and fuming and doing
nothing, to the delight of the anti-Western mullahs.
And frequently they ran photographs of crowds in the
streets displaying violent slogans against the erstwhile
benefactors of the Shah. The tide of anti-American
opinion had never been so strong or so virulent.

Ezra had decided to apply only on behalf of Esther,
Sepideh, and himself. Moosa might travel with them,
but he would do so with as little advance notice as
possible.

Rising from the small desk, Ezra walked toward the
embassy aide. Glancing up, the young man inclined his
head toward the consul's chamber.

Ezra laid the completed application on the Swiss consul's desk. The consul, a dapper, middle-aged man with
a carefully trimmed goatee, smiled perfunctorily at Ezra
and perused his application—the 400th he had reviewed that week.

"Hmm," he murmured, placing his finger alongside
one of the questions, "this says you have traveled to
Switzerland before, on business." Peering up at Ezra,
the consul asked in French-accented Farsi, "Can you
prove this, *Aga* Solaiman? As you must know, many people are applying for Swiss visas, and we must carefully
screen all applicants."

"Yes, sir," Ezra responded, placing his passport on
the desk while saying a silent prayer of thanks that he
had done frequent business with Ciba-Geigy and
Sandoz Corporation, two large Swiss firms.

The consul nodded slightly, studying the dated Swiss
stamps on the passport. "To what city do you and your
wife and . . . daughter intend to go?"

"To Geneva."

"You intend to stay for how long?"

"Two days at most."

"And your destination upon leaving Geneva?"

Ezra paused before answering. Glancing quickly about in habitual caution, he replied, "The United States of America."

The consul glanced significantly at Ezra. After his own thoughtful pause, he said quietly, "As you know, *Aga* Solaiman, we represent the American interests during these . . . these difficult times."

Ezra nodded.

The consul leafed idly through the stack of applications on the side of his desk before again meeting Ezra's eyes. "I'm sure you have your own reasons for not applying for American entry visas at this time."

Again Ezra nodded, silently.

"Do you have a green card?" the consul asked quietly.

"No," replied Ezra, averting his eyes.

Carefully spreading his fingertips atop Ezra's application, the consul asked, "Why do you think you will be granted entry into the United States?"

"I . . . I have a son who lives there."

"There is no assurance this will be accepted as a valid reason," the official warned quietly.

After another silent debate, Ezra asked, "What about money?"

The consul leaned forward on his elbows, making an arch of his fingertips. "You must have a minimum of $400,000 in American banks."

"We have that amount," Ezra replied carefully.

The consul's eyes widened slightly. "In American banks?" he repeated.

Ezra looked away, then back. "It is en route there now," he said. *If this works,* he told himself, *the money will be en route to the U.S., so I'm not lying. Not really.* He hoped that in convincing himself he would be able to convince the consul.

The official gave a Gallic shrug, arching an eyebrow.

163

"If it is as you say, *Aga* Solaiman, you will have no problem." He reached into the lap drawer of his desk and brought out a large stamp, which he inked from a pad on his desk. With the stamp hovering just above Ezra's passport, he glanced up a final time. "Good luck," he said, and stamped the passport, affixing his signature. As Ezra watched, his heart hammering with exhilaration, the consul repeated the process on the other two passports.

MOOSA WAITED in the green Volvo, its engine idling. Nervously, he drummed his fingers on the wheel, his eyes flickering back and forth, now in the rearview mirror, now through the windshield. The car was completely dark; not even the dashboard was illuminated. They wanted nothing to attract a random glance at a car parked in the darkness of an abandoned alleyway.

Nathan had organized this action. They were parked behind the home of a certain Mullah Hojat who headed one of the Revolutionary Committees. This particular committee had played a prominent role in the campaign to arrest and confiscate the estates of wealthy Jews and Christians. Nathan and the two with him had been gone perhaps fifteen minutes, stealing quietly away from the car, after checking their weapons and the clips of slugs they each carried.

Sitting in the dark alley, Moosa reflected upon the change—unlooked-for and, in his more reflective moments, unwelcomed—which had stolen over him since his return from America. He had come here only to help his parents and sister leave Iran; now he found himself involved in a deadly and probably futile effort to alter the course of the Islamic revolution. When he had flown into Mehrabad Airport, his only concern had been how soon he and his family could be on the next plane West. But now, despite his better judgment, he felt himself drawn slowly but surely into a tangled, dark maze of awful purpose. He could feel the heady wine of conspiracy working deep into his bowels, changing his mind and his will. Since his return to Iran, Moosa had begun a metamorphosis and what he was becoming, he was not certain. That from which he had originally sought to deliver his family—the curse of the Third World—had arisen to claim him as its true son. His father, Moosa knew, moved eagerly toward the gentle, commodious beacon of the civilized West, while he, the westernized, UCLA-educated son, became an unbridled throwback to some barbaric past, a saddle horse loosed into the wilderness.

Why? He couldn't put his finger on the precise moment when the change had begun. His father's arrest had something to do with it, the grinding, impotent rage he had felt at hearing those ignorant, unwashed *pasdars* haughtily accusing his father of wrongdoing. That and the double injustice done to the Moosovi family had kindled within him a desire to strike out— partly in anger and partly in fear—at the source of the wrong. Nathan Moosovi had been less recruiter than midwife to the birthing of something which was already fighting to emerge from within Moosa. Once the bloody, steaming child of his rage was born, he felt helpless to deny it life. Now it fed eagerly and grew apace, suckling eagerly at the thrill of fear which was becoming addictive, a loved and hated rush of sensation which he dreaded but couldn't deny himself.

Hearing the sudden scamper of feet behind him, Moosa jerked around to see several figures approaching the Volvo at a dead run. A surge of adrenaline tensed his sinews to a taut readiness.

Nathan and the other two yanked open the doors of the Volvo. "Go! Go!" shouted Nathan before they were inside. Moosa's hands flew to the transmission lever, the headlight switch. As the Volvo squealed away, rifle slugs spattered on the masonry walls beside them, followed instantaneously by the *crack!* of the pursuers' firearms.

Moosa's foot pinned the accelerator to the floorboard as they raced toward the end of the alley and onto Abbasabad Street. They were within perhaps fifty feet of the thoroughfare when three *pasdars* appeared in the opening. As if in slow motion, Moosa saw their arms rising, saw the quick blue-and-white spitting of their pistols.

The windshield shattered. Moosa heard someone screaming. He fell over in the seat, trying to dodge the hail of death. The Volvo swerved in the narrow alley, slamming against the wall on the right, caroming back toward the center. Raising his head as much as he dared, he aimed the Volvo toward the alley entrance, roaring toward the still-firing *pasdars*. One of them didn't dodge quite in time; Moosa heard him scream as the front fender of the Volvo clipped him at the waist, rolling him over the hood and roof of the car.

He careened onto Abbasabad, amid blaring horns and swerving headlights. Air was rushing through the smashed windshield; Moosa's lap was full of green pellets of safety glass. Only when he had driven perhaps half a mile, madly swerving through the traffic, did he realize that Nathan was slumped against him, blood pouring from a hole in his neck onto Moosa's shoulder.

"Aaron! Manuchehr!" he shouted, panic burning through him like an electric charge. One of the men in the rear roused, looked over the back of the seat, and gasped. "Nathan—we must get him to a doctor!"

"It's too late," said the other, who had risen from the rubble on the floor of the backseat and pressed a hand into Nathan's neck. Shaking his head, he pronounced, "Nathan is dead. Our only course now is to take his body to his family and then get rid of this car, before we are caught."

Forcing down the gorge in his throat, Moosa drove on into the night, seeking a place where they could stop long enough to assess the damage. A place where they might have the luxury to grieve. And to plot revenge.

EIGHTEEN

ESTHER CLASPED THE FOLDS of the *chador* about her face as she threaded her way along the crowded sidewalk. Like the other pedestrians, she had to step around and past the rabble of streetside vendors clogging the teeming walkway. Since the revolution, the Islamic government did not have time to tend to such niceties as business permits or regulation of vendors. In this vacuum of official attention, the hawkers had proliferated to the point that they now ganged constantly along Tehran's busiest thoroughfares, noisily offering their wares to passersby—when they were not fighting each other over the prime locations.

As Esther sidled through the mob, she felt the sweat running in rivulets down her back. The perspiration from her cheeks had drenched the folds of the garment, and her nostrils were filled with the smell of damp wool. For the thousandth time, she cursed the hateful black *chador* and the narrow-minded regime which forced her to wear it.

To her eye, Tehran was now a dirty, vulgar place. Where men once strode proudly in their well-pressed business suits, their silk neckties, and freshly shaved faces, all one now saw were bedraggled fellows in wrinkled, open-collared shirts, shuffling along with downcast faces, as if they sensed the embarrassment of the country. Shoeshine stands, once so prevalent along the side-walks of Tehran, were a thing of the past. Where once majestic statues of the Shah had stood, gazing serenely down at the people as they went on their way, now one saw ugly, jagged stumps, piled about with the rubble of Shiite vandalism. Instead of the patrician visage of the Shah painted on the sides of buildings, one now encountered the bearded, turbaned likeness of the usurper, Khomeini. It seemed to Esther that Tehran's pride of appearance had been replaced by statutory uncleanness, as if to be clean and proud was now a sin, another casualty of the Islamic revolution.

Reaching the lee of a building, she paused to take advantage of an eddy in the masses of people. The weight of her market basket was beginning to cut painfully into her palm. As she shifted it to her other hand, she felt a touch on her shoulder. Turning, she found herself gazing into the face of a handsome young man.

"Solaiman *khanom?*" he inquired. Not knowing what else to do, Esther nodded hesitantly.

"I am Khosrow Parvin, *khanom,*" he said. "Your daughter, Sepideh, and I are . . . or were . . . friends." A downcast look came over his face as he said it. "We went to school together," the lad finished, again looking into her eyes. "I am sorry to speak to you this way, on the street, but—" Again the boy's eyes dropped as he searched within himself for words which seemed to elude his grasp. "I wanted to ask . . . Sepi . . . is she . . . is she well?" he stammered at last.

Wordlessly, Esther looked at the abashed young man. Was this one of the "friends" who had cursed her daughter, called her names? Was this one of the boys who had laughed and played with Sepi in childhood, only to drive pins of spite and hate beneath her fingernails at the urging of the mullahs? "Why should I tell you?" demanded Esther finally, in a tone as cold and distant as ice on the dark side of the moon. "How do I know that you are Sepi's friend? What proof can you give?"

Khosrow's cheeks reddened as he continued to stare at his toes. Finally, he looked up at her. "It was I who called to warn *Aga* Solaiman of the mullahs who came to arrest him—and to tell of what happened to Abraham Moosovi."

Esther stared at him, mouth agape.

"Our house is not distant from yours," Khosrow explained in a low, cautious voice. "I heard the *pasdars* making inquiries at our front gate." Looking about him, he continued, "My father is very afraid of the mullahs. Being university-educated, he is afraid they will think him loyal to the Shah."

As Esther watched, a look of consternation, mingled with traces of disgust, trudged slowly across young Parvin's face. More to himself than to her, he murmured, " 'Stay away from the Solaiman girl!'—that's what he always says to me. As if Sepideh were herself to blame, and not the viciousness of the fanatics! I tried to do what he said, tried to keep away, telling myself it was for her benefit as well as mine." Once again the dark, smoldering eyes of the boy burned into her own. "But if we all give in to our fear, who wins except the greedy mullahs, and the stinking *pasdar* henchmen who do their dirty work?"

Esther allowed herself to be mesmerized by the defiant simplicity of this boy she had only just met—this angry innocent who, unknown to her, had been so intimately involved in the affairs of her family. Then, realizing that passersby were looking at them oddly, she stirred, breaking the grip of the moment. Under Islamic law, it could be worth her life to be seen conversing openly with a man not her husband. Pulling the folds of her *chador* close about her face she said, with eyes downcast, "Sepi . . . Sepi is well enough, under the circumstances." She dared a final glance at him. "But perhaps your father is correct in one thing: it is better for both of you that you stay apart." Then she turned away from him and was soon lost in the crowd.

THE BELL RATTLED above the door of the Nasser Pharmacy as Nader Hafizi stepped through the entrance. Glancing up, he was momentarily startled to see the studious-looking young man behind the counter. *Where is* Aga *Solaiman?* he wondered, even as he stepped tentatively toward the attendant.

"Yes, *baradar*," said the young man in a respectful tone, "how may I assist you?"

"Excuse me," began Hafizi hesitantly, "but where is *Aga* Solaiman, the gentleman who formerly ran this pharmacy?"

The young man smiled. "My father and I have purchased the pharmacy from *Aga* Solaiman . . . " he squinted upward in calculation . . . "some six months ago." He inclined his head toward the cleric. "I am your humble servant, Yusef Nijat."

A moment more Hafizi stared at him, then hesitantly proffered a crumpled piece of paper. Yusef took it, smoothing the creases. Presently he brightened. "Ah! A prescription! This is what you wanted?" he asked. Slowly, the mullah nodded. "Very well," said the druggist heartily, turning to seek the powders the doctor had noted on the paper.

Watching the young man work, Hafizi asked in what he hoped was a neutral tone, "So . . . do you hear from *Aga* Solaiman since . . . since he sold this store to you?"

Yusef glanced up quickly. "No, *baradar*, we have not heard from him. I, in fact, have never met the gentleman. My father handled the details concerning the purchase of the business, and was the one who actually dealt with *Aga* Solaiman." The youth's fingers moved nimbly, raking the proper number of capsules into a small medicine bottle. When he had worked silently for a few moments, he continued, "However, I have had many patrons of the pharmacy tell me what a good and kind man was *Aga* Solaiman. He had quite a loyal following, it seems." He drifted into a thoughtful silence.

"Yes," agreed Hafizi, after a period of reflection. "I would venture to say he had quite a number of loyal patrons. In fact, I was very surprised to come in here and find him gone. I had no idea he was selling his business. I . . . I certainly hope no ill has befallen him," the cleric finished quietly.

"Why should anything bad have happened to him?" Hafizi looked up quickly. These last words were spoken by an older man who had been seated at a desk in the storage room toward the rear of the premises. He came out now, fingering a string of orange worry beads.

"*Aga* Hafizi, please allow me to introduce my father, Ameer Nijat," the young man interjected.

"Why should anything have happened to Solaiman?" repeated the older Nijat, now standing directly in front of Mullah Hafizi.

Hafizi shrugged. "These are difficult days, *Aga*. So many changes, so much anger. . . ." He pulled back his coat, to show the holster he carried. "When an old man such as myself must carry a weapon on the street, the days are surely evil." Now he looked directly into the eyes of Ameer Nijat. "And there are some who would take advantage of such circumstances. Ezra Solaiman was a good man who took note of the needy. I hope the evil of these days does not overwhelm such a one. It would be a pity."

Ameer Nijat's eyes focused on a point just above Hafizi's left shoulder; his fingers furiously jiggled the worry beads. "Surely you concern yourself needlessly, *Aga* Hafizi. I know that *Aga* Solaiman had a wonderful business here—why else would I wish to buy it for my son?" He inclined his head toward the reflective Yusef.

"No doubt *Aga* Solaiman is busily and happily occupied in enjoying the fruit of his labor." Shifting uneasily under the cleric's gaze, Nijat added, "I paid him a fair price for the store and its inventory. He should be well situated for the rest of his days."

Yusef Nijat gave a little cough. "Will this be all, *Aga* Hafizi?" As the mullah's gaze shifted back to the son, he noticed the prescription, filled, labeled, and ready to be taken away. Looking from the pills to the young man, Hafizi nodded wordlessly.

"That will be . . ." Yusef scribbled a moment on a note pad, "135 *rials*," the druggist announced with a businesslike smile.

Pulling the notes out of his wallet, Hafizi remembered another time when a poverty-plagued mullah had offered payment for this same prescription and had been refused. Apparently, Ameer Nijat and his son did not trouble themselves as much as Ezra Solaiman about the circumstances of their patrons. Sighing, Hafizi laid the money on the counter and picked up his package.

"Thank you, *baradar*," said Yusef. "Please come again, whenever we may be of service."

Peering intently from the son to his father, the mullah nodded. Then he turned and walked to the door. The bell jangled at his departure.

A BAR OF brilliant moonlight fell across Ezra's face as he slept fitfully. His chest heaved, his fists clenched and unclenched as he struggled in mute terror against the demons inside his skull.

In his dream, he was driving through the streets in the north of the city, approaching the house of a friend. He was in the last car he had owned, a 1968 light-blue Chevrolet Impala. He had been especially proud of the pristine condition in which he had maintained the American car—rarely seen in Iran. Likewise he was especially loath to sell it and commit himself wholly to public transportation.

In the odd manner of dreams, however, he knew this was not the past, but the terrible present. The streets were dark, and frequent staccato bursts of gunfire could be heard, some frighteningly close at hand.

He had managed to get within one block of his friend's house, but could go no farther because of huge piles of rubble which littered the streets on all sides — as if a huge explosion had crushed the entire area. In some confusion, he parked his car and proceeded on foot.

Seeing a man standing near one of the houses, he walked over to ask if there was any way to get to the next street. "You can't drive to it," the fellow replied, "but you can walk. Leave your car parked where it is — no one is likely to disturb it."

Pocketing his keys, he climbed the heaps of rubble and came to the street on which his friend lived. To his horror, he saw that every house on the entire block had collapsed. Not one wall was left standing. How could anyone have survived such a tremendous calamity? Inexplicably, the yards of the destroyed houses were now pools filled with muddy water, like so many moats surrounding abandoned castles.

In the clairvoyance of dreams, he knew at once that his own house had been likewise destroyed. *Esther! Sepi and Moosa! I must get back immediately! I must find them!*

Sobbing with despair, he clambered back to the place he had just left, and discovered with shock that his car had vanished, along with the fellow who had sanguinely assured him of its probable safety. Compounding his consternation, he suddenly found himself bereft of clothing. He was at once bereaved, isolated, and exposed — his greatest terrors come to haunting realization.

Two men were unloading a truck nearby. Seeing no

175

recourse, he approached them and begged for some sort of covering. "An old shirt, a scrap of cloth, a towel—anything, please!" he appealed. One of the fellows grudgingly went into the house, only to reappear scant moments later, shaking his head. "Nothing in there. Just get lost, why don't you?"

Again he begged, only to be met by jeers and insults. "Get lost, old man," they laughed. Immolated in his shame, he fancied one of the voices scalding him with curses was that of Firouz Marandi. As he walked away, covered in disgrace, one name fell from his lips, again and again. "Yeshua!" he was crying. "Yeshua, have mercy on me!"

The face of Reuben Ibrahim rose up before him. *"Yeshua,"* he had breathed, *"Yeshua will protect them."*

Shaken awake by the sudden, vivid memory, Ezra felt his eyes snap open. That name! In the terror of his sleep, he had called upon the name of the Accursed One! In the moment of his utmost humiliation and extremity, this name had been on his tongue! What could it mean?

He was now wide awake, but it was several minutes before the flaring panic in his brain would allow his vision to focus, to realize that it was, after all, only a dream. *Only a dream,* he reflected, struggling to bring his breathing under control, *and yet spawned by a dire and unrelenting reality which will not evaporate with the coming of the daylight. A dream it may be, but the ordeal which made it so vivid is all too genuine.*

Carefully he rolled onto one shoulder, to see if Esther was awake. No, apparently his nightmare had disturbed no one else. He knew it would be some time before his agitated imagination would allow him to again fall asleep. Quietly he got out of bed and padded barefoot toward the stairs, while pulling on his robe.

Sitting downstairs in the moon-washed parlor, he looked about him, as if for the first time, at the room, the furnishings. The moonlight lent these familiar surroundings a freshness which struck him just now with an odd force. It had been his intention, all along, to make an orderly disposition of his property: the business, this house and its contents, some odds and ends of real estate he owned in another part of the city. He intended to liquidate everything, convert it to cash and thence to American currency.

But his arrest and imprisonment had jarringly interrupted his orderly plan. He had managed to sell the business, true enough, albeit for a price that he would scarcely have considered in normal times. And, he had managed finally to convert the entire sales proceeds to American dollars; well over a million dollars in United States currency lay concealed in the basement cache. He was uncertain how he would get all this money past customs. Sternly, he shoved that problem beneath the surface of his mind—best not to consider too many difficulties at a time.

But the house! How could he now take the time and care needed to dispose of it? To find a buyer who could afford it, to arrange the terms of the sale, to manage all the attendant details while simultaneously trying to arrange their departure from the country—the prospect daunted him, tangled him helplessly in complications.

He got up, pacing slowly across the floor toward his study. Leaning against the door frame, he peered down at the inexpensive rug they had gotten to replace the fine Kermani stolen by the mullahs who had "searched" the house during his arrest. Perhaps things would not go as badly as he feared; with all that had already happened, might he not expect that many of the difficulties were behind them? Perhaps he still suffered from the anxiety of his dream; perhaps the night-phantoms seeded his mind with doubts and fears which were really less formidable than they seemed in the hours of darkness and solitude.

Reluctantly, he felt the pull on his mind, an insistent tug turning him back toward the frightful recollection which had finally forced him awake. "Reuben, Reuben," he whispered, sinking weakly into the nearest chair. "Why did you have to be so good, so kind, and so deluded?"

"Protected by the same grace which shielded Reuben," his widow had said. Ezra remembered Jahan Ibrahim's quiet faith, the velvet-covered steel of her conviction, unshakable even in the face of the greatest tragedy which could befall a family. For a scant moment he allowed his mind to tease the corner of the possibility: *Is there anything to this Jesus business? If faith in Yeshua could sustain Jahan Ibrahim, might it not . . .*

Abruptly, he stood and walked back into the parlor, passing a hand through his hair, as if to wipe away the troubling thoughts which peered at him around the corner of his mind. *Why torture myself with such foolishness? I have problems aplenty to face, without trying to thread dreamghosts on a skein of uncertainty. What about the house? What will I do? What if the mullahs come back?*

The mullahs. He paused, cautiously scenting a possibility. Perhaps the mullahs were the solution to two problems; the house and the difficulty of customs. Not the mullahs, really, but one particular mullah.

Twining thoughts and strategies in his mind, he made his way back up the stairs. In the morning, he would begin making plans.

NINETEEN

WITH THE CAUTION NOW habitual on the streets of Tehran, Ezra looked behind him before turning aside into the small narrow way which was Javid Street. Finding the weatherbeaten number he sought on one of the gates, he rapped at the portal. He heard the slap of sandaled feet on the flagstone courtyard. Then the gate opened, and he saw the face of Mullah Nader Hafizi.

The cleric squinted in confusion, then smiled uncertainly. "*Aga* Solaiman! How good to see you! What brings you again to my poor house?"

"Good day, *baradar*," Ezra replied, glancing about him. "Perhaps we should go inside. It could be bad for you to be seen talking to a Jew."

Hafizi scoffed. "I need not fear the prattle of busybodies, *Aga* Solaiman. My standing with the Ayatollah is firm. He is a good man, despite what his detractors say. However..." A worried look crossed the older man's face. "I'm not too sure about some of the people around him. Sometimes I think...ah, well," he interrupted himself, "you have had a long walk. Come in and we can surely find you a glass of tea." Ezra stepped through the portal, and Hafizi locked the gate behind them.

"Now, then," asked Hafizi later, as they sat at the kitchen table in his small apartment, "why have you come? Your eyes tell of trouble, I fear. How can I help you, my friend?"

Ezra sighed gratefully, taking a slow sip of tea through the sugar cube in his teeth. With Hafizi's generous words, he felt a tenuous step closer to the resolution of his difficulties. Still, he considered carefully the words in which to couch his request, for much depended on the perception he created in the mullah's mind.

"Friend Hafizi," he began finally, "as you have seen, fear is a constant shadow on my days. It is my bedfellow at night, and it follows me in the streets each day, dogging my steps like a silent spy." Now he looked up at the cleric. "It is deliverance from this fear, this constant dread which withers me and my family, that you have the power to grant. That is why I have come here today."

Hafizi's eyes widened. "Ezra," he said, "you make me sound like one of the great and powerful! I am but a poor mullah, as you can see by looking around you." Hafizi spread his hands, taking in the small room where they sat and the tiny parlor adjoining.

The furnishings were few and threadbare. The floors were mostly bare concrete, covered here and there with an inexpensive rug. No television, no telephone, no artwork other than the obligatory portrait of Khomeini graced the Hafizi residence. It was painfully obvious that Nader Hafizi had not profited by the graft which had enriched so many of his less-scrupled peers. Looking about, Ezra thought of the proposal he would make to this good, honest man, and was both encouraged and fearful. Would a man who had steadfastly turned his back on the easy riches reaped by his colleagues be able to accept what he was planning to suggest?

"It is true," Ezra resumed, "that yours is not a position of power in the usual sense. Yours is a power of the spirit, *Aga* Hafizi, the indomitable power of purity of heart, of mercy, and of kindness to others. It is to this power I make my appeal today."

Hafizi bowed his head, humbled into speechlessness by Solaiman's lavish words.

"You have said that your standing with the Ayatollah is good," continued Ezra. "I know that this standing was earned not by bribes and flattery, but by the steadfast devotion you have shown to the teachings of the Prophet — blessings and peace be upon him — for so many years. And, because of this standing," Ezra concluded carefully, "you may be able to accomplish for me and my family the greatest desire of our hearts."

"What is this desire?" asked the mullah hesitantly.

"We want to leave Iran," said Ezra quietly.

"And go where?"

There was a long pause. "To America," replied Ezra, finally.

Hafizi looked at Ezra for almost a full minute, then looked away. "I understand your fear, of course. That a man such as yourself should have gone to Evin Prison is a dreadful wrong, but . . ." The cleric again looked Ezra full in the eyes. "To America? The heart and soul of Western decadence?"

Now it was Ezra's turn to level a steady gaze at the mullah. "There are those who say that all Jews are cheats and misers. There are others who say that all mullahs are thieves and murderers. Yet you and I know these sayings to be untrue. Is it not possible that there are those, even in decadent America, who strive for lives of purity and discipline?" He held Hafizi's eyes until the mullah gave a sardonic little smile and nodded his head.

"Well said, *Aga* Solaiman. I concede the point."

"And my stay in Evin isn't the only problem," Ezra continued. "My daughter has been attacked at her school. My wife was terrorized by *pasdars* who came to search our home during my detention, and while the rogues were there, they confiscated as 'evidence' some of our property."

"Anyone can wear a white turban and robe and call himself a mullah," commented Hafizi. "I am aware of such instances of impersonation. And unfortunately," the cleric continued sadly, "I have also seen the greed of some of my colleagues."

Ezra nodded. "You yourself know that the leadership changes almost daily; uncertainty is the only surety these days. Suppose another committee decided to arrest me again—or arrest my son. . . ." Ezra thought of Moosa's late-night forays into hatred and shuddered. "I can't go on living this way, *baradar*," he pleaded, reaching across the table to grip the mullah's forearm in a clasp of urgency. "I beg you, in the name of Allah the merciful and compassionate, help me."

MOOSA'S EYELIDS FLUTTERED. Sunlight lanced his blurred vision with sharp brightness, wrenching a groan from him as he rolled onto his stomach and pulled the pillow over his head. Surely it couldn't be daylight already! Blearily he rolled onto his side and sat on the edge of his bed, rubbing his sleep-webbed face.

The meeting had lasted until 4 this morning. Rubbing his eyes, Moosa felt as if he were changing into some sort of night creature. But the business the group was discussing was best left to the dark hours, when eyes were fewer and concealment was easier.

The latest plan was a campaign of terror against the mullahs. The group had decided to wreak such havoc on the clerics that the whole country, the whole world, would hear of it. For too long now, it was reasoned, the international community had assumed that the Shiite power structure had a monolithic grip on the hearts and minds of Iran. It was time, they decided, to prove otherwise.

Moosa ran a hand through his hair, rubbed his stubbly cheek. This new plan was bloody . . . and risky. Gunning mullahs down on the streets in broad daylight sounded like a recipe for disaster. He had voiced serious misgivings to the others, but he never seriously believed they would reconsider their plans. The duration of the meeting had proved his assessment correct.

He wondered why he didn't pull out. At certain moments when he looked at himself these days, he couldn't believe he was the same person who had blithely flown into Mehrabad Airport to help his parents leave Iran.

And the answer, of course, was that he wasn't that person anymore. The violence and brutality of Iran had altered him in some fundamental way. For the hundredth time, he asked himself why he was reacting as he was. His father saw the evil coming and made plans to get out of its path. Moosa saw it and felt compelled to challenge it, to spit in its eye and give it blood for blood. Why?

A knock came on his door. "Moosa?" His mother's voice. "Moosa, are you awake?"

"Just a minute," he grunted, reaching for the jeans he had dropped on the floor when he fell into bed earlier this morning. Pulling on a shirt, he called out, "All right, I'm dressed."

Esther entered her son's room, bearing a cup of steaming tea before her, like a talisman to ward off evil.

"A nice cup of tea," she beamed at him, a little too cheerily, he thought.

"Thanks, Mother," he said, looking out his window. From the corner of his eye, he saw her looking at him. *Here it comes,* he thought.

"Moosa, I know you're an adult, and what you do is your own business," she began.

Moosa sighed loudly, bowing his head. He knew what was next.

"But I can't help being worried," she said. "These friends that you spend so much time with, until all hours of the night —"

"Mother," he interrupted, "I'm very tired. I hardly slept at all last night, and I don't feel like—"

"Of course, you hardly slept," she retorted, her facade of forced cheerfulness dissolving instantly into a barrage of clipped words, a tight-faced glance of disapproval. "Anybody who comes in at 4:30 in the morning is going to be tired. Is that any reason to snap at me?"

Moosa buried his face in his hands. "Mother," he moaned, "let's not start this now."

"Fine, I'm leaving. Drink your tea before it gets cold." Pulling the door behind her, she paused, and then said in a low voice, "I pray to God you know what you're doing." The door closed, and she was gone.

"EVEN GRANTING WHAT YOU SAY," mused Hafizi, "what can I do? I have no authority with the emigration officials. I cannot get you a visa, nor can I approve your request to go to America."

"I have already...taken a number of steps," said Ezra carefully, picking an imaginary piece of lint from his sleeve. "My difficulty is in what I must take with me."

"You are surely not thinking of taking contraband out of the country!" interjected Hafizi, his eyes wide with alarm. "You must know I cannot be a party to anything illegal!"

"No, no. Nothing like that!" assured Ezra. Choosing his next words very carefully, he said, "I...have some things which are very precious to me, second in value only to my wife and children. Things which have been in my family for many years, which are indispensable to me wherever I may live. Things," he stated, looking Hafizi firmly in the eye, "which some in the government might confiscate from a Jew who was leaving the country. This I cannot accept. This is why I have come to you."

Hafizi returned Ezra's gaze, searching deep within the other's eyes for some confirmation, some assurance.

"Perhaps you know I have sold my business," Ezra said quietly, after some moments had passed.

"Yes," Hafizi nodded. "I only just found out. I went in a few days ago to have my wife's prescription re-filled." He smiled ruefully. "The new owners are not as kindhearted as the old. I paid full price."

Ezra shrugged, smiling. "The world has changed."

Hafizi nodded. "Yes—in some ways not for the better."

"At any rate," Ezra said, "I have spent all of my life as a loyal citizen of Iran. I was born here, have worked here, raised my children here, made friends here, buried family members here. It's not an easy thing to uproot one's existence. I don't intend to leave any more of my lifeblood in Iran than is already necessary."

Hafizi took a slow sip of the now lukewarm tea. "Forgive me for asking, *baradar*, but since my relationship with the Ayatollah is apparently to be put to the test, I must know—"

"I have some antique objects," Ezra answered, "a few fairly expensive carpets . . . and . . . some money."

Through the open kitchen window, the rattling of the latch on the front gate was heard. Nader Hafizi glanced outside to see his wife's *chador*-draped figure crossing the courtyard toward the front door.

Ezra got up to leave. "I'm sorry, *Aga* Hafizi. I should be leaving—"

"Please, *baradar*, sit down," urged the mullah. "You are a good man and I trust you. I want you to meet her."

The front door opened, and *khanom* Hafizi entered, carrying a market basket filled with bread, cheese, and fresh fruit. Seeing Ezra seated at the table, she paused, her eyes flickering from the stranger to her husband.

"Come in, Akram," the mullah said, beckoning to his wife. "I want you to meet a good friend of mine. Please," he urged, motioning with his fingers, "take off your *chador*. I want *Aga* Solaiman to be able to recognize your face when he sees you again." The mullah smiled from Ezra to his wife as she placed her basket on the table and gratefully removed the dark, concealing folds of the *chador*.

Akram Hafizi was a plump, jovial-faced woman. She smiled and inclined her head demurely toward Ezra as her husband said, "Ezra Solaiman, this is my wife, Akram. Akram," he continued, "this is the kind druggist who refused to charge me anything for the medicine you needed before our last trip to Isfahan."

"I am your humble servant," the mullah's wife murmured. "And I am grateful for your kindness to me in my illness."

"I am honored to meet you, Akram *khanom*," Ezra replied, bowing sedately. "Your husband has returned my small service tenfold." An idea, a refinement to his original plan, was unfolding in his mind as he spoke. He decided to pursue it. "Would you both do me the honor of being my guests for dinner at my house, say . . . two days from now? That is," he added, "if you have no compunctions about eating food prepared by non-Islamic persons."

Hafizi waved a hand in dismissal. "We're not as fanatical about food taboos as some," he said, looking from his wife to Ezra, "and I'm honored by the invitation." He gave Ezra a curious look. "But to what do we owe this unexpected privilege?"

Ezra shook his head, smiling enigmatically. "I have a proposal, in connection with our earlier discussion. One which will be more effectively made, I think, at my home. Will you accept?"

Hafizi looked at his wife, then back at Ezra. "Why not?" he shrugged. "On Thursday, then?"

"Yes, that will be good," said Ezra. "Just after the evening prayers." Inwardly, he felt a cautious confidence. He liked the way this plan tasted.

TWENTY

ESTHER JERKED THE SHEETS from the cedar closet, tossing them in a tangled heap atop the bare mattress. Going to the bed, she spread the bottom sheet, jabbing its ends savagely between the mattress and the box springs. She hurriedly placed the top sheet, and scattered the counterpane haphazardly over everything, pulling it this way and that, leaving a network of folds and wrinkles which she barely noticed.

As she dusted the furniture, she thought again of Moosa's intransigence, his refusal to listen to her. She swiped angrily at the dust atop the mahogany bureau and rehearsed the list of her grievances: her son was becoming a gangster who would not heed his own mother; her husband was embarked on a ruinous scheme which would probably not move them any closer to leaving the country; her daughter was sinking deeper and deeper into the mire of depression; her maid had abandoned her; it was summer, and she must wear the cursèd *chador* in the blazing midday sun if she wished to walk abroad. The maddening sum of her many frustrations and angers was an ache in her shoulders, a garrote about her throat. At times she felt she must scream aloud, pull her hair, give violent birth to the twisting, grinding rage which contorted her insides.

But instead, she sublimated the anger in activity. She

cast a *chador* of domestic normality over the blinding frustration she felt at the harum-scarum demolition of the safe world she had inhabited all these years. She dusted. She cleaned. She stayed busy. How much longer the *chador* would shroud the turbulence in her soul, she didn't know, and tried very hard not to speculate. But the rigid routine of running her household was the only antidote she had found for the helpless fury which threatened to poison her sanity.

Giving the top of the drapes a final, violent swipe, she left the master bedroom, walking down the hall to Sepi's door.

"Sepi, dear," she called softly, tapping on the door, "it's time to start dinner. I need your help in the kitchen."

A muffled, incoherent reply came from the other side of the door. *How long?* Esther wondered. *How long will Sepi remain withdrawn from life, a disinterested spectator to the events swirling about her?*

She tapped again at the door, urging her daughter in a gentle voice. "Sepi, dear. Please. Come to the kitchen." When she heard the sound of feet dragging across the floor, she turned and went downstairs.

The lamb had been marinating since this morning. Esther slid the lid from the pot and looked inside, satisfied with the appearance of the meat. Hooking the haunch with a long fork, she laid it on a board beside the sink and began slicing it.

She heard Sepi slouch in behind her. "There are onions, peppers, and tomatoes in the refrigerator," she said without looking up. "Begin slicing them into quarters. When you've finished, you can steam some rice."

From the corner of her eye, she saw Sepi move toward the refrigerator like a robot. She wanted to grab the girl by the shoulders, to shake her, to shout, "Come back! I need you! I need an ally in this insane world of men!" Controlling her indignation, she said quietly, "If you handle a knife with as little care as you handle yourself, there will be fingers in the kabob."

Sepi gave her a dead stare, then resumed listlessly quartering the tomatoes. "I'm fine, Mother," she said in a hollow voice. "Just leave me alone."

A few minutes passed, as mother and daughter toiled silently in the kitchen, their backs nearly touching and their hearts light-years distant. Not content to allow Sepi to continue in her passive refuge, Esther remarked, "I have heard that in America, boys and girls often go to a movie or a restaurant together, without a chaperone. Do you think that's a good thing?"

Sepi continued working without any response for so long that Esther wondered if she had even heard. Then, the girl shrugged. "I don't know," she responded, with a halfhearted effort at interest in the question. "If that's the way it's done over there, then . . . I suppose. . . ." The sentence trailed off into an obscuring mist of apathy, then evaporated into nothingness.

Esther felt her teeth grinding together as scolding admonitions crowded onto her tongue. "Do you suppose any American boy will want to date a girl who drags herself about like a household drudge?" she wanted to say. "Who won't even brush her hair unless forced? Who only comes out of her room to eat, and barely that?" Allowing the bitter tirade to die in her throat, she finally said, "That's enough tomatoes. You can start on the onions." Esther shoved the blade deep into the mutton haunch, viciously shredding the meat she would soon place before Nader Hafizi and his wife.

As THE LAST GOLD and rose hues of sunset faded into the long shadows on the streets of Tehran, the gate buzzer announced the presence of visitors. "I'll get it," Moosa shouted toward the kitchen as he stepped from the bottom stair toward the foyer.

189

"Moosa," called Ezra from the dining room, where he was assisting Esther with the table settings, "I'll get the door. I'm sure our guests are here."

"No, that's all right," replied Moosa. "I was on my way out, anyway. I can see who it is."

Ezra strode rapidly from the dining room and gripped his son's shoulder. Moosa spun around to face his father. "What?" he asked, in reply to Ezra's angry stare.

"You knew I had invited guests to our home," said Ezra through clenched teeth. "I intended for them to meet my family . . . my entire family."

Moosa turned his face aside, sighing and rolling his eyes. "Father, I . . . you know I go out with my friends most nights."

"And why can you not make a single exception for this occasion?" grated Ezra. "This is an important evening—perhaps the most crucial night we will have while we are still in Iran. It is my wish that you remain."

"No!" spat Moosa, his lips curled in resentment. His eyes blazed a hot challenge at his father as he zipped his jacket with a defiant, thrusting motion. "I have my own plans, and I'm not staying here to help you entertain your friends. Perhaps . . ." He faltered a moment, then surged ahead. "Perhaps my plans and yours no longer coincide. Had you considered that possibility in any of your scheming?" For fifteen seconds they glared at each other, before Moosa flung himself out the door.

He pounded down the walk toward the gate, muttering to himself. When he was five paces from the portal, he jerked to a halt, his heart leaping into his throat. Through the bars of the gate he saw the white-turbaned, robed figure of a mullah, a rifle slung across his back on a shoulder strap. *They are here!* he thought, as his hand darted beneath his jacket. *Who betrayed us? How did they know so quickly?*

As his fingers glided over the grip of the Beretta, he heard his father's voice behind him, calling out in greeting. "Ah! *Aga* Hafizi, *Khanom* Hafizi! You are here, as expected! I'm so glad to see you!"

His father strode around him, as Moosa slowly removed his hand from the pistol grip. Ezra opened the gate, and welcomed the mullah and his wife warmly into the yard.

"Please pardon the rifle, *Aga* Solaiman," the mullah was saying, "but it is an unfortunate necessity in these days. Many mullahs have been attacked—" The cleric broke off, peering at Moosa with a questioning look.

"*Aga* Hafizi, please meet my son, Moosa Solaiman," said Ezra, hurrying into the breach in the conversation. "Moosa, you perhaps remember *Aga* Hafizi, the mullah who saved my life when I was in Evin Prison?" His eyes delivered a veiled challenge to his son, who now bowed properly toward the cleric and his wife.

"I'm afraid your father makes it sound more heroic than necessary," chuckled Hafizi. "His own generosity saved his life; I was merely the messenger who made the announcement."

"I'm pleased to meet you," murmured Moosa, glancing tensely from the couple to his father. "I regret that I must be absent this evening, but I have a pressing engagement which, unfortunately, I can't reschedule."

"What a shame!" cried Hafizi. "Ah, well . . . it was good to meet you, Moosa. I hope we shall see each other again soon."

Moosa stared with a surprising intensity at the cleric for perhaps five long breaths, then nodded. "Perhaps we shall. And now, please excuse me." He stepped through the gate.

Ezra gazed after the vanishing figure of his son with an expression that appeared to Hafizi to be an amalgam of grief and anger. Then his host latched the gate and turned toward him, his face giving no hint of anything other than eager hospitality.

"Please! Come in! Esther has the table set, and the

meal is practically ready!" He gestured toward the front door, and they preceded him up the herringboned brick.

Hafizi paused in wonder beside the fish pond which lay beside the walk, illumined by the light from the front portico. "Never have I seen such a thing!" he remarked in astonishment. "Goldfish and blue glazed tiles! Beautiful!"

Ezra shrugged, smiling. "This house has been most comfortable, as well as enjoyable. Please . . ." He bowed them up the front steps, then opened the front door.

The mullah and his wife stood just inside the front door, staring about in openmouthed astonishment. Never had they imagined such lavish surroundings in the homes of anyone other than royalty! From the foyer, they had a partial view of the parlor with its parquet floors, its Louis XVI furniture. Looking to the left, they could see a huge dining table of polished mahogany, richly laid with gold-rimmed English bone china. Sparkling Waterford crystal glittered in the glow from the chandelier, eagerly giving back a thousand tiny reflections of each of the dozen brilliantly lit lamps. From the kitchen, the rich aroma of curried lamb cooked with vegetables spread its mouth-watering canopy throughout the house.

"Akram *Khanom*," said Ezra quietly, "would you care to remove your wrap? *Aga* Hafizi?"

Dumb with wonder, the couple let their cloaks slip into the hands of their host, who hung them carefully on the brass coat rack in the foyer. "Would you like to see the upstairs?" Wordlessly, the Hafizis nodded. Ezra led them to the staircase, grinning to himself. *They are plainly awestruck by the richness of the house and furnishings. So much the better,* he thought.

MOOSA ARRIVED at the meeting, ducking from the alley into the darkened doorway. Two heavily armed men stood just inside, flanking the entrance. Seeing Moosa's face, they nodded, motioning him toward the smoke-filled room where the others gathered.

The building was an abandoned warehouse. Ironically, it was located on a side street off Kurosh-e-Kabir, between the Military Garrison compound and the Qasr Prison. It stood in a row of nondescript corrugated steel sheds and warehouses, some of which were still in use. Stacked against the walls were pallets of warped, rotting wood and mildewed cardboard boxes. The leaks in the tarred roof had allowed moisture to spoil whatever had been left by the last tenant, and the interior smelled of dank paperboard and creosote. The group met in a plywood office in the northeast corner of the huge structure. A tiny splash of light came through the grimy windows of the office and reached feebly toward the shadows between the ceiling joists ten meters overhead.

As Moosa pulled a decrepit stool toward the scarred table around which they gathered, he noticed an unfamiliar man sitting in the place directly beneath the hanging lamp. The shaded 100-watt bulb made a shadow-mask of the stranger, even as its heat smeared his face with a sheen of sweat. He was pulling nervously at an unfiltered Turkish cigarette, glancing nervously at the group which had gathered to interrogate him.

"Who's this?" Moosa whispered to Manuchehr, jerking a thumb toward the unfamiliar figure in the hot seat.

Manuchehr shrugged. "Some guy who made contact with Ari," he murmured. "Says he was in the *mujahedin* fighting the Shah, but when the Ayatollah started squeezing them, he saw the light. Wants to come in with us."

"How did you hear about us?" Ari was asking the newcomer. "What makes you think we should trust you — we don't know anything about you. You could be a stooge for the *pasdars*, for all we know."

The stranger's gaze flickered nervously about the table. He took another drag at his cigarette, then dropped it on the bare concrete floor, grinding it with his foot. The smoke issued from his nostrils in slow streams as he looked briefly at Ari, then down at his scarred knuckles.

"I know where weapons are stashed," he said in a low, mumbling voice. "Unless the *pasdars* have found it all, I know where there is petrol, and some money. We didn't have much—there wasn't time—but . . ." He fell silent, his eyes shifting among them, then back to the table top.

"I don't like this clown," growled one of the men. "He walks out of the dark and asks to join up, like this was some kind of social club. I say we get rid of him." In this desperate circle, no one had any doubt what such a phrase implied for a rejected applicant. The stranger's hand shook visibly as he lit another cigarette.

"Look," he said, staring directly at his detractor, "I lost friends to the *pasdars* too! I've had mullahs lie to me, cheat me of what was rightfully mine. We of the *mujahedin* thought we had earned some consideration from the mullahs for our assistance in the overthrow of the Shah, but once they got in the saddle, they've done nothing but spit in our faces—and worse." His dark, furtive glance darted about at them. "I have no more love for them than anyone here."

"Guns . . . petrol . . ." mused Aaron, seated across the table from Moosa. Next to him, another member nodded.

"You need to know," cut in Ari, "that we in this circle are a . . . how to say it . . ." His fingers circled in the air as he searched for a phrase. ". . . a mixed bag. Some of us are here because we belong to minority groups persecuted by the new regime: Christian, Sunni Muslim, Jewish."

The stranger's eyes glittered upward, but he said nothing.

"Others," continued Ari, "are simply royalists, who wish and work for nothing other than the return of the Pahlavi monarchy. We each have our own reasons for being here, and no man has the right to question those of another. Understood?"

The fellow glanced at Ari, then back down, nodding.

"All right then," said Ari, looking about at the others. "Let's put him to a vote. All in favor?"

Members of the group studied the shadowed face of the newcomer, seeking any clue, any basis for a guess. At some point, their lives might depend on the actions of this man. If they guessed wrong, the mistake would almost certainly be one of their last. Slowly, hesitantly, seven of the ten raised their hands, voting the stranger in.

"Opposed?" Just as slowly, three hands went up.

"Majority rules," commented Ari, staring meaningfully at the one who had spoken against the newcomer. "He's in." The naysayer grumbled, but nodded his assent.

"By the way," said Ari, looking back at the stranger, "nobody here but me knows your name."

"Just call me Aziz," mumbled the relieved but still taciturn new member. Drawing smoke deeply into his lungs, the one who called himself Aziz stared into the darkness. Contemplating the group he had just joined, Firouz Marandi considered himself lucky to be alive. *The mullahs will pay through the nose for this job*, he told himself grimly. *When the time comes, they will pay off big.*

TWENTY-ONE

"PLEASE, NO MORE," begged Nader Hafizi, pushing his plate away and holding both palms outward in a gesture of surrender. "That is the most wonderful kabob I have had in some time." He looked at his wife. "Akram, you must get *khanom* Solaiman's recipe." His wife nodded appreciatively.

Esther inclined her head graciously toward the mullah. "You honor me, Aga Hafizi." She arose from the table. "Sepi, please help me clear the table."

"Would you care to take a cup of coffee in the study?" Ezra asked the mullah.

"The only improvement possible in such a meal would be a cup of coffee," agreed Hafizi. He rose from the table, clutching his stomach in mock agony. "Such a feast! I cannot imagine, *Aga* Solaiman, how you have stayed so slender all these years with meals like this!"

Ezra chuckled as he led the way to the study. As the two men settled themselves, Sepi entered, bearing a silver tray with two china cups on matching saucers. Quietly she set the service on her father's desk and returned to the kitchen.

"A memorable evening, *Aga* Solaiman," commented the mullah, patting his full stomach. "I have not enjoyed such a fine time in very many years!" As Ezra seated himself behind the teakwood desk, Hafizi set-

197

tled comfortably into one of the dark leather chairs across the polished surface from his host.

Ezra smiled, taking a careful sip of the steaming black coffee. Placing the cup gently back on its saucer, he looked meaningfully at Hafizi. "I am happy you and your wife accepted my spur-of-the-moment invitation. I have a reason for bringing you here to ask for your help."

"As I have said, I will do anything honorable in my power to aid you. You must only ask." A silence deepened between the two men as Hafizi waited to hear the shape of Ezra's request.

"The only way I can think of to clear customs smoothly is with a direct written order from the Ayatollah himself," Ezra said in a rush, before he could halt himself. "With such a document, no customs officer would dare impede our departure. Can you obtain such a thing for me?"

Hafizi swallowed the coffee in his mouth and replaced the cup, without taking his eyes off Ezra. He bridged his fingertips together, a contemplative expression on his face. "The Imam Khomeini is a very busy man, whose every word must be weighed thrice carefully," the cleric said, with long, thoughtful pauses between his words. "He will want a very good reason for issuing such an extraordinary instruction on behalf of an ordinary citizen."

Ezra took several deep breaths before replying. "What about my contribution to the cemeteries? I kept copies of the receipt."

Hafizi scratched his beard as he gazed up at the ceiling. His eyes narrowed to thoughtful slits.

IN THE KITCHEN, Akram Hafizi stood beside Esther at the sink, carefully wiping the chinaware with a towel. On her right, Sepi placed the plates and glasses in the cabinet. The women had been working together for some minutes, the only sounds the splash of water in the sink and the low mumble of the men's conversation in the study. Akram broke the stillness with an abrupt question.

"You are afraid and angry. Why?" Her eyes bore in on Esther's shocked glance with a startling intensity. Her quietness at the dinner table had not prepared Esther for such a direct, perceptive thrust.

So unnerved was Esther that she blurted a reply before thinking. "We are Jews in a land governed by Muslim fanatics. Why should we not be afraid?"

"Mother!" objected Sepi, glancing nervously at the mullah's wife.

"It's all right, child," said Akram Hafizi, laying a hand on Sepi's arm. "My question was a bit ill-mannered, perhaps even simpleminded. It's just that . . . I have lived with lack all my days. I can't imagine anyone living in such splendor . . . and being afraid.

"In my lifetime, I have known much fear," she went on. "I have felt the fear which comes with hunger pangs in my children's bellies; the fear of illness striking when there was no money for doctors or medicine; the fear of being left alone when Nader was late in returning home from the mosque. Did SAVAK have him? Had he said the wrong thing in the presence of the wrong person? These fears I have known. Perhaps," she said, smiling gently at Esther, "that was why I so readily recognized your symptoms, Esther *khanom*. I have wrestled often enough with the same opponent to know his holds."

Esther soaped a plate with an avid, jaw-clenched concentration. *What gives this woman the right to peer into my soul? Why am I the only one whose feelings are acceptable fodder for conversation? I live in a house full of concealed fears, hidden resentments. Why should mine alone be dragged mercilessly out into the open? Do I not have the same right as others to hide behind a shroud of depression or stubborn silence?*

An acrid resentment lodged in her throat as Esther stared fixedly at the plate she was scrubbing for a needlessly long time. Why did she feel the unbearable urge to let slip the veil, to unburden herself to this improbable Islamic confessor? Even now, Akram Hafizi studied her profile as if expecting something. As the last bolts ripped from the door frame of her heart, a flood of pent-up anguish gushed from her eyes in an irresistible flood.

"PERHAPS," MURMURED THE MULLAH after a very long pause. He began nodding slowly. "Yes, I think the Imam would be favorably disposed toward such an action. With my urging, and with the affixed signature and stamp of Ayatollah Kermani, the thing might be done. And perhaps, if his secretaries could be persuaded to draft the letter—"

"I was thinking," interrupted Ezra, "that I might impose upon you to draft the letter yourself. I thought perhaps if the document were in your handwriting. . . ."

Hafizi chuckled, shaking his head in admiration. "*Aga* Solaiman, your brain is never still, I warrant. As you say, it would be better to have the letter ready for the Ayatollah's signature."

"I realize," said Ezra, toying with the handle of his coffee cup, "that this project is no small inconvenience for you, *baradar.* I want you to know what I am willing to do in exchange for this lifesaving favor."

The cleric put down his cup, his eyes resting on Ezra's face with an attentive, questioning look.

Ezra felt his chest tightening with nervous apprehension. The next words he would utter, and the mullah's response to them, would determine the success or failure of his plan. If Hafizi agreed to the terms, they might depart Iran within the week. If he didn't, a bleak future stretched ahead; an endless round of fear, repression, and furtive efforts to survive in a hostile world.

Everything hinged on the next moments.

"If you can do this for me and my family," Ezra said, pausing for a deep breath, "I will make a gift to you and *Khanom* Hafizi." He stopped again, sucking in the air which was suddenly very rare in the study. "This house, and all its furnishings and grounds, shall be deeded to you. It will be yours to keep."

Hafizi's look of curiosity metamorphosed slowly into one of disbelief. His jaw slackened, his eyes widened. He had been sitting toward the front of the leather-covered chair across the desk from Ezra; now he slumped down into the cushions as if the wind had suddenly gone out of him. Almost involuntarily, he stared about the room, wildly calculating the possible worth of the offer he had just heard. "*Aga* Solaiman! I could never—"

"You don't understand!" urged Ezra, leaning forward on the desk and feverishly gripping the astonished mullah's eyes with his own. "I am not bribing you!" He searched frantically for the words to explain his actions. "What good will this house be to me if I am again dragged to Evin Prison and shot? What comfort will it bring my wife and children when the *pasdars* return — and return they will—and evict them into the street like stray dogs? This house is a wonderful thing, I admit," said Ezra, his eyes pleading with Hafizi for understanding, "but compared to the safety of my family, compared to freedom from fear, it is nothing. Can't you see the truth of what I'm saying?"

Hafizi stared at him for ten heartbeats, then nodded slowly.

Ezra let the breath leave his chest in a slow exhalation of relief. "Then you must see, *baradar*, that I consider this house to be a bargain in exchange for what I am asking you to do. And I cannot think of anyone I would rather see gain by its vacancy than you, who have already rescued me once. This is not bribery, *Aga*

Hafizi. It is a show of gratitude."

The mullah drew within himself for several moments. His brow furrowed as he pondered the complicated ethics of Ezra's proposal. To receive a reward for showing kindness to another human being—this somehow tainted the act. Compassion was not properly done for the sake of a payoff; it was its own justification.

And yet . . . what Ezra said was all too true. Many atrocities had taken place under the guise of the restoration of Islamic values to Iran. Doubtless this fine house would not long remain empty. Then there was the fact that Ezra had offered it of himself; Hafizi had had no inkling that such an invitation would take place. And Akram had gone without so many things during their difficult life together.

Ah, well, he decided at last, *Allah's ways are mysterious. If He wishes me to have this house, I shall have it. If not, I shall not.* He looked up at Ezra, a tentative grin teasing the corners of his lips. "Very well, *Aga* Solaiman. Perhaps I should call my wife in and explain things?"

SOBS TORE FROM Esther's throat in great, wracking spasms, shaking her down to the very center of her being. She was vaguely conscious of Akram Hafizi's arm across her shoulders, supporting and comforting her; she was less aware of Sepi standing in the background, as if uncertain or embarrassed. The grief and anger poured from her in a dark catharsis, punctuated by painful words and semiarticulate moans.

"Our lives . . . have been destroyed," she managed to choke. "My family . . . my place . . . my future . . . all ripped from me . . . without warning." She covered her mouth with her hand and squinted her eyes in pain.

"Gently, now, gently," soothed the mullah's wife. "Your future and your daughter's—and mine, and that of everyone in Iran—is in the hands of Allah, as they have always been. No one has ever known what He had in store until time unfolded. These troubles won't last forever."

"Akram?" came the mullah's voice from behind them. Nader Hafizi stood framed in the doorway, a concerned, confused expression wrinkling his brow. "Should I call your husband, *Khanom* Solaiman?" he asked.

Esther vigorously shook her head in refusal.

"It's all right, husband," assured Akram. "Esther *khanom* is overwrought, but she'll be better with some rest. Isn't that right, dear?"

Esther nodded with more conviction than she felt.

"Very well," said the mullah doubtfully, wincing as Esther's shoulders heaved silently. His eyes returned to his wife. "Akram, when it's convenient, please step into the study. *Aga* Solaiman and I have something to discuss with you." He turned slowly, looking again at Esther before going back toward the study.

"HERE'S WHAT I'VE FOUND out so far," said Manuchehr, pulling a wrinkled piece of paper from the pocket of his jacket and referring to it as he spoke.

"A couple of weeks from now, a Shiite holy man from the mosque in Karbala is coming from Iraq to pay a state visit to the Ayatollah. Something about the problems between our two countries."

As Manuchehr glanced at his notes, Moosa yawned widely. Rubbing his face, he filched a cigarette from the fellow sitting next to him, lighting it and drawing the sleep-banishing nicotine deep into his lungs.

"Anyway," continued Manuchehr, "there will be a big party of higher-ups from the Ayatollah's organization on hand to greet the man at Mehrabad." He looked cautiously about at the others. "Sounds like our best shot so far."

Ari scratched his cheek, deep in thought. A few heads

nodded in agreement with Manuchehr's assessment. A strike at the airport, with foreigners certain to be present, would have a good chance of attracting international attention. And the opportunity to eliminate a number of Khomeini's top aides was a tempting strategic bonus.

Moosa felt an icy twinge of apprehension prickling at his breastbone. An operation at Mehrabad Airport would be complicated. Security was tight there, and simply getting through the gate would pose a certain amount of risk. The logistics were sure to be intimidating. He looked up at Manuchehr. "What gate will this guy be using? Some of the gates are a long way from the airport exits. Getting back out could be suicide."

Manuchehr spread his hands. "They won't assign an arrival gate until one or two days ahead of time. There's no way to know any sooner."

Moosa grunted, shaking his head. No way to know. He should have guessed as much.

In the name of the Merciful Allah:
To all officials and departments of the Islamic Republic.
This is to certify that Ezra Solaiman, a Jew by birth, his wife, son, and daughter . . .

Ezra looked at the last phrase he had written, and slowly put down his pen. Again he heard the echo of Moosa's wrathful words, *"Perhaps my plans and yours no longer coincide."* He closed his eyes and drew a sharp breath as a nearly unbearable pang of grief shoved its dagger into his windpipe. As if he picked up a scalpel to amputate his own hand, he took up the pen and crossed out the words, "his wife, son, and daughter," and replaced them with the simpler, infinitely more painful phrase, "and his family." When he had blinked back the tears sufficiently to see his work, he continued the draft:

... are taking an extended trip to Switzerland for business and pleasure. Aga Solaiman has conducted himself with benevolence toward his Muslim neighbors, and has also contributed a large sum of money to a Muslim cemetery which was in need of repair and expansion.

It is our wish to be helpful to him in his journey, in return for his kindness toward Islam and its principles.

You are hereby instructed to expedite the departure of the Solaiman family from Mehrabad Airport. Affixed is our signature and seal.

Ezra read and reread the letter of instruction. He did not think Mullah Hafizi would find anything objectionable in it. They had agreed that under no circumstances should America be mentioned. Switzerland was neutral, and proceeding from there to America would be simple, despite the stamp routinely placed on Iranian passports which read, "Not Valid for Emigration." Once Ezra was on Swiss soil, no one could force his return to Iran. And once he was on American soil ...

He forced himself to halt his conjecture. One careful step at a time. He must deliver this draft to Hafizi's house. As he placed the note in an envelope, he smiled, remembering Akram Hafizi's reaction when she had stepped into the study the night before. ...

Her husband had said simply, "*Aga* Solaiman and his family are leaving Iran, and he wants to give his house to us. What do you think?"

The mullah's wife had laughed aloud at the rich jest her husband had just uttered, shaking her finger at Nader Hafizi. "Please forgive my husband, *Aga* Solaiman," she said, chuckling. "Sometimes his sense of humor borders on the bizarre."

Her eyes had stayed on Ezra's face as he slowly shook his head, a tiny smile flickering on his lips. "No, Akram *khanom,* your husband isn't teasing. He has told you the truth."

Her smile had evaporated by degrees, leaving behind a blank look of disbelief. She had stared from Ezra to her husband, who nodded, a broad grin striding irresistibly across his features. "It's true, my wife," he averred softly. "This house and its contents are to be ours."

Akram had dropped to her knees so quickly that her husband darted forward, thinking she had fainted. Instead, she clapped her hands together in front of her bosom and whispered over and over in wide-eyed wonder, "Praise be to Allah! How can this be? *Allahu Akbar!** I can't believe this!"

After many protestations of the seriousness of his intentions, Ezra had escorted the Hafizis to the front gate. As he closed the portal behind them and watched them walk into the darkness, he could still hear Akram softly saying, "This can't be happening! It can't be true!" He had felt a small bloom of pleasure at her ecstatic disbelief in her good fortune. That he could be the bringer of such unlooked-for joy was, in some small measure, a reward for his generosity.

His face fell with the memory of what happened next. When he came back into the house, Esther was standing in the foyer, her face a brooding composite of grief, resentment, and confusion. "My darling!" he exclaimed. "What is the matter?"

He would have felt better if she had shouted and raged at him. If she had torn her hair and cried aloud, he might have been able, when her wrath had spent its fury, to calm and comfort. To console.

But instead, she had stared about the foyer and into the rooms on either side. Her eyes had glided coldly over the things she would be leaving, the things he had

*"God is great!"

206

ceded to the Hafizis. Then her gaze had returned to him, and a single tear, soulless as the path of a snail, traced a shining trail down her cheek. She turned away from him without a word, and walked away.

Am I destined to save my family, only to lose it? Will any of them come through this dreadful ordeal with heart and soul intact? His fingers curled into a fist, pounding at first softly, then harder and harder atop the desk. A strangling cry of dismay struggled at the back of his throat. He longed to shout at them, at the world, *Can't you see what I'm doing? I want only to do what's right, and be left alone! Is this so much to ask? Isn't there anyone who understands?* In an instant, the voice of Reuben Ibrahim was whispering in the ear of his memory, *"Yeshua ... Yeshua will protect them."*

A wave of dizziness swept over him, as emotions surged through him he didn't understand. For a moment, Ezra Solaiman cradled his head on his forearms, pondering the hapless condition of a man whose only desire was for order, yet whose every action spawned chaos.

After several minutes, he raised his head, wiping his face on the sleeve of his shirt. Then he did the only thing he knew how to do: he set about taking the next carefully planned step. He would deliver this note to Nader Hafizi, so that the cleric might copy it in his own hand and submit it for Khomeini's signature.

He looked about him at the house he would be leaving behind, shedding it as a serpent doffs an outgrown skin. Pruning.

TWENTY-TWO

NADER HAFIZI STEPPED OFF the bus, which roared away in a swirl of dust and diesel smoke. The *pasdar* commanding the guard detail at the gate of the Ayatollah's residence scrutinized him, then patted him down perfunctorily. With a jerk of the head, he motioned the gray-bearded mullah through the gate.

Khomeini had his lodgings in Jamaran, a small village in the hills on the outskirts of Tehran. The approaches to the place gave it the appearance of a command center in wartime, with tanks and machine gun nests bristled along the roads. Heavily armed *pasdars* scowled at any vehicle that hove into view, and this was no small task, for a steady stream of supplicants, sycophants, and functionaries wound up into the hills to court the endorsement of the India-born octogenarian, who had returned from exile in the suburbs of Paris to lead this nation of thirty-five million souls.

Upon his arrival from France, the Ayatollah had at first lived in the poor southern precincts of the capital city, but had since moved to an aging villa in Jamaran, whose elevated terrain made it far more comfortable in summer than the crowded, broiling streets of Tehran. Still, the Imam remained true to his image: he reportedly preferred this down-at-the-heels structure to anything newer and more modern which might smack of Western decadence.

Hafizi gave his name to the young mullah at the gate of the courtyard, who sent a runner inside. Presently the boy returned, motioning the gatekeeper to allow Hafizi to enter. Crossing the courtyard to the main doorway, he bowed to the mullahs waiting there, and received their respectful bows in return. Once more patting his breast pocket to make certain the letter and receipt were still there, he took several deep breaths as the doors opened and he was admitted to the presence of the Ayatollah Ruhollah Khomeini.

The Imam was seated on a simple straw mat, eating a pear he had just selected from a plain ceramic bowl in front of him. It was odd, reflected Hafizi, how fame changed the way one looked at a person. He had known Khomeini for many years, and for all that time, the man seated on the mat had worn the same garb: dark camel-hair robe, sandals, black turban. Yet, Hafizi could not help comparing this man with the countless portraits one now saw on posters, on the sides of buildings, in every Islamic home. Since the revolution, Khomeini had become more than a man, more even than the most revered mullah in Iran. He was now an icon, a symbol. It was oddly disconcerting to see him seated on a mat in a sunlit room, chewing on a bit of fruit. The reality was disappointing when compared to the image. In this moment, the Ayatollah was diminished by his fame.

He glanced up at Hafizi, and his dark, quick eyes flickered from the mullah's face to that of his aide.

"This is the honored mullah Nader Hafizi, your excellency," intoned the assistant in a soft, well-modulated voice.

"Of course," replied the Ayatollah, smiling softly at Hafizi as he indicated a place near him on the mat. "*Aga* Hafizi and I are old friends, are we not? Please, *baradar*, come in."

The two clerics exchanged the traditional Islamic ceremonial greeting, each brushing his lips lightly on the other's cheek. "Tell me, then, *Aga* Hafizi," said the old man with the snowy beard, "what brings you up to my perch in the hills?" Licking the juice from his fingers, Khomeini gave Hafizi a quizzical look.

The Imam's voice was soft but deep, and his eyes were flinty beacons of the quick intelligence behind them. This man bestrode center stage in the drama of world events because of his agile mind and his fierce, uncompromising devotion to Islamic and Shiite doctrine.

Though he had known Khomeini for many years, Hafizi found himself sweating beneath his robe, and not entirely because of the summer heat. He knew that no word, no nuance of this conversation would be overlooked. He carefully gathered himself to speak.

"Ayatollah, I have come here today for the sake of our friendship, and in the name of Allah the Merciful." The older man bowed his head slightly as Hafizi invoked the name of God. "I seek assistance for a man who, though not a Muslim, has shown much kindness and respect for the true faith, and who, I believe, merits the favor of any right-thinking disciple of the Prophet—blessings and peace be upon him."

"Blessings and peace," responded the Imam impatiently. "Perhaps it would be best to state this man's case, *Aga* Hafizi, and allow one to decide for himself the fellow's merits or lack of them."

Hafizi inclined his head, accepting the muted rebuke. "I'm sorry, Your Excellency. Forgive me if my heart intruded upon my tongue."

The older man shrugged, taking another large bite of the pear. "Tell me more, *baradar*," he urged, speaking around the plug of fruit in his mouth. "By the way, would you like a pear? They are exceptionally sweet—and fresh fruit is a necessity for an old man such as myself."

"No, thank you," said Hafizi, reaching into his breast pocket.

The aide's eyes widened, then returned to normal when he saw that all Hafizi retrieved from his pocket was paper. The mullah spread the sheets on the mat before Khomeini.

"I hold here a receipt signed by Ayatollah Kermani, for a million *tomans* donated by the man of whom I speak. He gave the money for the refurbishment of a Muslim cemetery near Mossadeq Boulevard. He did this," said Hafizi, pausing significantly and fastening the Ayatollah with an intent look, "even though he is Jewish."

The Imam's thick eyebrows arched. "Indeed?" he responded in an impressed tone.

Hafizi nodded his head. "In addition, I can give you several instances—some from personal experience—where this same man has shown great generosity to the poor. I will personally vouch for the sincerity and quality of this man, Your Excellency," concluded Hafizi earnestly. "In light of what he has done for Islam, and the trivial nature of what he is asking, I urge you to help him."

Khomeini chewed slowly and quietly, staring intently at a place on the mat just beyond the rim of the bowl. At last, his raven-bright eyes glittered up at Hafizi. "What is it that he wants us to do for him?"

Hafizi drew a quiet, deep breath. One hurdle overcome. "He wishes nothing more than to leave the country with his family," the mullah answered.

"And go where?" asked the Ayatollah quickly.

"To Switzerland, Your Excellency."

"And for this, he must personally petition me?" rejoined the Imam. "For a man of such excellent report, it is surprising that he would feel the need to leave Iran. But granting that," said Khomeini, glancing sharply at Hafizi, "why does he require my intervention in the normal process?"

"He wishes the procedure expedited," explained Hafizi carefully. "Unfortunately, there have been misunderstandings in the application of certain laws and procedures. This man—"

"What is his name?" interrupted the Ayatollah.

"I'm sorry, Your Excellency, I should have mentioned that earlier. Solaiman. Ezra Solaiman."

The older man grunted, nodding slightly.

"At any rate," continued Hafizi, "Solaiman has, because of such mishaps, been arrested and placed in Evin Prison as an enemy of the state—which clearly he is not."

"Is he still in prison?" queried the Imam.

"Fortunately, no. I . . . I intervened in his behalf with the trial committee, using this very receipt as evidence. He was released, but he is in some anxiety to leave the country."

Again the Ayatollah grunted quietly, rubbing his beard in a calculating manner. Presently he gave Hafizi another of his incisive obsidian glances. "Is this—what's his name?"

"Solaiman, Your Excellency."

"Yes. Is this Solaiman trying, for some illegal purpose, to circumvent the controls we have placed on emigration? How much money is he taking with him?"

"I don't know. Presumably he will take enough to permit his family to survive until he is settled in his new country." Hafizi looked diffidently at the mat between his knees, then back toward the older man. "This seems only fair," he added softly.

Khomeini squinted at Hafizi, then away. Thoughtfully he toyed with the core of the pear he had consumed, as his mind scampered to and fro along paths of probability and conjecture. For almost two full minutes the two mullahs sat silent, the Ayatollah engaged in tacit analysis, Hafizi feverishly wishing for some indication of which way the die would fall. Finally, Khomeini reached forward, dropped the core into the bowl of fruit, and fixed Hafizi with an intense stare.

"You will personally vouch for this Solaiman's intentions, you say?" the Imam asked.

"With all my heart, Your Excellency," replied Hafizi, returning the Ayatollah's level gaze.

"Very well then," said Khomeini. "It is not our wish that anyone remain in Iran against his will. I will have my secretary draw up something suitable."

"If I may, Excellency," put in Hafizi, again reaching into his pocket, "I have taken the liberty of drafting a letter which I hope will meet with your approval."

GRUNTING WITH THE EFFORT, Ezra pulled the canvas bag out of the hole in the basement floor. Briefly he peered inside, seeing that the bundles of American dollars had not diminished in size. *Except for inflation,* he thought wryly, as he started upstairs, lugging the bag of money with him.

The box built for him by Ahmed Dabirian sat in the middle of the floor of his study. He reached inside, removing the false bottom. Hefting two of the bundles of dollars in each hand, he remembered the awkwardness of his interview with the cabinetmaker, and the skepticism of his wife and son regarding the effectiveness of the box as a hiding place. *"My uncle is a mullah,"* Ahmed had said. *"I was able to get an appointment as a special agent for the government."* Sighing a silent prayer that he was doing the right thing, he placed the currency in the bottom of the box.

A few moments later, Esther walked past the study door and glanced in his direction. He had just finished rolling up the Isfahan carpet, and was thrusting it down into the box. He looked up and met the eyes of his wife. For a moment she looked at him, then at the box. Her glance accused him silently of ruinous folly. Without a word, Ezra returned to his work. Esther shook her head and walked away.

The phone rang. Placing the cover on the shipping box, Ezra walked over to the desk. "Yes?" he said, placing the receiver to his ear.

"This is Hafizi," crackled the voice on the other end. "I have the letter signed."

Ezra's heart raced with exhilaration. "My friend, this is the best news I have had in a while!"

"There was one problem, though," cautioned the mullah.

Ezra's heart fell into his stomach. "What?" he asked, sudden fear almost choking the word.

"Not to worry, my friend," calmed the mullah. "The difficulty is slight, and easily remedied. Ayatollah Kermani, whose signature appears on your receipt, has died these two weeks past. I had heard the news, but had forgotten. The Imam has stipulated that you must be willing to take an oath on a holy book that the signature is genuine. Since I was present when you gave the money, I have already taken such an oath on the Koran, in the Ayatollah's presence."

"*Aga* Hafizi, I would take such an oath in the very courtyard of the Ka'aba itself," asserted Ezra fervently. "How soon can you get here?"

"I'm on my way now," answered the mullah. "Take heart, *Aga* Solaiman. Your troubles are almost over."

"*Inshallah*," whispered Ezra hoarsely, as the line went dead.

TWENTY-THREE

As they hurried down the corridor toward their departure gate, Ezra noted pasdars stationed at ten-meter intervals, nervously fingering their weapons and looking over the heads of the crowd as if awaiting a signal.

"Ezra," Esther whispered as they paced quickly along, "why are there so many pasdars about? Are they always here in such numbers?"

"Quiet," he urged, "and don't look at them. If they read doubt or fear in your face, they will stop us for questioning." Ezra was beginning to feel a cautious confidence: the Ayatollah's signature was like a magic talisman, granting them safe passage through the maze of customs. Was it actually going to work? Were their trials nearly over?

Ahead of them, Hafizi had also noticed the inordinate number of guards. "There is a mullah arriving today from Iraq for a conference with the Ayatollah," he explained over his shoulder as they walked along. "Security is somewhat tighter because of this, no doubt."

"No doubt," agreed Ezra, his eyes steadfastly fixed toward the space in front of his striding feet. "Just keep walking," he tersely whispered toward his wife and daughter. "And don't look at them." Surely they couldn't get this close to their destination without being successful, he thought. Surely . . .

"Which gate is ours?" panted Sepi, pulling the strap of her shoulder bag back into place.

217

Ezra consulted the boarding pass stapled to his ticket. "Twelve," he said, replacing the ticket in his pocket as he walked. "Our plane boards from Gate 12."

. . . .

ARI CLOSED THE COVER of the trunk and nodded to Moosa, who started the engine of the black Ford and backed the car into the concealed bay at the rear of the warehouse.

After the fiasco on Abbasabbad Street, they had abandoned the Volvo in a remote area on the outskirts of the city. One of the men found this aging Ford Fairlane parked on a dark side street, and summarily appropriated it for use by the group.

Aziz had proved as good as his word. Locked in the boot of the car was a box of gleaming rifles and automatics. They had crept into the center of the city late last night and found the cache still concealed where the newest member of the band said it would be.

Unfortunately, as they exited the area, they had met a patrol of *pasdars*. Moosa drove slowly, as if he had no reason for alarm, but still the jeep swung around in a U-turn and zoomed up behind them, its searchlight raking across the rear windshield of the car. As Moosa pulled over to the curb, the two men sitting beside the front and rear passenger-side doors rolled out onto the sidewalk and came up behind the Ford, firing their pistols at the *pasdars* from point-blank range.

The gunfight was quick and deadly, for the guerrillas had the advantage of surprise. Three of the occupants of the jeep fell onto the street, their bodies riddled with bullets. One of the *pasdars* somehow managed to get the jeep into reverse and screamed away backward down the street, the gunfire from Moosa and his accomplices following him in a deadly farewell salute until the vehicle squealed out of sight around the street corner.

When the jeep had gone, and just before they left the

scene, Ari had ordered them to strip the dead *pasdars* of their guns and ammunition. Moosa had hurried to the nearest bloody corpse. In the red glow of the Ford's tail lights, he saw the face of the one he plundered. It was a boy—not yet old enough to have a beard. Swiftly Moosa unbuckled the bandolier of cartridges from about the lad's torso and tugged it free. He grabbed the pistol from the youth's gory fingers and rushed to the car, trying to forget that here too was some mother's son, some sister's brother.

The face of the slain boy still haunted him as he switched off the engine. Handing the keys to Ari and walking toward the warehouse office, he wondered how many more children would die—with or without guns in their hands.

The men gathered about the table. Smokes were passed around. "Those *pasdar* pigs never knew what hit them," bragged one of the men who had been in the car the night before. "The stupid fools didn't even have their guns cocked."

"Most of them are morons," agreed another. "They think a uniform and a gun is all the protection they need."

"All right, enough," called Ari. "Let's get down to business. We've got an operation to pull off in three days, and it'll be a lot tougher than ambushing *pasdars* in a jeep. Let's get started."

The room quieted. "Manuchehr," called Ari, "what have you found out about the arrival arrangements?"

"He's coming in at Gate 13," Manuchehr responded, unfolding a schematic drawing of the main terminal building of Mehrabad International Airport. "Here," he said, putting his finger on the map. The men gathered behind him and looked over his shoulder, studying the map silently for a few moments.

"Gate 13 will be unlucky for him," jested one of the men, sotto voce. Some chuckles greeted the joke.

"The plane is supposed to land around 10 in the morning," finished Manuchehr.

"Not too far from this service road here," mused Ari, his finger tracing a possible escape route.

Moosa nodded his head in agreement, chewing his lip in thought. "Better to cut across the runways here than back out the main gate. If we hit quickly and keep moving, we can be almost to the Tarasht Highway before the *pasdars* can mount much pursuit."

"Very well, that's it, then," announced Ari decisively. "Everybody sit down." The men shifted slowly back to their seats, waiting to hear Ari's further orders.

"The car stays here until 9:30," he began. "We don't want anyone recognizing it from our little scuffle last night. Aaron will drive it to the service road beside the runways, where we will regroup after the action. Manuchehr and . . ." Ari's eyes roamed the group. ". . . and Hafez will have the other cars waiting there. Everyone is to take a bus or a cab to the airport. And make sure there aren't more than three of you together on any single bus." The men nodded, taking in the instructions.

"When you get to the airport, don't cluster together. Stay in ones and twos, until . . ." Ari looked at the center of the table, a calculating expression on his face. ". . . until 9:45. Then start moving toward Gate 13. When the Iraqi mullah comes through the door and greets the first member of the delegation, that will be your signal to act."

With a sinking feeling in his chest, Moosa realized that he was included in the group inside the terminal. This time he would not be waiting in the car when the shooting started. He would be in the thick of it.

Firouz Marandi was impassive as he evaluated the probabilities. *It could be chancy,* he thought. *But not impossible.*

"I'm sure I need not say this," finished Ari, "but

caution compels me. If anyone here says anything to anyone outside this group—be they wife, mother, sister, father, or brother—we could all be dead." He paused, as the finality of his words reflected leadenly from each face in the circle. "Trust no one. Confide in no one." For ten heartbeats his will gripped them with the severity of the upcoming mission. "That is all," he said at last. "You may go."

EZRA SOLAIMAN AND NADER HAFIZI walked out of the escrow office. Ezra turned, smiling, to the mullah and gripped his hand. "Congratulations! You are now the owner of a fine house which will serve you well for many years to come!"

Hafizi shook his head in wonderment. "I still cannot comprehend such good fortune," he breathed.

"It would be a great convenience to us," Ezra said, "if we could remain in the house until the day of our departure from the airport—three days from now. Will this be possible?"

The mullah looked at Ezra reproachfully. "How can you even ask such a thing?" he scolded. "When a diamond falls from heaven into a man's lap, does he upbraid Allah because it is not an emerald?"

Ezra laughed. "I apologize, *baradar!* And thank you for your kindness."

"I'm sure I don't need to caution you," said Hafizi, as they walked toward the nearest bus stop, "not to tell anyone else about what I have done for you. When you have gone, I could still be accused of accepting a bribe."

"I will tell no one," promised Ezra. "But," he added after a pause, "I would beg of you a final boon."

"What else is left, my friend?"

"Would you and your gracious wife accompany us to the airport? It would be a tremendous comfort to us to have your companionship and—I will say it—your protection until we are finally on our way."

The men took several paces as Hafizi mulled the idea. As they reached the bus stop, he looked up and gripped Ezra's hand. "I will come with you, at least," he said. "Akram dislikes the noise and bustle of the airport, and I would not willingly compel her, but I will come. I promise."

"Thank you, *baradar*," said Ezra gratefully. A bus roared up, and Ezra glanced at the placard on its front. "This is my bus," he said, turning to go. As he stepped into the dark interior, he turned again toward the mullah. "I will never forget this," he promised.

"Go in peace," answered Hafizi, as the doors closed, and the bus pulled away.

As ESTHER FOLDED THE CLOTHES into her suitcase, she suddenly realized that she ought to be crying, or at the very least feeling despondent. She felt nothing. She watched her hands as if they were the hands of a stranger: folding the clothes, arranging them, like the faded souvenirs of a forgotten holiday, into the valise atop her unmade bed.

Something final had left her at the relinquishment of the house. As if realizing at last what the departure from Iran was to cost, she had looked deep within herself and found a part of her which was reluctant to pay the price. The knowledge by turns sickened her at her own weakness and angered her at Ezra and the events which forced him to such desperate generosity.

She wanted to take the samovar, but Ezra said it was too cumbersome to lug on and off the airplane. The heavy, kerosene-heated samovar had been a gift from her mother on the day she and Ezra wed. It had belonged to her grandmother, and Esther begged as much as her shredded pride would allow, but Ezra remained adamant. "Nothing we cannot carry with us," he had said. "One valise and one shoulder bag apiece. I will check nothing except the carpet...."

The carpet! That ridiculous trojan horse of a box with all their money hidden in such a childishly obvious fashion! Esther wanted to shout aloud at him, "You fool! Do you imagine that your stupid little plan is going to work? You will succeed only in having all our remaining sustenance confiscated and ourselves arrested as smugglers!"

But the numbness within her would not allow such a venting of rage. He was locked away from her, inside the shell of his futile machinations. She, in turn, was frozen into the barren cocoon of her depression. Their worlds did not intersect. She went along with his plans as one riding a raft over the edge of a cataract: she could hear the roaring of the falls, feel its death-mist on her face, but she was too surely snared in the current to resist.

She heard the bell downstairs announce the presence of someone at the front gate. Her heart turned to ice. *Someone knows! They've come back for us!* Her breath trembling in and out of her chest, she crept to the window and peered out the space between the curtain and the window frame. Even as she did so, the bell rang again, evidencing the impatience of the unknown caller.

The shape was that of a man. Through the open window, she heard Marjan half-barking, half-growling at him. Remembering the instinctive hostility of the dog toward the *pasdars* who had come, she felt her face blanching with dread. The bell rang again as she madly pondered what to do.

"Mother?" Sepi's voice sounded at her elbow. "Who's at the gate? Aren't you going to answer it?"

"How do I know it isn't the mullahs, come back to carry us away?"

"Let me see," said Sepi, elbowing her aside and craning her neck to see the stranger at the gate. "He looks familiar, he..." Sepi suddenly gasped. "It's Khosrow!"

223

She looked at her mother, her face a shifting map of uncertainty, as if her heart dared her eyes to believe.

The girl whirled about and raced for the stairs. "Sepideh!" Esther called after her. "Stop! You don't know why he's here!" But the footsteps never slowed, pounding down the staircase and slapping into the marble-tiled foyer. Esther heard the front door flung back against the wall and an instant later saw her daughter racing down the walk toward the gate. "Quiet, Marjan!" she heard her shout, then, "Khosrow! I thought I'd never see you again!" As Sepi opened the gate, Esther turned away from the window.

Sepi came through the gate toward Khosrow, her steps slowing with indecision as she stared intently at him for some sign. And then, heedless of who might see, he took two quick steps toward her and enfolded her in his arms. Neither of them spoke for a full minute. Then, he held her shoulders and looked into her eyes.

"Sepi, I am so sorry. I'm ashamed of the way I've treated you these past weeks. And . . . I admit it . . . I tried to forget about you. I tried to listen to my father and have no more to do with you, but . . . it just wasn't right, Sepi. I was wrong to—"

"I understand," she softly interrupted. "These are terrible times, Khosrow. People do things out of fear and prejudice that they wouldn't do if they weren't so frightened. You at least tried to defend me from those . . . those boys. I am grateful for your courage."

"Courage!" Khosrow barked the word derisively. He could not meet her eyes. "No, Sepi, I am not brave. If I were, I wouldn't have spent the last weeks trying to pretend you don't exist. If I were brave, I wouldn't have listened to my father telling me to blend in, to go along and avoid the notice of the fanatics. If I were brave," he said, finally turning to look at her, "it wouldn't have taken me this long to decide to ask for the privilege of seeing you again."

She looked at him, uncomprehending.

"Sepi," he said, taking her hand in his, "I want to see you again. I don't care what the others think, what my father thinks. I . . . I care very much for you, and—"

"O Khosrow," she said, biting her lip and looking away. "I . . . you can't." Tears of frustration burned the corners of her eyes and spilled onto her cheeks.

"Sepi! What is it? What did I say?"

She shook her head, her hand covering her mouth. "It's not what you said," she managed. "It's just that . . ." She clenched her jaw against the sobs that begged for release, took several deep shuddering breaths before facing him again. "Khosrow, I . . . we . . . are going away."

"What?"

"My family is leaving. Leaving Iran. We are going to America."

His face wore the expression of someone who has just been stabbed by his closest friend.

She took his hand. "Come inside," she said, leading him toward the gate. "The street isn't a good place to talk."

He allowed her to lead him through the gate, still not quite believing what he had heard. It was impossible! He had finally resolved to become a man, to use his own mind and set his own course, and Sepi, his intended destination, was leaving?

She sat on a chaise of whitewashed ornamental wrought iron and beckoned him to sit beside her. "Khosrow. Listen to me. Sit down here."

Woodenly, he obeyed.

"Someone once told me," she began, "that when bad things happen, there are three ways to react. You can give up, you can adapt, or you can become angry. I don't think you should give up, Khosrow. And anger won't do any good, in this case." She placed her fingertips on his chin and gently guided him to look at her. "I think you and I must adapt. At least, that's what I'm trying to do about our leaving."

He felt as if all the air had left his lungs. He thought of the way he had felt at the beginning, when he knew he was beginning to care for her, how the exhilaration of his emerging feelings had transformed every moment of those days. Life had seemed bigger, colors were brighter, smells were richer. Now he knew he would never again experience those feelings in that same way, and he resented the loss. He groped for words which would change things, which would set them both back at the beginning, would erase all the harm which had intruded on their blossoming relationship. But such words didn't exist. He knew deep within himself, though he loathed admitting it, that Sepi was right. The world had changed . . . for the worse, probably. But still, they had to adapt.

"I will never forget you," he said, finally. "And, perhaps—who knows? I may come to see you in America someday."

She smiled at him through the tears cascading down her cheeks. "Perhaps." But in the silence they both knew the possibility was remote.

"Sepi, I . . . I want you to know that . . ." He swallowed drily, then went on. "I want to tell you that even though I behaved badly toward you—"

"But, Khosrow—"

"Even though I did," he persisted, "you have helped me learn a valuable lesson which I desperately needed. And for that reason too I will remember you."

Wiping her eyes with a palm, she asked, "What did you learn?"

"I learned that no one can make you into someone you don't want to be . . . unless you allow it."

She looked into his eyes for a long moment, then smiled again. "I think I learned the same thing," she whispered.

"YOU TOLD HIM *WHAT?*" Ezra exclaimed, his eyes wide with disbelief. He held a butter knife, and the skin of his knuckles whitened as his fist clamped tighter about its grip.

"I told him . . . that we were leaving," gulped Sepi, her nostrils flaring with the panic spawned by her father's suddenly wrathful visage. "I . . . I care for him, Father," she explained guiltily, dropping her eyes to her plate and kneading her hands in her lap.

"And do you care nothing for your family, that you would place our safety in jeopardy?" grated Ezra through clenched teeth.

"Father!" exclaimed Sepi in consternation. "It's only Khosrow."

"And has he no parents, no family to whom he may tell this news you have passed on?" demanded Ezra hotly. "And is this one to whom you have confided our plans not a Muslim?"

"What about the Hafizis?" interrupted Esther in a brittle voice. "Are they not Muslims?"

Ezra's eyes bulged outward at his wife and daughter, the first challenging him with a stony stare, the second weeping softly into her plate. With an inarticulate groan of strangled rage, he rose from the table and stalked out of the room.

Moosa, who had been sitting with his eyes carefully averted during the foregoing exchange, swallowed the bite of veal he had been chewing, following it with a long draught of water. Carefully replacing the glass beside his plate, he asked softly, eyes still downcast, "When will . . . when do you leave?"

Esther, hearing her son's implied exclusion of himself, whitened visibly. There was no reply for perhaps a full minute. Suddenly, Sepi realized what her brother had said.

"Moosa! You're coming too . . ." The question died in birth, as Moosa looked steadily at his sister, shaking his head. Like her mother, Sepi's face blanched, her eyes widened in horror at the understanding that there would be three passengers on the departing flight, not four.

"Moosa, why?" The last word was scarcely more than a whisper, a throttled plea for something Moosa knew he could never deliver.

Thrusting another morsel of food in his mouth, he mumbled, "It's just . . . something I have to do." A host of tangled feelings twined about within him, but he could never hope to frame them in words that would make sense to them. Instead, he shrouded his face in silence, chewing food he couldn't taste in a house filled with emotions he couldn't allow himself to feel.

"The day after tomorrow," whispered Esther, in answer to her son's question, as if the reply had only now managed to sunder itself from the frozen despair of her consciousness. "The flight leaves the day after tomorrow."

Moosa's knife fell from his suddenly nerveless fingers. *The day after tomorrow!* "What time?" he asked, his abruptly louder voice betraying the steel band of panic clamping his chest.

Ezra stepped into the doorway of the dining room. "Why do you ask, Moosa?" he demanded. "What's the matter?"

"What time?" Moosa shouted, suddenly standing and knocking over his water glass in his startling frenzy. "Tell me!"

Esther involuntarily jerked her forearm in front of her face, as if to fend off an attack. "Our plane leaves at 9 o'clock in the morning," she gasped, realizing with horror that she was terrified of her own son.

Moosa stared at them, his fists clenching and unclenching. *Nine o'clock. They should be long gone before . . .* As his breathing slowed in the silent room, he became acutely conscious of their eyes—wide, staring, frightened, and fixed with a horrid fascination on him. How to explain to them, to defuse the effect of his inexplicable anxiety?

"Tell no one," came Ari's warning in his ear. *"We could all be dead."*

"Never mind, I . . ." He groped about for some plausible explanation for his outburst. "This decision about staying here . . . it has been very difficult for me, and . . ." His mouth opened and closed a few more times, but no more words came to him. "I'm very tired. I've had enough to eat," he mumbled, crumpling his napkin and tossing it on his chair. He strode to the doorway, past his father, and up the stairs.

The quiet darkened as the unmoving occupants of the dining room silently contemplated the desolate shape of private despair.

TWENTY-FOUR

AKRAM HAFIZI SIGHED as she set the plate of rice and cold mutton before her husband. "I can't help it, husband," she said, wiping her hands on her apron as she fetched the tea glasses. "I can't escape the feeling that something is going to happen."

"What would you have me do," questioned the mullah, allowing more than a hint of impatience in his voice, "renege on my promise to Solaiman? After all he has done, all the turmoil he and his family have suffered?"

Sadly she shook her head. "No, no." She heaved another deep sigh as she sat down across the table from her husband. "You must perform for them the things agreed upon. And it is certainly a wonderful house," she wavered wistfully. "Still . . ."

They bowed their heads for the benediction. "In the name of Allah the Merciful and Compassionate," Hafizi intoned. He tasted the first morsel of rice, a thoughtful look on his face.

"And getting the Solaimans out of Iran is not the only concern," continued Akram, after she had taken a swallow of tea. "Even after we move into the house, the problems won't be over."

"What do you mean?" asked her husband finally, unwilling to continue the conversation, but wearily accepting the fact that his wife had more on her mind—words which would be uttered.

"You know how things can change," replied Akram, carefully scooping a spoonful of rice atop the portion of meat on her fork. "Look at the Islamic revolution which has just taken place. Decades of Pahlavi rule vanished without a trace; everyone associated with the Shah is dead, imprisoned, or in hiding."

"*Allahu akbar,*" commented Nader Hafizi, wryly.

"What I'm saying," pressed Akram, giving him an admonitory look, "is this: how are we to know the same thing could not happen again—only in reverse? Look at the violence in the streets! Still mullahs and *pasdars* are attacked by secret supporters of the Shah and groups of radicals."

"Not without justification, in some cases," observed the mullah, scraping the last of the rice onto his spoon.

"Granted," countered Akram, waving her fork like a pointer at Nader, "but entirely beside the point I'm making. Who knows when a counterrevolution may occur? If such a thing happens, do you imagine there will be no retribution taken against anyone deemed to have profited from the Ayatollah's rule? And what more visible target than two old people living in a sumptuous house earned by nothing other than the emigration of those who bought and paid for it?"

"But that's not the way—"

"I know that!" she interrupted. "I'm not talking about fact; I'm warning you about perception."

Nader Hafizi took a slow drink of tea.

"The next time, it could be you sitting in Evin Prison instead of Ezra Solaiman," she said quietly. "And who will come to your defense?"

THE PHONE JANGLED in its cradle. Mullah Hassan swiveled about in the chair behind his desk, picked up the handset, and placed it to his ear. "Yes?"

"When the Iraqi mullah arrives, there will be trouble," murmured the voice on the other end. "Be ready."

"Of course," responded the mullah. "And may Allah bless you for your help."

"Forget that!" snapped the voice. "When do I get my money?"

"*After* your information proves correct," growled the mullah. "You will be met in the usual place."

"The house on Avenue Ismaili?"

"That's what I said, isn't it?" snarled Mullah Hassan.

The line went dead. With a look of distaste, the mullah pressed the switchhook button, then dialed another number.

"Yes?" came the answer.

"Our source has communicated with me again," said Hassan, quietly.

"Shall we make the usual arrangements for payment?" asked the voice.

"I think not," replied Hassan. "I believe his usefulness to us has neared its end."

"What will you do, then?"

"I think we should make an alternate settlement this time—a permanent one."

There was a pause. "Understood," said the voice, finally.

"Good," said Hassan. "See to it." He hung up the phone and swiveled his chair away from the desk, to gaze out the window into the Tehranian dusk.

"PUT ALL THE VALISES and handbags at the foot of the stairs," Ezra said. "Everything else is done." He looked at his wife and daughter, their faces scored by stress. "Then go to bed and try to get some rest. It's already close to midnight, and tomorrow is a full day." *Surely the understatement of the year*, he thought.

After they had gone upstairs, he sat alone in the study. A single desk lamp illumined the room, casting a pool of cheerful, yellow light about his desk, but shrouding the rest of the study in an indistinct darkness. He stared in thought at his hands folded on the desk top.

What else was to be done? Nothing that he could see. Every preparation, every precaution that he could imagine had been taken. Everything now rested in the hands of fate. What was the Arabic word? *Kismet.* Everything now depended on *kismet* or Allah, whichever one preferred to call it.

He ground the heels of his hands into his eye sockets. A deep weariness, one which sleep could not remedy, had been slowly seizing him these past days. Now that he was near the end of his journey, it had all but mastered him.

He was tired—and not only from the final preparations for departure. He was bone-weary of the constant caution, the never-ceasing need for watchfulness and alertness. He was fatigued by the endless cycle of taut expectation and numbing depression, of heartbreaking hope banished by the nagging crone of fear who wrapped her limbs about him in an embrace that could not be dislodged. Having reached the ragged end of his own inner resources, he longed, more than anything, to lay his burden somewhere else, on someone else—but on whom?

Esther? Hardly. He was not even certain their marriage would hold together, once the crucible of Iran no longer bound them in an uneasy alliance. He had heard that in America, divorce was far more common than in the East. Perhaps Esther would seek such a permanent exit from his presence, from the reminder of the turmoil for which he knew she blamed him. He longed to reach out to her, to bridge the chasm gouged between them by their troubles. But she was too tightly bound by her own pain, her own sense of loss, to grant any foothold on her side of the abyss. He dangled helplessly in the darkness of her mistrust, suspended on the fraying rope of his own good intentions.

And Sepi. A bubble of grief burst in the back of his throat at the memory of the carefree, dark-curled child who had toddled happily about their lives—wasn't it only yesterday? Of all the bitter prices demanded of them by the trouble in this country, he most regretted the loss of Sepi's innocence. She was slowly beginning to mend, and he hoped desperately that the process would continue. But never again would she be able to see the world with a child's acceptance and lack of caution. And, he feared, his last chance for such a vision vanished with hers.

Moosa. A melee of anger, bewilderment, and distress rioted within him as he contemplated leaving his son in Iran. Indeed, he had no choice, for Moosa had made it more than plain that he rejected any notion of return to America.

How had it happened? Ezra had tortured himself repeatedly with this question since the first night on the stairs, when he had seen the butt of the revolver smirking at his son's waist. He and Esther went to great pains, even in the days of the Shah, to secure Moosa's passage to America. To support him while he was a student there had meant a ceaseless series of logistical and financial obstacles, but it had been well worth it—or so he thought until now. Their son was a professional; he had a place and an identity in the free haven of the West. But now, through some bizarre incongruity, he chose to turn his back on all the opportunity and potential that America offered him.

What witchery had beguiled Moosa? What siren song had captured his will, that he could choose the violence and cruelty of Iran over tolerant, democratic America? Was it the unfortunate death of Nathan Moosovi which

whispered in his ear a dark chant of revenge? Or was it
Iran herself calling out to Moosa? Demanding the life of
the son as the price of his father's passage?

Ezra laid his head on his arms and sobbed silently in
the tiny circle of light atop his desk. Whatever else he
managed to take from Iran, he could never recover what
he would leave here.

Blearily he raised his head from his arms. His eyelids
were sticky, his back stiff. He looked at his wristwatch—2 A.M.! He must have fallen asleep. He rose,
wincing as the kinks of sleep twanged along his arms,
back, and legs. Slowly he paced from the study to the
foyer. He stood in the semidark beside the luggage and
the carpet box. A deep sigh wrenched loose from the
weariness in his chest. *Only one thing left to do,* he
thought. *Then, to bed.*

MOOSA LOOKED for the thousandth time at
the clock beside his bed. Six o'clock. Morning scratched
feebly at the window; it was barely light enough to
announce the coming of dawn.

He had lain awake all night, his mind endlessly gnawing at the possibilities of what the next day might bring.
His family was leaving, and he was going into the most
dangerous situation he had yet faced.

"Tell no one . . . father, mother, sister."

He sat up on the side of his bed, still wearing yesterday's clothing. Considering the day's plan of action, he
saw little need to tend his appearance. Rubbing his
face, he decided to get out of the house. *Better to be gone
when they wake. Better not to have to face them.*

Feeling more alone than ever before in his entire life,
he tiptoed to his door and eased it open. He held his
shoes in his hand as he crept toward the stair. *Yes, better
this way,* he told himself again. *No need to prolong the pain.*

"Moosa." He stiffened. It was his father's quiet voice.

Turning, he waited in dread.

Ezra stood outside the closed door of the master bedroom. He too, despite his fatigue, had been unable to sleep. "Where are you going?" he asked his son.

Moosa hunched his shoulders defensively. "Out," he grunted, with a terse jerk of his head. *"Tell no one."* "I didn't want to wake you."

"I was already awake," replied Ezra.

A long silence ensued, dropping between them its dead weight of unspoken words and sundered dreams. At last, Moosa moved toward the stairs. "I've got to go," he said, his eyes refusing to meet those of his father.

"Moosa!" The word was quiet, but the echoes of grief and loss made it ring in the dead air of the stairwell. The son halted a final time, without turning around.

"Whatever happens," Ezra whispered around the anguish swelling in his throat, "remember that I love you!"

Moosa wavered atop the stairs. *"We could all be dead."* Slowly he turned his face toward his father and, as if lifting the weight of the entire world, raised his eyes to Ezra's silently pleading, mortally wounded face. The son nodded once, blinking back tears, and hastened down the stairs and swiftly out the front door. He closed it as quietly as an apparition and was gone.

EZRA PACED BACK and forth in the foyer, looking at his watch every thirty seconds. It was almost 8 o'clock, and still he had not heard from Hafizi. The mullah was essential to his plans—he had to come! He felt the nibbling of nervousness in the pit of his stomach, the tense cramping of his bowels as apprehension mounted with each passing moment. Traffic was always heavy on Eisenhower Boulevard, the main thoroughfare to Mehrabad International. Their plane left at 9:05. To miss the flight and be forced to reschedule their departure was unthinkable!

Esther, sitting on the bottom step of the stairway, watched her husband pacing like a lion in a cage. For a fleeting moment, she caught a whiff of his nervousness, felt the glimmering of ... anticipation? Fear? Then the faint sensation was gone, swallowed by the dull ache of her anger at the unfairness of life. She turned her head and stared out the window of the dining room. Small green cherries were forming on the trees in the side yard—the immature fruits clustering in profusion on the trimmed branches of the trees. *So*, she thought sardonically, *Ezra's pruning was successful. But he will not enjoy the benefits of his success. When the fruit ripens, we will be more than halfway around the world, a universe removed from everything familiar.*

Removed also from the danger that is here, the nagging voice within reminded her. Esther clamped a tight lid on the annoying whisper of truth. She couldn't let go of her anger just now. She needed it to carry her through the ordeal of the next few hours. She needed its spur to goad herself and her daughter through the obstacles which lay ahead.

Ah, well, she conceded to herself, *we're in the thick of it now. Best to go along. Pulling backward won't change anything—might get us arrested.*

The crunch of gravel was heard, and the scrape of tires on the curbside. Ezra leapt to the door, flinging it open. A cab had pulled up out front, and Hafizi was getting out of the front passenger side.

"Come, *Aga* Solaiman!" he called, beckoning with his arm. "I have taken the liberty of bringing a cab for us!"

Ezra thought his grin might split his head open, so relieved was he to see the mullah. He waved and dashed inside. "Come!" he urged the women, "grab your things and let's go! We mustn't be late!"

By the time they reached the gate, the driver had opened the trunk of the battered yellow Audi. There was room only for the valises and shoulder bags. "Is this all, *Aga?*" the cabbie asked in a bored voice.

"No, I have one more item in the house," said Ezra. "I'll be right back." He strode toward the house, then halted suddenly, turning back toward the cab.

"*Aga* Hafizi," he called, "could you come here a moment, please? There is something we ought to do before we go."

The mullah walked slowly toward Ezra. "What is it, *baradar?*"

"I want you to hold this for me," Ezra said, handing Hafizi the Ayatollah's letter. "Officials will be more inclined to believe it's genuine if a mullah hands it to them. Of course, I would like to have it back before we board the plane."

"Certainly," agreed the mullah, placing the document in his breast pocket. "If you think this will help."

"Come with me," Ezra said, leading him toward the kennel where Marjan lay, his tongue lolling in the morning heat. When the dog saw Hafizi approaching at the elbow of his master, his ears perked forward, and he arose in one uncoiling motion—instantly alert, his nose tasting the scent of this seemingly friendly stranger.

Ezra walked over to the dog, knelt down, and fondled him behind the ears. "Marjan, you have served us faithfully. Now we are going away. This," he said, motioning Hafizi to extend his hand for the dog to sniff, "is your new master. He is a good man, worthy of your service. He will take care of you."

Marjan cautiously tested the scent of Nader Hafizi's open palm. Without dropping his guarded pose, the dog wagged his tail slowly, once . . . twice. Hafizi scratched him beneath the chin.

"He knows you now," observed Ezra. "He won't forget." For a moment more he scratched the dog's back, then stood. "If you wish, you may wait in the cab. There is one more piece of luggage in the house."

Ezra walked into the foyer and hefted the carpet box. He looked quickly about, then went back outside, kicking the door shut behind him.

The cabbie stood listlessly beside the back door of the vehicle as Ezra approached. "The trunk is full," he drawled, looking at Ezra with half-lidded eyes. "You'll have to hold that box in your lap."

"I prefer it so," said Ezra, climbing into the backseat beside his wife. He pulled the carpet box in with him and the cabbie shut the door, then went around to get in the car. They pulled away from the curb, and the house vanished behind them, lost behind the high brick walls which protected it.

Ezra heard his wife weeping softly, her sobs muffled by the folds of her *chador*.

TWENTY-FIVE

MOOSA LIFTED the ammunition clip doubtfully, looking askance from it to the short, snub-nosed automatic weapon he held in his left hand. "Where does this thing fit?" he asked, as the handful of men standing about the table inspected the weapons from Aziz's cache.

"It goes here," said Aziz, his eyes flickering toward Moosa with a flash of veiled contempt. *Stupid Jew.* He pointed to the opening, then demonstrated with his own gun, shoving the clip into place with a deadly click. "You pull this back like this," he continued, snapping back the bolt. "Then," he deadpanned, "Allah help anything in front of you."

"Hey, Aziz! Put your safety on in here!" barked Ari in annoyance. Marandi shrugged and complied, thumbing the lever from red to green.

The atmosphere reminded Moosa of the locker room before a big soccer match. He saw the same taut nervousness in the other faces, felt the same tension in his gut, smelled the same sour stench of anxiety hanging in the room, mingled with the odor of cigarette smoke and stale coffee. *But after this game,* he reflected dourly, *the losing team won't walk away.*

"Is everyone straight on the details?" asked Ari, his cheek twitching with a nervous tic. The men nodded.

Ari looked at his wristwatch. "Everyone set your watches. On my mark, it will be exactly . . . three minutes until 9 o'clock. Ready . . . Mark!"

Moosa clicked the stem of his watch. *They're probably backing away from the gate by now.* Again, loneliness washed over him in a heart-stopping wave, before he sternly choked back the emotions he could not afford to acknowledge.

"Moosa, you and Manuchehr should get going. Don't want you to miss your bus," he joked weakly, as a smile died uselessly on his face. Moosa and his partner tucked their weapons beneath their clothing and made ready to leave.

"Aziz," added Ari as an afterthought, "why don't you go along with them? Don't act like you know each other. Split up once you get near the bus stop—come in from different directions. Got it?" The three men nodded and walked toward the door of the warehouse office.

"And don't forget," said Ari, as Moosa's hand paused on the doorknob, "when the Iraqi shakes the first mullah's hand . . ."

THEY ARRIVED AT GATE 12, all of them panting from the exertion of their rapid walk down the corridor. Ezra peered out at the ramp, noting to his horror that no aircraft was visible. Had the flight left early? Frantically he looked at his watch: 9 o'clock exactly. They should have had five minutes to spare. Wiping the sheen of sweat from his forehead, he approached the ticket counter, looking in confusion at the marquee behind the bored attendant. The sign was blank: it displayed no departure time for the flight they were supposed to board.

"Excuse me," he said. The attendant peered up at him disinterestedly.

"The 9:05 SwissAir flight to Geneva—is it on time?"

Despite his attempt to remain calm, he heard the edge of panic in his own voice. As the attendant, heaving a sigh, keyed the computer terminal, Ezra looked about at the departure area.

Perhaps thirty people lounged about the gate, some in the few metal folding chairs available, the rest squatting on the floor or leaning against the walls. Were they waiting for the same plane? His eyes returned to the attendant, who was now studying the greenish glow of the computer screen.

"Your ticket, please," he intoned, taking Ezra's ticket and thumbing through it, matching it with the information displayed on his screen. Presently he looked up. "Your flight was delayed. It will be here, but it's running late."

Ezra breathed a sigh of relief. At least they had not missed the plane! "When will it arrive?" he asked the attendant.

The man looked again at his terminal. "Looks like it should be in here about an hour from now." He looked up at Ezra. "Somewhere around 10 o'clock."

AHMED DABIRIAN SHOWED his identification badge to the official guarding the luggage handling area. The man glanced at him, nodded, and turned away. The carpenter entered the large room, piled from end to end with the checked baggage of departing and arriving passengers. He motioned to an attendant. The fellow sauntered over, an irritated look on his face.

"I wish to locate a piece of luggage," he told the man. "It belongs to a departing passenger, and it is a matter of some urgency."

Dabirian showed the attendant his badge. The man's eyes widened in respect. Instantly, the irritation was replaced by alert officiousness. "Where is the passenger going?" he asked.

"I'm not sure," mused Dabirian. "Probably France —
or Switzerland. The thing I'm looking for is slightly
unusual," he added. "It's a plywood box with leather
handgrips attached. About so big — " Dabirian motioned
with his hands.

The porter thought. "Switzerland, eh? Hmmm. Let's
try over at SwissAir. I think they've got a 9 o'clock flight."

THE BUS SLOWED at the gate, its air brakes
squawking as the passengers wedged themselves against
the jerky stop. The door opened, and two *pasdars* came
aboard, their fingers curled through the trigger guards of
the submachine guns hanging from the straps about
their shoulders. They looked the passengers up and down,
moving deliberately down the center aisle of the bus.

Moosa was seated in the middle of the left-hand section, looking out the window with an air of affected
boredom. He huddled within the loose, shabby clothing
he wore and forced himself to pay as little attention to
the guards as to the rest of the passengers. From the
corner of his eye, he thought he noticed one of the
pasdars peering at Aziz, who was three seats ahead, on
the aisle. But then the fellow moved on toward the back
of the vehicle. In a moment the guards had satisfied
themselves, stepping off the bus and motioning it
through the gate.

When the acrid black fumes of the diesel exhaust had
dissipated in the air beside the gate, one of the *pasdars*
motioned to a jeep, parked inconspicuously a few yards
away. He pointed at the departing bus and nodded. The
jeep pulled out and followed the bus toward the main
terminal building.

ESTHER SHIFTED UNCOMFORTABLY on the seat
of the metal folding chair, wincing as she rubbed the

small of her back. She glanced over at Sepi, then reached to adjust the folds of her daughter's *chador*. Sepi's eyes flickered toward her, then back to their resting place in the empty space between her face and lap. Esther gave Sepi a tremulous, unheeded smile of encouragement, then sighed, looking about the area where they waited for their flight to arrive.

At an adjacent gate, a group of mullahs was gathering. They milled about, talking and laughing with each other in low voices. As the clerics filtered in by ones and twos, some of them recognized Hafizi, nodding cordially. Hafizi returned the greetings, but continued to converse with Ezra in low, guarded tones. Esther saw some of the mullahs peer quizzically at Hafizi, then at Ezra.

She reflected that as long as he remained with them, Hafizi was isolated, an anomaly. Iran was not a safe place for the unusual these days. It was a time for homogeneity, for anonymity. Grudgingly, she admitted that Hafizi was placing himself in no small risk to aid their departure. There was always the possibility that they might be detained, despite the intricate precautions taken by her husband. If that happened, how could Hafizi avoid being tainted by association with them? The prospect of obtaining their house would not be enough to induce this man to place himself in harm's way, would it? If he had coveted their house, why had Ezra emerged from Evin Prison?

She remembered the night in the kitchen, when she had sobbed on Akram Hafizi's shoulder. Why, if she couldn't unburden herself even to her own husband, was she able to spill her emotions to a mullah's wife — a woman she had only just met? What was it about the Hafizis that caused her, despite her experience and inclination, to trust them? And what was it about her husband which enabled him to identify Hafizi's trustworthiness so long before?

Reluctantly, she felt a tendril of self-examination

thrusting through the crusted soil of her conscience.

A static-laden burst of words flared from the loud-speaker in their waiting area. "Passengers on SwissAir Flight 702, nonstop service to Geneva: your aircraft has landed and will be at Gate 12 shortly. We will begin boarding this flight in approximately fifteen minutes." The message repeated in Farsi-laden Arabic, French, and English.

Esther heaved a sigh. One way or another, the ordeal would soon be behind them. When they were settled in . . . wherever, then she would try to piece together the scattered fragments of her feelings. For now, better to tend to the immediate.

She heard the whining glissando of jet engines as an aircraft taxied to the gate where the mullahs waited. The clerics gathered about the door where the deplaning passengers would soon emerge. Idly she wondered who the dignitary was that commanded such a greeting.

MARANDI SURREPTITIOUSLY SLID his hand be-neath his caftan, his fingers curling around the rubber-ized grip of the gun. The attendants were wheeling the boarding ramp out to the airplane. Without moving his head, his eyes sought the locations of the other mem-bers of the guerrilla squad. The Jew who had ridden the bus with him was standing to his right, about ten me-ters down the wall. Good. He had hoped to kill a Jew. Since Ari wasn't nearby, this one would do.

He had made good money by acting as informant for the revolutionary committees. This particular job was a little more dangerous than most, and he would choke plenty of *rials* from them in payment. But so far, every-thing was going as expected. Unseen by the rest of the squad, the *pasdars* filtered into the area from the side corridors. They wore plain clothes, so they were as un-obtrusive as the guerrillas themselves. But Firouz saw the bulges beneath their clothing as they closed in on their targets.

There would be a lot of lead in the air in a few moments. *What a tragedy if a few mullahs catch a stray bullet,* he smirked inwardly. *This is going to be amusing as well as exciting.*

ESTHER FELT HER BREATH catch in her throat. That man lounging against the wall by the mullah's gate looked like—he *was* Moosa! Instantly, she scented danger in the air. His late-night forays, his obstinate silence, the gun, the proximity of so many mullahs.... Nauseated by a sudden rush of adrenaline, she scurried to Ezra's side.

He looked at her, apprehension starching his features. "What is it, Esther? What's wrong?"

"Look there!" she pointed. Ezra's eyes followed her trembling finger. When he recognized his son, a loud gasp of panic rushed in through his gaping mouth. He strode toward the slouched, watchful figure of his son.

"Ezra!" his wife moaned at his back, "be careful!"

"Moosa!" he called, closing rapidly with the gangster disguised as his son.

Moosa's head jerked around at hearing his name, and his face slackened in shock when he saw his father approaching. Over Ezra's shoulder, he could see the dismayed faces of his mother and sister. *Why are they still here? Their flight was to have left an hour ago!* As his mind raced in frenzy, he saw the SwissAir jet only now approaching their gate. A delayed flight! *Why on this, of all days ...*

"Father!" he hissed, white-eyed with horror, "get away from here! You don't know—"

Marandi almost laughed aloud. *So! This Jew is the son of that one!* Who wouldn't assume that the father was a collaborator? He would kill two Jews today!

The first passengers from the jet were approaching the entrance to the gate as Marandi unslung his semiautomatic from its hiding place beneath his caftan. Yanking back the bolt, he grinned as he aimed the muzzle at the two Jews.

Moosa heard the click of the weapon. From the corner of his eye he saw the dark hole of Marandi's gun pointed at him. He shoved his father violently in the chest, flinging him hard onto his back with the unexpected thrust. He charged Marandi, shouting, "No! He's my father—"

Marandi's burst caught him in the chest, just as the nearest *pasdar*—who had slipped unseen behind the informant—opened fire. A spray of blood spewed from Moosa's chest as he fell, wide-eyed with the tragic surprise of the betrayed. Lying on his back in the echoing, darkening world, he saw Marandi fall, the traitor himself a victim of treachery.

The crowds in the gate areas screamed and fell to the floor as the first shots erupted. All around the perimeter of Gate 13, guerillas died in short, thrifty bursts of gunfire as the *pasdars* acted on the information supplied to them by the now-dead informant.

Esther clambered to her feet, her legs wobbling with terror. "Ezra!" she screamed, racing madly to where he lay, spattered with the blood of his son. His eyes were open wide, his mouth moving. *"Moosa..."* his lips framed in silent urgency. *"Moosa..."*

She looked up, her eyes drawn in horror to the splintered chest of her son. She crawled to him, vaguely aware of a distant ululating wail—her own voice. Cradling his head in her lap, she moaned the timeless, wordless dirge of the bereaved mother, a sound that rose up from the darkness of forgotten time like a death-groan from a well.

Moosa's eyes flickered open into her face. His lips moved. She bent near.

"Go."

Dumb with grief and confusion, she looked into his eyes. Feebly his fingertips brushed her *chador*, as if to push her away. "Go!" he whispered, his voice quiet with the urgency of the dying.

Feebly he turned his face to peer toward Gate 12, even as his soul shuddered from his body. With tears flooding from her eyes like rain, she turned her gaze in the direction, it seemed to her, that Moosa's spirit had yearned in its final flight. Toward Gate 12. Toward freedom.

As she stood, she felt hands on her shoulders. She turned, thinking to see Ezra beside her; but it was Nader Hafizi who gripped her arms and peered into her face in urgency. "Esther *khanom*, hurry! It is now more important than ever for you to leave Iran at once! Come!"

The mullah had raised Ezra to his feet, stiff-limbed and dumb with shock. Through the wailing maelstrom of confusion which had descended, he herded the two of them toward Gate 12, where Sepi stood trembling, unable to remove her face from her hands.

"Esther *khanom*," the mullah murmured tersely, "quickly turn your *chador* inside out. The blood stains will attract attention."

An insane cry—half laugh, half sob—sprang from her throat, before she clapped a hand over her mouth. *No, indeed!* she thought, *we surely don't want to attract attention!* Unnoticed in the general hysteria, she adjusted her garment.

The mullah guided the three blind, staggering wretches toward the door of Gate 12, even as *pasdars* poured into the area, swiftly imposing order on the frenzied, shrieking crowds. The bodies and blood stains of the guerrillas were removed, the area efficiently secured, and the patrons calmed. Within thirty minutes, the only evidences of the foiled ambush were the muted murmurs of the bystanders, the edgy glances and wan faces of those who had lived through the one-sided melee.

Looking somewhat befuddled at the unexplained delay, the Iraqi mullah came through the door of Gate 13 and was welcomed—in a slightly wilted fashion—by his greeting committee. At almost the same instant, the door to Gate 12 was blocked by three *pasdars* and an officious weasel of a man who announced in a reedy voice, "Unfortunately, we must reinspect the passports of all those wishing to leave the country. Please form a line."

TWENTY-SIX

AFIZI STEPPED UP to the official, pulling the Ayatollah's letter from his pocket. "These three people," he said, gesturing toward the Solaimans, "are, by order of the Imam himself, not to be detained on their way out of Iran. I am charged with expediting their journey." He thrust the letter in the man's face as he concluded, "I assume you will honor the wishes of the Ayatollah Khomeini?" He glared at the sweating inspector, whose Adam's apple bobbed repeatedly as he scanned the document.

In half a minute, the official handed the letter to Hafizi, a nervous twitching across his face. "Allow these people into the boarding area," he snapped. One of the *pasdars* opened the door.

"You," snapped the mullah at one of the *pasdars*, "fetch their luggage." He jerked a thumb imperiously at the valises and handbags beside the door. Grumbling, the soldier stooped to comply.

Hafizi shepherded his three blank-eyed charges through. The official stared after them, his expression of awe mingled with traces of suspicion. The *pasdar* tossed their luggage in a heap just outside the doorway.

The door closed behind them, and they stood on the tarmac of the airport runway. Although the steps had been wheeled to the door of the SwissAir craft, because

251

of the disturbance inside the terminal, no one had yet been permitted to deplane. As they waited for the hatch to open, Hafizi gripped Ezra by the shoulders and shook him like an errant child.

"*Aga* Solaiman! *Aga* Solaiman! Wake up! You must come back! Someone must take charge!"

Ezra's eyes twitched toward the mullah, then away, back into the trackless abyss of sorrow where he wandered.

"Ezra!" By now Hafizi was shouting. "Moosa is gone! Neither your death, nor that of your wife and daughter, will bring him back! Do you wish all this to have been for nothing?"

In a blinding, rending rush, the world snapped back into place within Ezra Solaiman. In sudden recognition, with instant, horrified memory, his eyes leapt out toward the mullah. "My son!" he gasped, clenching Hafizi's upper arms with a desperate grip, "my son is dead! God in heaven, how can this be?" He sobbed aloud, his face raised blind to the sky, his fingers digging into the mullah's flesh, seeking some mooring, some point of anchorage against the storm of madness which dragged at him.

Hafizi pulled him against his breast, hugging him fiercely as if attempting to hold down a wild, winged thing which strained to spring into the air. "Yes, *baradar!*" he said, teeth clenched, into Ezra's ear. "He is dead! But you are alive, and your wife and daughter. You deserve a future, a chance to live past all this hatred, this mindless violence! Be strong, now! You must have strength enough for the three of you." Hafizi stepped back, took Khomeini's letter out of his pocket, and carefully placed it in Ezra's. Looking at Ezra, he said, "I have come as far as I can!"

As Ezra's eyes locked with his, an understanding beyond words passed between them. Just then, the door to the aircraft opened. Arriving passengers, complaining loudly about being delayed inside a cramped, stuffy cabin, began descending the stairs.

WHEN THE AIRCRAFT was cleared, the Solaimans were permitted to board. They shouldered their handbags and valises. After clasping Nader Hafizi in a final, firm embrace, Ezra guided Esther and Sepi up the steps, toward the small, dark doorway to freedom. They were greeted atop the stairs by a smiling, efficient flight attendant who glanced at their boarding passes and gestured toward their seats. Sidling down the narrow central aisle of the 707, they arrived at their places. Numbly, Esther began to heave her shoulder bag into the luggage rack above, but Ezra stayed her.

"Put the valises in the racks," he told them, "but not the handbags. They should stay beneath the seats . . . where they'll be easy to reach."

Their eyes stared blankly at him; then they turned to comply.

For ten or fifteen minutes, they were the only ones on the plane. Then the other passengers, who had been unable to avoid the tedious passport checkpoint, began trickling into the cabin. Esther and Sepi were seated next to each other, Ezra just across the aisle. Presently, the occupant of the window seat arrived, glancing from his boarding pass to the vacant place beside Ezra.

Ezra glanced up, wincing inwardly. Inevitably, the man was corpulent, laden with baggage, and perspiring heavily. Quietly Ezra got out of his seat, managing a polite smile as his seatmate began unloading and arranging his paraphernalia. After he had stowed his baggage in the rack, grunting heavily as he shoved and pushed the things into place, he managed to wedge himself between the armrests of the window seat.

The cabin was nearly full. Ezra edged into his seat, trying to avoid contact with the sweaty bulk of the man next to him. As he was buckling himself into place, he glanced up and dropped the ends of his seat belt from suddenly nerveless fingers.

Ahmed Dabirian had just entered the cabin, after showing some sort of badge to the flight attendant. The cabinetmaker was making his way down the center aisle, swiveling his eyes this way and that, carefully inspecting the face of each person he passed.

There was only one reason that Ahmed Dabirian could be on this aircraft. With a dull pounding in his ears, Ezra watched the approach of the carpenter. Unaccountably, he found himself slightly amused by the sawdust in Dabirian's beard. He imagined the ludicrous picture: himself handcuffed and led off the plane by a ragtag Islamic official who looked as though he had only just left his work bench.

Dabirian saw him, elbowed his way past the squirming passengers, and came to stand over Ezra, his face grim with purpose.

Esther felt the presence of someone standing beside her in the aisle longer than should have been the case. She stirred from her dark trance to peer upward and recognized the figure of Ahmed Dabirian looming above her husband. She closed her eyes and bowed her head. *This is surely the end.* Without consciously willing it, she began silently cursing Ezra's stubborn insistence on his own cleverness.

"*Aga* Solaiman," Dabirian was saying in a quiet, serious voice, "you have done a bad thing."

Ezra felt his heart twisting inside him, as if someone had reached through his ribs and clamped it in a steel-fisted grip.

"You thought, perhaps," continued Dabirian, "that an uneducated man, such as myself, would not be clever enough to discover the purpose for the empty space at the bottom of your so-called shipping crate." The carpenter stared down at Ezra in silence, slowly shaking his head from side to side.

Any minute now, thought Ezra with the fatalistic clarity of the doomed, *the* pasdars *will come up the aisle and take me away. Can they be persuaded to allow Esther and Sepi to go on their way?* He began composing a plea in his mind—some entreaty which would influence Dabirian to allow his wife and daughter to go to safety. He realized the cabinetmaker was speaking again.

"This hurts me deeply, *Aga* Solaiman. I have had many dealings with you, and always we have treated each other with complete fairness. That you would presume to take advantage of our friendship wounds me deeply."

The area of the cabin immediately around them had grown very still; Ezra was acutely aware of the eyes, the silent faces of the other passengers. The man sitting beside him had not moved since Dabirian had arrived. From the corner of his eye, Ezra sensed the fellow staring, open-mouthed, as Dabirian reached into an inside pocket of his coat and drew out two bundles of American dollars.

There was an audible intake of breath as the currency came into view. It was not difficult to see the numbers printed on the topmost bills in the stacks. The man standing in the aisle was holding some $20,000!

"Because of my personal regard for you, *Aga* Solaiman," Dabirian was saying, "I am not going to arrest you." He paused, as if in debate with himself. "I have prayed much about this matter," he muttered, "and I have decided that to show mercy in such a case is not an altogether bad thing. . . . But my duty will not permit me to allow this money to be taken out of Iran. It will be given to the poor—so perhaps my act of mercy will not, after all, be fruitless. No one will know the source of the money. I will see to that."

Ezra realized that Dabirian was not going to send him back to Evin Prison. He felt a slight breeze of hope wafting through his mind, then remembered Moosa's bloodied body, lying on the floor of the terminal.

"I wish you well, *Aga* Solaiman," finished Dabirian. "I mean this with all sincerity." Gravely he bowed toward Ezra, turned and nodded toward Esther. Then he strode down the aisle to the front of the cabin and was gone.

This is a tragic exodus, thought Ezra, as he surrendered to the dark, gauzy curtains of exhaustion falling across his vision. *This time, the blood of the firstborn is on us—and we must hide it at all costs.* Then he was unconscious.

HE WAS AWAKENED by the landing gear, the grinding rumble of the jet's wheels as they slammed into the tarmac of a runway. He clawed his way out of the darkness of sleep and looked across the aisle at his wife.

"We're in Geneva," she announced in a voice devoid of all inflection.

The taxi dropped them in front of the nearest hotel. Wearily the three refugees leaned against the walls of the elevator cubicle. Wearily they slogged down the dark hallway to the door whose number matched that of the room key the desk clerk had issued.

They went inside. "Place the shoulder bags on the bed," said Ezra. Esther and Sepi shrugged their satchels onto the bed beside Ezra's. He unzipped the nearest one—Esther's—and unceremoniously turned it upside-down, dumping the contents in a tangled heap atop the bedclothes.

Tumbling from the bottom of the bag came just over $300,000, done up in the same neat bundles as those confiscated by Ahmed Dabirian. Ezra repeated the process with the other two bags, with the same result.

The three of them gazed silently at the money—the sum total, Ezra reflected, of his life of careful planning and toil. He had managed, despite everything, to bring this out of Iran.

It was not enough.

TEHRAN

NADER HAFIZI smiled as the small child dipped his hand in the pond beside the front walk. The toddler was fascinated by the goldfish and had inched closer and closer to the water, his chubby hands twitching, as if they longed to touch the shining ornamental fish which swam gracefully to and fro in the blue-tiled pond.

He managed to brush one of the fish with his fingertips and it wriggled away with a sudden burst of speed. The child gave a little yip of alarm and yanked his hand back, losing his balance and sitting down hard on the herringboned walkway. Hafizi laughed aloud.

"*Aga* Hafizi, the midday meal is prepared. Will you come and offer the blessing?"

The mullah looked over at the shy young woman who had spoken. "Yes, Maryam *Khanom*, I will come." He gestured toward her son, who still sat dazed on the sidewalk. "If young Akbar has his way, we will eat fish for supper." Hafizi winked at the child as he rose from his seat on the front steps.

The young mother shook her head as she hurried to gather her son. Together they went into the dining room.

The boarders were already gathered about the large table, Akram standing in her habitual place beside the kitchen door. Hafizi beamed at her as he sat down.

Their guests were the dispossessed, the downtrodden, those with no place to go. He found them in the streets and alleys of Tehran, and brought them here to Solaiman House — the refuge he had created on this spacious, beautiful site. It was a place of peace, a place of healing. A place of hope reborn.

There had been suspicions, at first. From time to time, officials and mullahs came poking about the premises, looking for any sign of double dealing or suspicious goings-on. Hafizi endured these visits good-naturedly, knowing he had nothing to hide. It was, as he told Akram, as if a thief returned from a long journey, to find that one of his cronies had become a holy man. He would be bound to search diligently for some evidence of an ulterior motive for his former colleague's inexplicable behavior. To the hypocrite, Hafizi well knew, nothing is so baffling as sincerity.

He raised a morsel of bread in his hand. "In the name of Allah the Merciful," he intoned, "may He bless this house and its occupants.

"And may He also," the mullah continued, as was his habit, "bless the house of Ezra Solaiman, the generous and gracious man whose good will made this place and its mission possible."

PLAINSBORO,
NEW JERSEY

AS EZRA TURNED the key in the lock, the door to his apartment swung open. He went inside, tossing the package from the drugstore on the table of the kitchenette and tugging open the drapes. He sat down on the couch and looked out the front window.

The view led across a blacktop road into a cornfield, framed in the distance by stands of hickory and ash. The idyllic setting pleased Ezra; it was the main thing which had drawn him to this semirural community south of the loud tangle of New York City. Sometimes the quiet, the sibilant rustle of the wind through the corn leaves, could almost make him forget. . . .

He looked over at the package on the table—Demerol, prescribed by his doctor for the raging headaches which had tormented him of late. Sometimes the pain was so fierce he woke in the middle of the night, writhing and squeezing his temples in a futile effort at relief. But the headaches paled beside the nightmares.

He rose, walking over to the kitchenette. Almost offhandedly, he picked up the cylindrical brown plastic bottle of Demerol. How well he knew what too many Demerol could do.

Esther and Sepi lived nearby, in an apartment much like his own. Esther called him sometimes, and they made small talk around the shouting silences between their words. He was lonely, and he often thought she was too. But he couldn't blame her.

Shaking the pills in the bottle like a child shakes a rattle, he drifted again toward the couch. He looked down, his eye lighting on a book he had recently purchased.

There was a growing Iranian community in these parts as many others followed Ezra's path out of turmoil. Businesses were springing up to cater to the needs of the refugees. One of these, located in a small strip center half a mile from Ezra's apartment, was an Iranian bookstore.

As he had browsed through the meager offerings, he had noticed the book which now claimed his view. A New Testament translated into Farsi.

Telling himself he was motivated by mere curiosity, he had bought the book. When he came in that day, he had flung it on the coffee table in front of his couch, where it had lain undisturbed. Until now.

He picked up the thin volume, thumbing through the pages. "Nothing remarkable here," he told himself aloud. "Just a book. A waste of money."

And then he was back in Evin Prison, among the emaciated, stinking bodies of the breathing dead. Reuben Ibrahim was beside him, weeping and praying. *"Yeshua . . . protect them."*

The book fell open and his eyes lit halfway down the page: "Anyone who loves his son or daughter more than Me is not worthy of Me. . . . Whoever finds his life will lose it, and whoever loses his life for My sake will find it."

A harsh grace, that of this Jesus. And yet . . .

To find a life . . . wasn't that his goal? Hadn't it been for that very purpose he had fled Iran? And had he succeeded? Was he now living—what was the American phrase—the good life? He had left Iran a millionaire. Had it made any difference?

In one hand he held the Demerol, in the other the book. His eyes flickered back and forth between them.

"Whoever loses his life for My sake..."

Or sleep and nothingness. Which? How to know?

The phone rang. He set the book and the pills on the table as he rose to pick up the receiver. "Hello?"

"Ezra." Esther's voice. For ten, twelve heartbeats there was silence on the line. Then she said, "I...I have been thinking. Perhaps..."

"...loses his life for My sake will find it." The phrase tugged at him like a lodestone.

"Perhaps we should talk," Esther was saying.

"Yeshua...He will protect..."

Ezra cleared his throat. "Yes. Perhaps we should."